Praise for *To Kill a Troubadour*

'The gorgeous scenery and delicious meals provide as much entertainment as the action'

Sunday Times Crime Club

'*To Kill a Troubadour* is a pleasant summer treat . . . melds together the bucolic and the political with an enviably steady hand'

Crime Review

'While a brilliantly conceived plot builds up to a climax that James Bond might envy, there is pleasure to be had in Martin Walker's sensitive portrayal of a tight-knit community . . . Bruno is a hero for our troubled times'

Daily Mail

'Martin Walker once again delivers a delightful potpourri of southern French *la vie en rose* and tense action'

Irish Independent

'This is the perfect summer escape novel, with a cracking crime at its heart'

Sun

A Chateau Under Siege

Also by Martin Walker

Martin
WALKER

A Chateau
Under Siege

The Dordogne Mysteries

QUERCUS

First published in Great Britain in 2023 by

QUERCUS

Quercus Editions Ltd
Carmelite House
50 Victoria Embankment
London EC4Y 0DZ

An Hachette UK company

A CIP catalogue record for this book is available
from the British Library

HB ISBN 978 1 52941 368 7
TPB ISBN 978 1 52941 369 4
EBOOK ISBN 978 1 52941 370 0

10 9 8 7 6 5 4 3 2 1

Typeset by CC Book Production
Printed and bound in Great Britain by Clays Ltd, Elcograf S.p.A.

Papers used by Quercus are from well-managed forests
and other responsible sources.

For Natalia Antelava and the team of journalists
at Codastory.com

A MAP OF

BRUNO'S PERIGORD

~FRANCE~

PERIGUEUX

CENDRIEUX

SAINTE-ALVERE

château de tiregand

ST DENIS

BERGERAC

LALINDE

DORDOGNE RIVER

LIMEUIL

BERGERAC AIRPORT

château de monbazillac

château de hautefort

O R D

VÉZÈRE RIVER

LASCAUX
(CAVES)

CAP BLANC
(ROCK SHELTER)

château de commarque

LES EYZIES

SARLAT

BEYNAC

château castelnaud la chapelle

Chapter 1

Bruno Courrèges, chief of police for the Vézère valley in the Périgord region of France, was deeply fond of the medieval square of Sarlat but he had never seen it from this angle before. He was seated among his friends on one of the top rows of benches and it felt uncomfortably high. Erected each year for the town's theatre festival, the benches were being used for a new venture, the re-enactment of the battle of Sarlat in 1370, when the town had been liberated from English rule. As a former soldier, Bruno was interested to see how this mock battle would unfold.

'Sarlat was the traditional capital of the Périgord Noir, dating back to Gallo-Roman times. Charlemagne himself donated holy relics to the abbey here,' said Pamela. She sat on Bruno's left and was reading aloud from a guidebook as Bruno gazed fondly at this former lover who had since become the closest female friend he'd ever known. 'It seems that's how it became rich, attracting pilgrims who ensured its growing prosperity. Over time, the monks established eighty-five daughter churches whose parishes by the year 1200 stretched nearly two hundred kilometres to Toulouse.'

'All while preaching the virtues of poverty,' grumbled Gérard

Mangin, sitting on Bruno's right. As the Mayor of St Denis, Mangin had hired Bruno to be the town policeman a dozen years earlier and Bruno, an orphan, sometimes thought of him as the father he had never known. The Mayor was a staunch Republican who only went to church when baptisms, funerals or his civic duties required. Weddings, he believed, were civic events for him to officiate rather than any priest.

Bruno's friends from St Denis were clustered around them. The Baron, one of Bruno's hunting partners, sat on the far side of Pamela. Fabiola, a local doctor, and her partner Gilles, a journalist, were on the bench below, beside Bruno's cousin, Alain, and Rosalie, the woman Alain would marry later that year once their twenty years' service in the armée de l'air was complete. On the row below them were Miranda – Pamela's partner in the riding school – and Miranda's father, Jack Crimson, a retired British diplomat. The only one missing was Florence, a local science teacher, who had lost the toss of a coin with Miranda to see which of the two mothers would babysit their young children, all of them exhausted after a long day around Pamela's pool.

It had been for Bruno a perfect day, undisturbed by any of the sudden crises that had ruined his previous Fridays and Sundays, nominally his days off. Three traffic accidents, two lost children and a drunken duel between two Dutch tourists in kayaks had consumed his supposed free time. But today had been spent in and around Pamela's swimming pool with his friends, and while preparing a huge salad lunch for them all he'd enjoyed showing the children how to make devilled eggs.

They had watched him halve the hard-boiled eggs, scoop

out the yolks and crush them with a fork. Next he made mayonnaise, added a generous spoonful of honey mustard and paprika, then used a fork to mix in the crumbled egg yolks before spooning the egg and mayonnaise mix into a dozen of the eggs for the grown-ups. He asked the children how they liked their eggs. 'With tomato ketchup,' they replied, so Bruno put the remaining mayonnaise into a dish and showed them how to stir in ketchup until it turned pink. He added the crumbled yolks and scooped the mixture into the halved whites and grinned as the kids darted off to show off their pink devilled eggs. He smiled to himself at the memory, until Pamela interrupted his thoughts to ask whether today's planned re-enactment was historically accurate.

'As usual, that depends whose version of history you read,' the Mayor said. 'Only later did English and French historians make it a matter of national patriotism. At the time, most people in this region accepted that their local lord was the Duke of Aquitaine who happened to be half-English. And if he didn't speak their language, nor did the King of France because everyone around here spoke Occitan. The English duke's taxes were usually lower and England was the main market for our wines.'

'Whoever built Sarlat, they left us a lovely place,' said Bruno. He never tired of visiting the old town, a jewel of medieval and Renaissance architecture so well preserved that it had become a mainstay of French historic films. Its markets and festivals for the local delicacies of truffles and foie gras were renowned. Sarlat was woven deeply into the history of France. It was lost and then liberated in the Hundred Years War against the English. It had again been a battlefield in the sixteenth century in France's civil wars when Catholic fought Protestant so long and so bitterly that more than two million – a tenth of the French population – died, not only from war but also the plagues and famines the marauding armies brought in their wake.

Sarlat's launch of this new event of the tourist season had certainly attracted great interest. There were TV cameras, radio and press reporters, and not an empty seat in the giant array of benches that had been erected in the main square. The town had provided a lavish budget for the medieval costumes and musicians to commemorate the great patriotic occasion. The townsfolk of Sarlat had risen against the English from within while French troops stormed the gates.

The idea had been borrowed from the annual re-enactment of the battle of Castillon in 1453, when the English army led by the renowned John Talbot, the Earl of Salisbury, had been decisively defeated. The *rosbifs*, as the French called their traditional enemies from across the Channel, had finally been ejected from southern and western France for good, with only the Channel port of Calais remaining in English hands for another hundred years. Every summer, the people of the town of Castillon, now known as Castillon-la-Bataille in commemoration of the victory, mounted a popular pageant. It featured crowd scenes and parades, knights in armour charging on horseback, picturesque tents and flags, and the roar of the cannon that had been the key to the French victory, opening the way for the French to take the strategic port of Bordeaux, just a day's march away.

As a former soldier, Bruno had always wondered why the

name of Jean Bureau had been forgotten, since the great victory of Castillon had been his. As Master of the Ordnance for the French king, Bureau had assembled three hundred cannon, and mounted them behind a defensive ditch. The guns had a greater range than the longbows of the hitherto invincible English archers. It was, therefore, a battle which lent itself to re-enactment. The English stopped to shoot their longbows, the guns roared out and the archers began to fall. Then the English infantry launched their doomed assaults and the guns roared out again, and finally the French knights emerged on horseback for a triumphant charge.

It was all very simple for tourists to understand, all very scenic and with powerful sound effects. No wonder it was a success, thought Bruno. But of course the actual mock-battle lasted for barely twenty minutes and the tourists wanted more than that. So there were scenes in the French camp: the delivery of herds of sheep and cattle to feed the French troops; the market with milkmaids; the country-dancing and the musicians; the solemn blessing of the French troops by the patriotic churchmen; the donning of armour. These scenes were balanced by the absurd overconfidence of the English archers, unaware that the storm of arrows that had won their battles for the past century was about to become obsolete as the cannon announced their new dominance over battlefields. It all made for a grand and dramatic evening.

Knowing something of the confusion of urban warfare, Bruno wondered how this re-enactment of the liberation of Sarlat would be stretched out for the planned two hours of spectacle. There was no ditch to be attacked and defended, no

5

roar of massed cannon, no flights of arrows, and in the narrow streets of the medieval town that led to this main square, little prospect of a scenic cavalry charge. Instead he could hear the sound of cattle and the bleating of goats as the livestock were prepared for their walk-on parts. This being the Périgord, the noise was echoed by the honking of geese and the clatter of barrels of wine being rolled over cobblestones.

These had been the sounds that had greeted Bruno and his friends when they had arrived late that afternoon to stroll through the medieval market that had been erected as part of the entertainment. The stalls offered the usual souvenirs of knightly helmets, plastic swords and bows with rubber-tipped arrows for children, sold by men in leather jerkins and women dressed as tavern wenches. Entering into the spirit of the event, they watched the staged sword fights and bought overpriced glasses of something called mead which Bruno recognized as the semi-sweet Rosette white wine that was unique to Bergerac. They had dined cheerfully on overpriced barbecue, followed by paper cups of fresh strawberries. Finally, at eight thirty, as that lovely soft twilight that the French call *le crépuscule* began to fall, a peal of trumpets summoned them to their seats.

A man dressed as a medieval herald appeared on one of the balconies on the far side of the square. He was flanked by two musicians bearing long trumpets who sent out another peal that made everyone sit up. It lasted until the first long roll of the drums and then the herald spoke.

'France groans beneath the English yoke,' he announced. 'Ever since the battle of Poitiers, when the English archers under their notorious Black Prince mowed down the flower of French chivalry, the English have occupied half of France. From Anjou to the Pyrénées, from Bordeaux to the Auvergne, the English ruled. But now, in the summer of 1370, ten years after the hateful treaty was imposed on our captured king, liberation is stirring here in the lush valleys and forests and vineyards of the Périgord. Bertrand du Guesclin, the Constable of France, is preparing to restore France to herself.

'The symbol that du Guesclin chooses for the great mission to recover France's freedom is here, the cathedral city of Sarlat, its prosperity founded by the great Charlemagne and its renowned abbey. An army has been raised and brought secretly through the woods and hidden ways to the heart of the Périgord. Secret agents have been dispatched to make their way into Sarlat, disguised as peddlers and merchants, to make contact with the consuls and the people of Sarlat and prepare the way for the audacious stroke that will launch the fight for the liberation of France.'

On a balcony across the square, curtains were being drawn back to reveal a group of men in period costume, evidently conspirators, gathered around a glistening candle and making angry speeches about Sarlat being crushed beneath the English boot.

'We'll come in for the market dressed like peasants but with our swords hidden in a farm cart,' said one of the conspirators, a hidden microphone sending his stage whispers through the loudspeakers that carried every word to the audience. 'We seize the town gate and hold it for du Guesclin and his troops to ride in, while more of our men ambush their archers and our townswomen distract the enemy with their charms.'

Bruno had expected the market scene to follow. No, declared the herald. It was still night-time in Sarlat, and the English troops were thronging the taverns and – his voice deepened ominously – molesting the womenfolk.

'And, of course, no French soldier has ever been known to molest a woman,' came Pamela's voice. She threw Bruno, the only Frenchman she knew who'd been a soldier, a friendly glance and gave his hand an affectionate squeeze.

He admired Pamela's energy, her intelligence and her kindness. She always had time for her friends, and when on occasion she let him know that she would enjoy his company for a romantic evening, he always found time for her. They exchanged a fond look before the sudden sound of uproar drew their attention back to the square before them.

English soldiers, dressed in chain mail, leather hauberks and characteristic soup-plate metal helmets, thronged out from a side street, most of them holding a leather tankard in one hand and a wench in the other. Bruno assumed the women were supposed to be tavern girls. They were all wearing low-cut dresses and most of them seemed content to join in the party. But one young woman with flaming red hair was clearly being dragged along against her will, weeping and begging to be released from the clutch of an apparently drunken English thug who was groping her.

'This is going a bit far,' muttered the Mayor. 'There are children in this audience.'

As he spoke, the group of English soldiers and the women passed beneath a balcony not far from where the conspirators had clustered around their candle. A young man in hose and doublet appeared, looked down into the street and immediately launched himself from the balcony to drop down onto the shoulders of the drunk. The youth must have been a skilled gymnast since he landed on the Englishman's burly shoulders and at once somersaulted from them to land lightly on his feet on the cobblestones. The woman, who had evidently been expecting this manoeuvre, tripped the drunken soldier so that he stumbled across the feet of his fellows as she cried, 'Down with the English tyranny!' She then seized the young gymnast's hand and they disappeared together into the maze of alleys in the old town.

The audience applauded, many of them like Bruno and Alain leaping up from their seats to salute this theatrical coup. But the applause subsided as the English troops began taking their revenge, kicking in doors and rousting out the townsfolk in their nightshirts to the sounds of breaking crockery and furniture and screams. At last a patrol of sober soldiers appeared to restore order, to shepherd the weeping citizens back into their homes and to escort their drunken comrades to their barracks. When all was still again and the streets empty, the flame-haired young woman and the agile youth re-emerged into the main square, peeking around the corner to be sure they were alone.

'It's all clear,' the youth said, his whisper carrying to the audience over some hidden microphone. 'We plan to seize the gate and charge in just before midday, when the English gather to eat before the market closes.'

'The people of Sarlat are ready, my lord,' she replied. 'We'll make the *rosbifs* drunk on wine before you come. The fools cannot resist the fruit of the grape.'

'Nor can they resist you, *mademoiselle*, we saw that tonight.

But then who could? Your beauty puts the stars to shame and your eyes fill me with more light than the moon.' He knelt to kiss her hand. 'And I am no lord, just a simple chevalier, a squire to the great Constable du Guesclin. When I get back over the town wall, I shall tell him that Sarlat will be ours by midday tomorrow.'

He gave her hand a final kiss and she unwrapped a scarf from around her throat and handed it to him.

'May the good Lord and the Blessed Virgin hear my prayers and watch over you in the fighting tomorrow,' she said, before the young squire darted away.

Silence fell until a church bell gave a single toll and the herald emerged once again, to announce: 'Sarlat sleeps, her last night under English rule. Bertrand du Guesclin and his troops stand watch behind the heights to the west of the town. Du Guesclin's trusty squire, Philippe de Périgueux, has returned from his bold mission inside the walls of Sarlat and reported that the town's patriots are ready. In the darkness beyond these walls, du Guesclin and his men are kneeling at prayer, and the hopes of all France must wait through the long night for dawn.'

There was a lengthy pause, then through the loudspeakers came the sound of a cockerel crowing to greet the dawn, and suddenly all was bustle as spotlights came on to light the scene with a flood of artificial day. Escorted by young girls and boys, a small herd of cows emerged into the main square and young women appeared carrying stools and sat down as if ready to milk them. Market stalls were being set up and housewives came out to buy food, amid sudden smells of fresh bread and of the pickled herring the English loved. Over the loudspeakers came the cackling of far more ducks and chickens than could be seen in the cages being unloaded, while wooden carts with squeaky wheels and hauled by donkeys were bringing fruit and vegetables to the market.

Then came the musicians, playing their citoles and tambours, singing the old troubadour songs while jugglers tossed two and then three hatchets into the air and kept them all spinning. A one-legged man dressed in rags and leaning on a wooden crutch, holding out a bowl and begging for alms, limped around the crowd.

The English soldiers came out to patrol two-by-two, never alone. The richer citizens paraded in their finery, silks and embroidery, leather boots and shoes rather than the wooden sabots of the peasants. The square filled steadily with the market, the people, and the cries of the street vendors, the knife sharpeners, the wheelwrights, shoe-menders and wood-turners. The high voices of the women called on people to feel the quality of the linens they had spun.

Children darted between and beneath the stalls, picking up scraps, their little hands creeping up from below to steal pastry. At every corner planks were being laid across two upright barrels, making stalls that bore jugs of wine and clay mugs, and the winemakers cried out that they had to sell their stocks cheaply to make room in their *chais* for this year's harvest.

'A jug of wine for only two deniers, milords,' called out one of them to the English troops. 'Last week it cost three deniers so it's a special price today.'

Soon the Englishmen had taken off their soup-dish helmets and were leaning against the church wall, swilling jugs of wine as they watched the jugglers. Then a horse-drawn cart, piled high with firewood, came down the hill and two peasants began to unload it. Bruno noticed that once emptied, the floor of the cart seemed distinctly higher than it should have been. A church bell began to toll, slowly and solemnly. The church doors opened and a priest emerged first, six peasants following behind him carrying a coffin while the bereaved family trudged sadly in their wake, heading for the town's main gate and the path that led to the cemetery.

The herald emerged to announce that there was no funeral and no corpse. The mourners were the assault team that would attack the gate guards and open the gates for du Guesclin and his armoured knights.

From the direction of the gate came the sound of cheering, the clash of swords, cries of pain. The funeral party put down the coffin, wrenched off the lid and pulled out their hidden weapons. The peasants who had brought in the cart filled with firewood levered off the boards that made the cart's false floor and began handing out the swords and pikes that had been hidden there to the musicians and jugglers who at once attacked the English patrols. Milkmaids who had been flirting with the soldiers plucked daggers from inside their robes and stabbed at the nearest English men-at-arms who were hurriedly putting aside their jugs of wine.

Then the thundering clatter of horses' hooves on cobble-stones announced the arrival of the French knights, led by a big man on a white horse wearing a black surcoat over his armour, evidently intended to be Bertrand du Guesclin. With him were three knights in red surcoats, one of them carrying a fleur de lys banner, and three more in white. More horsemen were coming in their wake and after a triumphant ride along the front of the benches to the Church of Sainte Marie, du Guesclin turned his horse, roaring out, '*Vive la France!*', and ordered his cavalry to charge the English troops guarding the Hôtel de Ville.

Suddenly, du Guesclin's horse seemed to skid on a heap of straw that had been placed on a pile of fresh manure and went down hard, whinnying in pain and sprawling on its rear legs. But du Guesclin scrambled free and, with his fellow knights, he continued the charge on foot, his great broadsword held high. The newly armed stallholders and some of their womenfolk followed him and his knights in the attack along the thin line of Englishmen. From one side, a brawny milkmaid swinging a pole swiped at the legs of the English man-at-arms at the end of the line. At the other end, the beggar balanced perilously on his one good leg used his crutch to sweep away the feet from beneath another *rosbif*. Swords clashed against swords and slammed into shields while pikes and battleaxes were brandished, but the French knights were steadily driving the enemy back up the steps where the English defenders acted out dramatic deaths, one by one.

Turning to the sound of more trumpets from behind, Bruno saw a squad of French soldiers marching into view from the direction of the town gate. Disarmed English prisoners, their hands bound behind their backs, trudged in their wake. The stalls selling wine hastened to offer mugs to the new French arrivals as the townsfolk began to celebrate their liberation. One of the town's consuls was trying to make a speech of welcome as the cry went up for the hero of the day – 'Du Guesclin, Du Guesclin.'

But there came no answer. As the English troops lay faking death in front of the Hôtel de Ville and the French knights and townsfolk backed away, a solitary body remained, sprawled face-down on the steps, wearing a black surcoat. A pool of blood was spreading ominously beneath him.

As Bruno and the rest of the audience watched in stunned silence, the first drop of blood overflowed the marble step beneath the figure and dribbled down slowly to the next. At the moment of his triumph, du Guesclin had fallen.

'Another travesty of history,' murmured the Mayor. 'Du Guesclin lived on for ten more years before dying of illness.'

'I don't think this is in the script,' said Bruno.

Chapter 2

The first to react was the young squire who had been playing the tambour, no longer in time to any music but to beat out an insistent martial rhythm, the *rat-a-tat-tat* of the charge. Now he stopped, put down his drumstick and turned to address the audience on their benches, calling out to ask if there was a doctor among them. Fabiola rose and raised an arm in reply when a man in the second row and much closer to the place where the knight lay still shouted, 'I'm his doctor.' Brandishing a black medical bag he vaulted down to trot to the steps where the wounded man lay.

Fabiola began squeezing her way to the end of her row. Bruno, Gilles and Alain helped clear her path down the side of the benches, pushing slowly through the crowds despite Bruno's best parade-ground voice demanding they make way for the doctor. It took not much more than a minute to cross the square but it seemed much longer. The other doctor was bent over the fallen du Guesclin, avoiding the spreading pool of blood. He had two fingers on the man's neck as Bruno turned to the crowd and shouted, 'Police – get back.' Bruno raised his hands and made pushing motions to get people to clear the steps and make way for Fabiola. Alain and Gilles were still having trouble trying to help her to squeeze her way through the crowd.

The men who had just an instant before been playing the role of soldiers and the women who had been the murderous milkmaids, along with the apparently slain English troops now coming back to life, had all been transformed into a horrified and curious crowd of civilians jostling to get a view. Bruno took out his phone, brandished it so all could see and shouted, 'I'm calling an ambulance. You men dressed as soldiers, please form a line below these steps. We don't want a crowd coming up here. Does anyone know who this man is?'

'There's an ambulance on standby around the corner,' said the unknown doctor quietly before anyone could reply. 'It could be too late, there's hardly any pulse and he's lost a lot of blood.'

He started pumping the man's chest anyway as one of the soldiers called out that the victim's name was Kerquelin. That was a Breton name, Bruno knew, and it sounded almost identical to the French pronunciation of Guesclin.

'What if we get some plasma into him before we start resuscitation? He's still breathing,' said Fabiola, kneeling beside him.

'There's an ambulance coming,' the doctor replied. 'They have plasma and I'll start a transfusion right away.' As he spoke, two medical aides in fluorescent gear and carrying a stretcher trotted around the corner.

'I'm a doctor at the medical centre in St Denis,' said Fabiola by way of introduction.

'My name is Barrat and he's my patient,' the doctor replied as he began helping the ambulance men to place the stretcher alongside the stricken man. 'I work at the Domme facility,' he added.

Bruno was about to call the town's commissariat of police when someone dressed as a French soldier joined him on the steps. As soon as the man removed his helmet Bruno recognized him as Messager, a colleague of equal rank, the head of the municipal police for the town. He was a taciturn man, close to retirement, who shrank from responsibility and spent most of his spare time fishing. Bruno's relations with him were businesslike rather than cordial, and Bruno wondered why he'd volunteered to be part of the show. It seemed unlike him.

'Everybody, please stay where you are,' Messager called out to the crowd.

'We can't keep hundreds of people here for hours,' said Bruno quietly, into the man's ear, not wanting to question his authority in public. 'We don't have the manpower to process them. But we're going to need all the video of this that we can find. That includes phones. Could you use a bullhorn to ask people to save any images on their phones until we can put up a special website to receive them? And can you officially identify the wounded man? I think he was playing du Guesclin?'

'Bruno,' Fabiola called out before the police chief could reply, a quaver in her voice. Her face had gone white beneath some streaks of blood. He looked and saw that the casualty was now on the stretcher with an oxygen mask applied to his face but a much larger pool of blood had spread around the spot where he had been. 'It just started flooding out when we put him onto the stretcher and then it splashed into my face . . .'

Fabiola's voice was rising in pitch and the other doctor put an arm around her and used his handkerchief to clean her face as Fabiola burst out, 'His heart or the aorta must have been slashed wide open.'

She took a deep breath, pressed her face into her colleague's chest for a moment, and then said in her normal voice, 'And now look at this.'

She pointed to the body on the stretcher as the ambulance men began to lift it. She had ripped away the black surcoat and cut away the leather straps attached to a metal breastplate. On the man's left-hand side, the handle of what looked like a stiletto protruded. Bruno assumed the blade had slid between two ribs to penetrate the heart. Could that possibly have been some kind of accident?

'*Putain de merde*,' muttered Messager. 'Does this mean we've got a killing on our hands?'

'Don't touch that dagger,' said Barrat as Bruno bent down to examine the hilt. 'It may be helping seal the wound.'

'Where are you taking him?' Fabiola asked.

'Just up the hill to the hospital so we can get some plasma into him straightaway and we have resuscitation gear in the ambulance,' he replied. 'I'll try to call in a helicopter if one is available. Meet us there if you want but it may be too late. And if he's holding on, even without a chopper we might need to get him to Bergerac.'

He led the way for the ambulance men, and as they disappeared around a corner with the stretcher the young, red-haired woman who had been rescued from a drunken soldier by the squire in the night scene now pushed her way through the soldiers. Nervously she called out 'Papa', her rising voice making it a question. When she saw the blood on Fabiola's hands and face she gasped and tried to get past Bruno.

'I'm sorry, *mademoiselle*, but the wounded man is in the ambulance, on his way to the hospital,' Bruno said, rising to block her way.

'Is it my father?' she said. 'He's playing du Guesclin. Is he hurt?'

'The doctors are doing all they can,' Bruno replied. 'Can you contact your mother? Is she here?'

'They're divorced, she's in Paris.' She put her hands to her face and turned away, sinking into the arms of the young man playing the role of squire who had appeared at her side, the shock apparent on his face.

'Can you take me to the hospital?' she asked, and then Fabiola was at the girl's side, putting an arm around her and leading her to one side while speaking urgently of helicopters.

Thank heavens for that, Bruno thought, pulling out his phone to call his friend Jean-Jacques Jalipeau, the chief detective for the *département* of the Police Nationale, and known to all as J-J. Lowering his voice and turning his back to the crowd, Bruno explained that they seemed to be faced with an accidental death – or something worse – in front of probably a thousand potential witnesses.

'In the main square of Sarlat?' J-J asked. 'With TV cameras and medieval costumes?'

'Yes, and I assume it's already on the radio and most of the people here seem to be talking on their mobile phones,' Bruno replied. 'We've asked them to stay but some may have gone already. There aren't enough cops here to establish a proper cordon but we're trying to use the actors.'

'Who is the victim? Do you have a next of kin? Could this have been an accident of some kind?'

'Possibly, but I doubt it. It looks as though somebody slipped a knife between his ribs, somebody who knew where to find the gap in the armour he was wearing. His name is Kerquelin and his daughter is here. We'll get all the details from her. Apparently he's divorced. When can you get here? I doubt we can treat this as a crime scene. An ambulance has already taken him to a hospital.'

'I'll be there in about forty minutes and I'll bring a forensic team. Do you need help with crowd control? And see who might be missing a dagger.'

'That's up to you,' Bruno said. 'If you want to keep the audience here so you can collect their phones for any video evidence we'll need a lot of reinforcements, but I don't think there's enough time. I imagine you'll have enough eyewitnesses with me and the locals who took part, not to mention the TV cameras. I think we'd be better off just asking people to send in their videos if you can set up a special postbox on your Police-Dordogne website. We can get local press and broadcasters to publicize it.'

'I agree,' J-J replied. 'Let's not make any more of a drama out of this than we need. You'd better start by making lists of witnesses, anybody who was near enough to the dead man.'

'From what I could see that would only include people who took part in the re-enactment, so the Sarlat organizers should have all the details,' Bruno replied. 'What we'll need from the crowd are any videos they might have taken. We can always put out a public appeal. Hold on a moment, J-J.'

Bruno put out a hand to grab Romain, the deputy Mayor of Sarlat, by the shoulder. Not one to be left out of any civic activity, Romain was dressed as one of the peasants who had been offering wine to the soldiers.

'The victim, Kerquelin, what can you tell me about him?' Bruno asked. 'That's a Breton name, so he's not from around here. Does he live here in Sarlat?'

'No, near Domme, just down the road. His name is Brice Kerquelin, and with a name like that he claims to be descended from the great man, du Guesclin himself. But it's complicated,' Romain replied, and then hesitated and lowered his voice. 'There's a security aspect to this that we're not supposed to talk about, but I guess it's all right to tell you.'

'Okay, noted. Can you take care of his daughter? She seems to be in shock.'

Romain nodded and Bruno returned to his phone, hearing J-J's tinny voice demanding to know if he was still there. 'I'm here, J-J. The deputy Mayor says the victim, Brice Kerquelin, is supposed to have some security connection. Can you check out the name?'

The names and addresses of people in the *département* with links to the security services, or of special interest to them, were filed on a restricted list to which senior police officials like J-J would have access. Bruno could see the list, but only by going through the secure link on his office computer.

'*Bordel de merde*,' said J-J after a few moments. 'He's at the top of the damn list, with three stars and authorized to carry weapons. He's DGSE, senior staff at Domme. I have to call La Piscine first but after that I'm on my way.'

DGSE was the Direction Générale de la Sécurité Extérieure, France's foreign intelligence agency. La Piscine was the slang name for the headquarters on the Boulevard Mortier in Paris, named for the nearby public swimming pool. The DGSE also ran Frenchelon, the nickname of the French version of the Anglo-American electronic intelligence and global surveillance system. Its largest base was at Domme, just ten kilometres south of Sarlat.

Best known as one of the region's finest *bastides*, the fortified towns that date from the Middle Ages, Domme occupied a hilltop with spectacular views over the Dordogne valley. It was usually crammed with tourists at this time of year, although few of them were aware of Domme's pivotal role in French intelligence. The antennae and radar dishes could be seen but most of the facilities were buried deep underground, supposedly secure from anything but a direct hit by a nuclear weapon. Like most people in the region, Bruno knew of its existence. He knew that its role was to monitor and record communications of interest to the French security services, by phone and internet, and that it also had something to do with the communications of France's nuclear submarines. He had no idea how many people it employed, nor the degree with which it cooperated with its British and American allies in NATO.

He did know that it ran a number of language schools for its staff because Pamela, during her first years in France, had worked at one of them. It was based in a gently decaying nineteenth-century chateau in the hills west of Sarlat, where she helped the students decipher various accents of English from all over the world.

Bruno, now aware of how serious this attack might be, called the office of General Lannes in Paris, whose role was to coordinate the various arms of French security for the Minister of the Interior. Bruno's call was answered by the duty officer, the discreet button on his official phone glowing green to show the call was secure. Bruno gave his name and location and said he had an urgent message for the general. He was put through at once.

'*Bonjour*, Bruno. What's happening in Sarlat?' came the familiar voice.

Bruno explained, adding that he had informed J-J who was briefing La Piscine before joining Bruno in Sarlat.

'Brice, *mon Dieu*,' said Lannes, evidently shocked.

'You know him?' asked Bruno.

'Know him? I'm godfather to his daughter,' Lannes replied, his voice ending in what might have been a suppressed sob. It betrayed his grief in a way that Bruno had never heard from this hitherto calm and commanding official. Bruno did not know what to say, whether to ask for instructions or offer comfort. Perhaps he should ask whether he should alert anyone else in officialdom.

'*Mon général* . . .' he said, unsure whether Lannes was still listening to him. He heard the man murmur, '*Mon Dieu*, poor Nadia. She's so close to him.'

Then came the sound of a throat being cleared, a nose being blown and the efficient general that Bruno knew was back and speaking almost normally.

'You're sure it was deliberate?' came the question. 'Possibly even enemy action? He's an important man, a genius in his way.'

'Too soon to say for sure but it's hard to see it being an accident – a stiletto slid between the ribs into his heart through the only gap in the man's armour. A doctor who said he was a colleague at Frenchelon thinks he is dying but he's called for a helicopter and meanwhile taken him to Sarlat hospital in an ambulance.'

'Right, I'll get onto Domme and La Piscine. Leave that with me. You stay until J-J can take over and I can get some of my people there. I'll call you back. There are some things I'll have to count on you to do. And if you can, Bruno, please take care of his daughter.'

As Lannes ended the call Romain arrived with three other men carrying two tall stands of the kinds normally used to display local announcements, and erected them in a V-shape around the steps to keep the steps and bloodstains from view.

'We can't touch anything until Commissaire Jalipeau arrives with his forensics team,' Bruno said. 'This now has to be treated as a possible crime scene. Thanks for bringing the screens. I've informed the right people in Paris about the security aspect. What about his daughter? Are there any other close relatives?'

'The girl is now with my son, who was playing the squire. She has a brother but he's away on vacation somewhere,' Romain replied. 'The gendarmes are sending a couple of trucks to reinforce the town police.' He turned as the Mayor of St Denis was approaching them.

'*Cher collègue*,' the newcomer murmured to Romain. 'My commiserations, it is terrible that your remarkable spectacle should be marred by this tragedy. A heart attack, was it? I just heard the man playing the role of du Guesclin was dead.'

24

'I'll explain fully later, but he's on his way to hospital and may not be dead yet,' Bruno said. 'This may have been a tragic accident. J-J is on his way so I can get a lift back with him if you want to take our friends back to St Denis. I thought I saw Gilles taking photos or maybe video – can you check with him to make sure he saves it? We might need it. That goes for anyone else you might know who was filming the event on their phones.'

'Philippe Delaron is here and asked me to tell you that he needs an official statement, preferably from you,' Bruno's Mayor said. 'He's just done a story live for the radio: "tragedy strikes Sarlat re-enactment". But he wants more for his article for *Sud Ouest*. And someone from France-3 TV was filming the event and they want you speaking on camera.'

'Tell Philippe and the TV crew to try the town mayor or the *commissariat de police*,' Bruno replied. 'I haven't got the time and anyway, Sarlat isn't in my jurisdiction. You know that.'

'Well, jurisdiction or not, Bruno, it looks like you're in charge. And when you suggest this may even be a crime scene . . .'

'Sorry, I can't say any more at this stage. Security is involved. I'll tell you what I can when I get back to St Denis. In the meantime, if you could get some damp cloths or hand towels for me and Fabiola to clean ourselves of the blood, that would be a help.'

'Jacqueline always carries some in her handbag, so consider it done. I'll be right back.' The Mayor turned away to find his partner.

'There's something odd about this,' said Fabiola quietly, taking Bruno's arm and pointedly ignoring Gilles who was standing hesitantly at her side. 'I know most of the doctors around here, but not that man who went off in the ambulance.'

'It's a security matter,' Bruno said. 'The wounded man is some sort of high-up at Domme. I presume they have their own medics there.'

'Not that I've heard of,' said Fabiola. 'And I wouldn't take a resuscitation patient to Sarlat, it's no longer for serious patients these days. I would have taken him to Bergerac and given him a blood transfusion in the ambulance. Maybe they went to Sarlat for extra blood.'

'He said he was trying to call a chopper,' Bruno said, trying to keep the impatience from his voice. 'Did he seem like a real doctor to you?'

'Yes, but . . .' Fabiola paused. 'It just doesn't feel right.'

A group of gendarmes arrived from the rue Salamandre, led by a sergeant whom Bruno knew, and who asked for orders. Bruno asked him to keep the steps clear and then the Mayor returned and handed Bruno a pack of wet-wipes. He took two for himself to clean his hands and gave the rest to Fabiola, helped her clean up and asked if she could continue to take care of du Guesclin's daughter. Fabiola nodded dully in reply. Then he and Messager began taking the names and statements of the men dressed as soldiers, English and French, who had been part of the confused struggle where Kerquelin had fallen.

The third man he interviewed, dressed as an English soldier, was a professional actor in his forties who explained that he had been the coordinator of the day's battle scenes. He had a brisk, efficient manner, brown hair cut short and keen blue eyes with crinkles that suggested he smiled a lot. Or perhaps he was just making an effort to be pleasant.

'You don't know me, Monsieur Bruno,' he began, his voice affable but respectful. 'But I know you, and so do all the other people who are attached to the chateau of Castelnaud after you helped save the place from that forest fire. Thank you for that.'

He gave his name as Bernard Guyon, with an address in Bordeaux and a job each summer giving sword-fighting demonstrations at Castelnaud, the castle that boasted a museum of medieval warfare. The rest of the year, he said, he taught stage-fighting techniques at a theatre school in Bordeaux and directed fight scenes for TV and films. A man who took evident pride in his professional skills, he began by offering to help review any video of the event to see exactly what had gone wrong.

'It shouldn't have happened. Kerquelin was in good physical shape and a quick learner,' Guyon said. 'He told me that he used to wear the armour around the house and in his office to get accustomed to the weight. Of course, it wasn't the heavier armour they had back in the fourteenth century, thirty kilos and more, but it showed how seriously he took it. We must have spent hours on his swordplay. He even took up weightlifting to increase his upper arm strength.'

'Are accidents common in these re-enactments?' Bruno asked.

Guyon shook his head. 'Not if they're properly organized and the troops trained by people like me who know what they're doing. There's a drill: overhead downstroke right, overhead downstroke left, then leg stroke right, leg stroke left, and no thrusting. That's what causes accidents, not because you get stabbed in a thrust but you can lose your balance and fall over.

I've been doing this for more than twenty years and this is the first disaster I've seen.'

'Is there any way this could have been an accident?'

'I've been thinking about that,' Guyon replied. 'The answer is yes. It's not likely but it's certainly possible. I was against using that scene because of the steps and the crowd. Normally we prefer simple duels, one man against another. Crowd scenes can easily get out of control. But the director really wanted it, the massed fight on the steps. He said the different height of the steps would give the audience a sense of perspective. Anyway, after I'd given my warning as a professional the decision was his to make. So, yes, one of the actors could easily have tripped on the steps, cannoned into somebody else who was carrying a poignard, and if Kerquelin was doing an overhead stroke at the time, an accident could have happened. You can't rule it out.'

'If that happened, wouldn't the man with the poignard have known that he'd stabbed someone?' Bruno asked.

'You'd think so, but I know you were in the military so you'll understand that strange things happen in combat, even in mock-combat,' Guyon replied. 'Somebody cannons into you and you're off-balance, and maybe you're crossing swords with someone else and then you trip and put out an arm to save yourself. If there's a dagger in that hand ... well, you can imagine. You can get into a kind of mental overload and then it's easy to panic and not know what you're doing. It's like in real combat, some men freeze and some go berserk and win medals. That's why we do so many rehearsals.'

'How many people carried poignards?'

'Almost all of them but they were supposed to stay in their

scabbards. The knights on foot were carrying longswords, two-handers, but all the archers had some kind of long knife in their belts. In the fights I stage I always ban the use of a real knife in any kind of crowd scene. It's just too easy to have an accident, and I certainly didn't see anyone carrying one in their hand.'

'Am I right to presume that after your rehearsals you know all the men who were in the scuffle on the steps?'

'Indeed I do,' said Guyon, nodding cheerfully in his eagerness to help. 'Back in the changing room I have my stage directions and diagrams that show where each man should have been at each phase of the fight, both the English archers and the French knights. I know we started out in the right order, but then when Kerquelin's horse went down, he decided on his own to join the knights on foot, and that threw things off. I'd planned everything with just six knights on those steps and two civilians to join them at each side at the end, when the English tried to rally.'

'So Kerquelin shouldn't have been on the steps at all?' Bruno asked. 'I suppose that means if there was a deliberate attack on him it can't have been planned, it must have been more a seizing of an unexpected opportunity.' He scratched his head as another thought struck him. 'Could somebody else have been the knifeman's target and Kerquelin stabbed by mistake?'

'Not wearing that black surcoat that identified him as du Guesclin. We all knew that the only one wearing it was Kerquelin.'

'Did he have any enemies that you know of, men he might have quarrelled with?'

'No, he seemed to get on with everyone. After rehearsals

we'd usually have a drink together and we all liked to hear him talk about the mock battles he'd been in. Kerquelin was really keen on old warfare, all of it. He told me he'd tried it with seventeenth-century weapons in England, and he'd done re-enactments in America, of their own Civil War, where the women can get dressed up as Southern belles. He showed us a video of one of the mock battles in Virginia somewhere, all brilliantly organized with rows of tents and cannon. They even had a banjo band. He was one of a group who were trying to put together a future project for Roman legionaries under Julius Caesar fighting the Gauls at the battle of Alesia. Several of us were interested in that.'

Just then, Bruno saw J-J's portly figure making his way through the square towards him, Yves and the forensics team following in his wake. He turned back to Guyon. 'Could you go and get those diagrams you mentioned and can we present the chief detective in charge of this case with a list of all the men who were on the steps?'

'There were a couple of women there, too,' Guyon said. 'One of the milkmaids was supposed to hit an archer with her milking stool, and another one, a washerwoman, was there with the big pole she used to stir the linen in the wash tub. That was the stage director's idea.'

'Could you also find that director for me and bring him back here with your diagrams?' Bruno asked. Then he scribbled down Guyon's mobile phone number. 'Commissaire Jalipeau has arrived and he'll want to interview both of you. But thanks, Monsieur Guyon, you've been very helpful.'

Bruno turned to greet J-J and Yves, who headed the crime

scene and forensics teams. He explained briefly what he'd learned from Guyon and then his phone vibrated at his waist with the little green light that indicated the caller was on General Lannes's secure network.

'Bruno,' came Lannes's voice, 'I don't need to tell you that the need to avoid public embarrassment is the prime objective of any bureaucracy, the DGSE included. So rather than let them secure Kerquelin's house I'd like you to do it, and not let any of them inside to do any house-cleaning that might somehow lead to the disappearance of anything that could embarrass them. My people from Bordeaux will be with you in a couple of hours but get over there to his home and hold the fort. You're attached to the staff of the Minister of the Interior as of now and there's a letter being sent to your Mayor and to your own phone to say you are acting with his full authority, just in case Kerquelin's colleagues are a little too enthusiastic.'

'What's the address?' Bruno asked.

'He's in a manor house in some *lieu-dit* called Giverzac, just outside Domme. Call me when you get there.'

'I know it, the local tennis club is there. There's one problem, his daughter who lives with him. I presume you won't want her there while the search is going on.'

'I'm sure you can arrange something, Bruno. It's your turf, but securing that house is the priority. Take a look around once you get there, see if there are any signs of anyone else searching the place or any break-in. I very much doubt you'll find anything sensitive inside; Brice has been in this business too long for that.'

Once Lannes ended the call, Bruno told J-J that he'd need

a car to take him to Kerquelin's place. He then called Fabiola to make sure she was taking care of Kerquelin's daughter for the night.

'I'm with her now,' she said. 'I know Nadia from our executive women's group. We'll take care of her.'

'I knew I'd seen her somewhere before,' said Bruno. 'Fabiola, see if you can get hold of her brother and her mother. The parents are divorced but I think her mother lives in Paris. We might have to put Nadia up in St Denis for a couple of nights. I suspect the security services will be all over her home for a while.'

'That's fine,' Fabiola said. 'I presume you'll be stuck here on the police work. Call me when you can.'

Chapter 3

Kerquelin's house was a *gentilhommière*, a country house for the rural bourgeoisie. Its pleasing proportions suggested the place had been built in the eighteenth century, perhaps for a lawyer or doctor or some other local notable. Such buildings usually had four bedrooms upstairs, dining and sitting rooms, and a study or consulting room for clients or patients on the ground floor. Rooms for maids and servants would be in the attic. The kitchen, larders and wine cellar were below in a half-basement. The front garden was well planned with trellised roses, two lawns and box shrubs marking the stone path to the steps that rose to the double entrance doors at the front of the house. A gravel drive to the right led to stables and outbuildings. The front doors were locked and Bruno got no reply from his knocking. He went around the back, where the kitchen door was locked but there were shallow steps up to a terrace, where the latch that closed two French windows gave way to his knife. He went back out front to inform Gaston, one of J-J's detectives, who had given him a lift from Sarlat.

'Leave the car there, please, blocking the driveway,' Bruno said. 'And don't let anyone in. I mean anyone. Are you armed?'

Gaston stared at him, uncertain how to react. 'Sure, but the gun's locked in the safe in the back of the car. Regulations.'

'Please get it out, check the magazine and keep it ready,' said Bruno. 'Just in case.'

Gaston looked at him coolly and said, 'I know you're a friend of J-J but we're only supposed to unlock that safe when in imminent danger or under orders from a superior officer.'

Bruno pulled out his phone, opened the minister's letter of authorization that Lannes had sent him, showed it to Gaston and asked, 'Will this do? Or do you want me to call J-J while he's in the middle of a murder investigation?'

Gaston climbed out and opened the safe in the hatchback. He pulled out a standard Sig-Sauer handgun and inserted a magazine.

'Thank you,' said Bruno. 'I think it might be better if you waited outside the car. And, again, nobody gets in without my approval.'

He returned to the back of the house, pausing to look at an impressive *potager*, filled with lettuces, tomato plants and aubergines. Maybe forty metres away was a small single-storey house in Périgord style with its own *potager* and patio. No lights were showing. Maybe a place for a housekeeper or gardener, he thought.

Bruno went into the main house, relocking the door behind him. He went downstairs and began to search. The kitchen had been fully modernized with a Smeg stove and fridge, and there was a handsome old dresser against one wall. In a cupboard full of cleaning gear he found a pack of rubber gloves, and not having any evidence gloves in his pockets he pulled on a pair.

The larders were almost empty and the door to the wine cellar was locked. The dining room had a table that could seat a dozen people and another, even finer dresser, a serious antique. The sitting room had oriental rugs on the original wooden floor. The furniture consisted of two chaises longues and four Louis Seize armchairs. There was a pile of glossy art books on a low table, a handsome fireplace that seemed unused, and several generic landscapes on the walls. Above the fireplace was a charming eighteenth-century oil painting of a pretty young woman on a garden swing being pushed by an admiring beau who wore knee britches and a tricorn hat.

In the hall was a row of portraits of men in uniform from each of the world wars, another from the Franco-Prussian war and two more from Napoleonic times. There was one general, three colonels, one major and a very young lieutenant, with a caption painted in black script along the bottom of the frame to say that the lieutenant had been born in 1892 and died in 1914. The moustachioed man in the last of the portraits was on a horse and wearing a cloak that marked him as an officer in one of the Spahi light-cavalry regiments the French raised in North Africa. Kerquelin either came from a prosperous and successful old military family, or he wanted to suggest such an auspicious ancestry to his visitors.

The study contained a fine old desk, wide enough for two to work at it, a chair at each side. It held a big Apple computer and a small, government-issue laptop which looked identical to the highly secured one that he'd seen his former lover Isabelle use on her occasional visits to the Périgord. It came with her job, running the security-coordinating committee for France and her European partners, with one office in Brussels and another in Paris.

One of the photos on the desk, each of them in a silver frame, was of Nadia, and another of a young man who could have been her brother. A third photo showed a tall, middle-aged man, his arm around each of the two young people. That must be Kerquelin. There was a fourth, of another attractive young woman in a sailing boat, her dark hair blowing in the wind, her shoulders tanned. On it was scrawled a line with a felt-tip pen, *Cher Papa, bisous, Claire*. Did Kerquelin have another daughter?

On the walls were old glass-fronted bookcases, rather than plebeian shelves. They held matching leather-backed sets of Dumas, Victor Hugo, Montaigne and Proust. A similar bookcase on the opposite wall held leather-backed editions of Shakespeare, Gibbon, Dickens and Conan Doyle. He opened that one and leafed through two of the books. They were in English. Another shelf held editions of Goethe, Schiller and Thomas Mann, all in German. Volumes of Clausewitz on war and Bismarck's memoirs looked wellused.

There were two new-looking books in French, one by a man called Thomas Kerquelin, *The Future of French Energy Policy*. The flap copy said the author had studied engineering at the *polytechnique* and had just retired as one of the directors of Electricité de France. The photo of the elderly author bore a strong resemblance to the photo of Kerquelin. Perhaps it was Brice Kerquelin's father.

The other book was also by a Kerquelin, but this time an older woman called Clarisse, and from the biographical note beneath her photo she had taught feminist history at the University of

Vincennes. She was the author of a book that Bruno had heard of, but not read: *Pourquoi la France est Femme*: Why France is a Woman – a study of the symbols of France through the ages, apparently by Kerquelin's mother.

Bruno scanned the flap copy. Why did Germany have a Fatherland and the United States Uncle Sam and Britain's symbol was John Bull, but France had la Patrie? Why was the symbol of La République always a young woman named Marianne? Why did no other country name its symbol of patriotic courage for a young woman, while France had Joan of Arc? Interesting questions, thought Bruno, which made him ponder once again something that had often struck him on his visits to the decorated caves of his region: why was it that almost all modern sexual graffiti portrayed the penis, while those of France's prehistoric caves repeatedly featured the female pubic triangle?

The biographical note said that the author was the wife of Thomas Kerquelin and the mother of Brice, who was described as 'a leading French internet pioneer in Silicon Valley'. Well, well, Bruno thought, Brice had done more in his life than state security and intelligence. Bruno wondered if the parents were still alive, and if so that Lannes might be able to inform them before the news of their son's fate became public.

Another antique cabinet had been converted to hold files, mostly personal ones: insurance, banking, household bills and the like. One was marked 'Divorce', and contained some wedding photographs of a much younger Kerquelin and a very pretty young woman, photos of her pregnant, and with small children, vacation snapshots of the family on beaches and ski

37

slopes. The divorce had taken place three years earlier, when the two children were grown. There was a copy of a property agreement in which Kerquelin kept the house in Domme and his wife kept the apartment on the rue Truffaut in the newly fashionable Batignolles district of Paris, just west of Montmartre and the Sacre-Cœur. They also shared the use of a holiday home near Dinan in Brittany.

That sounded amicable enough, thought Bruno, until he saw a copy of the divorce court's ruling that Kerquelin's wife had been responsible for the break-up of the marriage by 'a serious and renewed violation of the duties and obligations of marriage, making the maintenance of a shared life intolerable'. The uncommon ruling stemmed from the husband's claim that the wife had for almost a year been refusing his sexual advances. He knew that a similar divorce case had recently been upheld by the Cour de Cassation, France's highest court of appeal. Women's groups had been outraged by the decision, which was based on two articles in the Code Civile, first enacted by Napoleon in 1804, which stated that spouses must 'pledge mutual help, respect, fidelity and a communal life'. Kerquelin's wife's counter-claim that her husband had been guilty of repeated infidelities had been rejected by the court for lack of evidence. That must have made quite a stir among their colleagues at La Piscine, Bruno thought.

The next file he looked at was labelled 'Testament'. It contained one folder that named as Kerquelin's trustees his mother, his daughter Nadia, the mysterious Claire, General Lannes and an Angus McDermott with an address in San Francisco. Neither his son nor his ex-wife were mentioned. Two lawyers were listed, one in Paris and another in New York. Four investment accounts were listed: one in Pierre, in the American state of South Dakota; another in Wilmington, Delaware, also in the United States; a third in Luxembourg; and a fourth in Taipei, the main city in Taiwan. This seemed very complicated for an employee of the French state, even in the intelligence services. On an impulse, Bruno pulled out his phone and took photos of these documents.

Bruno then found several family photo albums on the lower shelf, one of them marked 'Claire'. He opened it to see a photograph of a much younger Kerquelin, probably in his twenties, standing beside an attractive young woman with lustrous black hair and dark eyes who was several months pregnant. His right hand was on her swollen belly, his left around her shoulders hugging her to him. They both looked very happy. Then there were photos of a newborn baby girl, more of the same woman breastfeeding the baby, and then more photos of the baby growing, becoming a toddler, starting to crawl and to walk. There was a photo of mother and child on an outing in an American sports car, the mother offering a hot dog to the little girl in the parking lot of some fast-food joint in what looked to be California or maybe Hawaii.

There were more framed photos on the lowest shelf, mostly of Kerquelin's time in California. One portrayed him and some other young men holding a banner marked Stanford. Others showed him with some young faces Bruno recognized, including Steve Jobs of Apple, Bill Gates of Microsoft, and another of Kerquelin opening a large bottle of Champagne with some other young men beneath a banner reading 'Google is born – September 4, 1998'. There were more official photos of him in France, shaking hands with Jacques Chirac at the Elysée, and with presidents Sarkozy, Hollande and Macron.

Above this cabinet hung a shield bearing a double-headed black eagle with red beaks and claws, beneath it the name Du Guesclin, with a birthplace of Motte-Broons, Bretagne. On top of the cabinet itself was a bust of a plump-faced man with short, curly hair. An engraved plate below said it was a copy of the head above Bertrand du Guesclin's tomb in the royal Basilica of Saint-Denis outside Paris, a likeness commissioned by King Charles V. Bruno pursed his lips; Kerquelin evidently took his supposed link to the fourteenth-century French hero very seriously indeed. The connection might even be genuine. The name Guesclin sounded to Bruno like a Frenchified version of the old Breton name of Kerquelin.

Upstairs had been modernized. Each of the four bedrooms now had its own bathroom. The master bedroom was for Kerquelin, and bore no sign of a woman's presence. The waste-paper basket beside the small desk was empty and the main drawer contained only pens and virgin notepads. One lower drawer held maps and tourist brochures about the Périgord. Another held assorted plugs to convert to British, Swiss and American electrical grids. The drawer of the bedside table held massage oil, condoms, packs of tissues, a book of expert sudoku games, half completed, and a well-thumbed guidebook to Taiwan.

What looked to be the daughter's room was pleasantly messy, with a lovely, springlike scent that lingered. There was a crammed bookcase and several opened books on a desk, another on the bed and more on the floor with bookmarks between the pages. The one on the bed was an illustrated work on the frescoes in Périgord churches. What clearly was the son's bedroom looked unused since schooldays, full of sporting trophies, framed photos of soccer and swimming teams, framed paintings of sailing boats. The spare bedroom looked anonymous, as bland as a hotel room. In the attic he found a small gym, a games room with a big TV screen on the wall, a bar, comfortable modern sofas – and a locked door that he could not open.

Bruno went back down to the study and looked more closely at the big desk. The drawers were unlocked and revealed the usual office tools: staplers, pens, engraved notepaper, envelopes. There were several box files on a bookcase, one of personal letters, another of Christmas cards, and another titled 'Investments'. It contained only names, phone numbers and email addresses of banks, accountants and investment advisers in Paris, Geneva, New York and London. There was no indication of how much money Kerquelin controlled.

On a lower shelf were more box files, the first titled 'Sarlat', which seemed to concern the mock battle. The second was identified as 'Sealed Knot' and the third, 'PA Volunteers'. This turned out to be a regiment of Civil War enthusiasts in Pennsylvania of whom Kerquelin had been a member. There were photos of him dressed in a dark blue federal uniform and carrying a musket, others with him beside some wheeled cannon. The Sealed Knot file referred to an English group that re-enacted the battles of Oliver Cromwell's New Model Army in Parliament's wars against King Charles in the 1640s. Again, it contained photos of Kerquelin, with a pike, another with a matchlock musket, and on horseback, wearing a breastplate and a lobster helmet, so named for the long lobster-like tail that covered the back of the neck.

A serious enthusiast in three different countries, Bruno thought to himself, wondering why Kerquelin had chosen this form of play-acting rather than following the family tradition of a military career. The man was in his fifties, so born sometime in the late 1960s. Perhaps he had been at university when the Berlin Wall came down. That was a time when the military may have had less appeal than a career in intelligence. Another box file was marked GCHQ and when he opened it Bruno found mementos and photos of Kerquelin's time at Cheltenham in England, where he had spent 2005 at Britain's government communications headquarters, which was their equivalent of the kind of work that Kerquelin and his colleagues were involved in at Domme. Another box file was marked NSA, and carried souvenirs of the year he had spent at Fort Meade, Maryland, with the much larger American version, the National Security Agency. Presumably they were also the years that he took part in the military re-enactments.

There was yet another file, marked BND, which testified to the year he had spent at Pullach, near Munich, with the Bundesnachrichtendienst, the Federal Intelligence Service, before it moved its headquarters to Berlin in 2017. There did not seem to have been any German re-enactment group that had appealed to him. From the evidence of the bookshelves, however, it would seem that Kerquelin was fluent in German as well as English. The man seemed to have been some kind of roving ambassador for this arm of French intelligence and his fate would probably start alarm bells ringing in Berlin, London and Washington, or at least provoke some questions. Of course, that was why General Lannes had wanted Bruno to get to Kerquelin's house first, so that the routine checks would be made by his own team rather than by Kerquelin's colleagues in the DGSE.

Suddenly the blare of a car horn broke into his thoughts, sounding very close. Leaving the front door locked he went out through the back and peeked out to see a big black Renault trying to enter the property, its path blocked by Gaston's vehicle. There was a man at the wheel, two more in the back and a woman who emerged from the front passenger seat, marching angrily to Gaston's car as the horn continued to blare. She gave a curt wave of her hand and the horn went silent.

'Who the hell are you?' she demanded of Gaston, who was standing beside a tree in the garden, his gun held discreetly by his thigh.

'Police Nationale, and on the orders of the Minister of the Interior no one is to enter,' Gaston said.

'We're DGSE, the owner of this house, and the Interior Ministry does not have authority over us,' she said, and made another gesture at the black Renault. The two men emerged from the back of the car and came up to stand beside her. Big and burly enough for a rugby team, they were wearing jeans and denim shirts beneath quilted jackets. If they were armed, their weapons had not been drawn. Bruno ducked back behind the side of the house, pulled out his phone and called General Lannes. The duty officer told him to stay on the line. When he was put through to Lannes, Bruno explained the situation.

43

The general told him to keep the line open and check the documents of the newcomers.

'*Bonjour messieurs-dame*,' Bruno said, emerging from cover, the phone to his ear. 'I'm Bruno Courrèges, chief of police for the Vézère valley, and I'm acting under the orders of General Lannes for the Minister of the Interior. I'm sorry, but nobody is allowed in here until his team arrives. May I see your identification, please?'

The woman was in her thirties, perhaps a little older, with well-cut black hair, a clear, slightly tanned complexion, and no make-up. Strongly built and looking as if she kept herself fit, she was wearing a dark blue trouser suit, flat shoes and a plain white blouse. When she pulled from her jacket pocket a DGSE identity card with its red, white and blue stripes, Bruno saw that her nails had been recently manicured.

'Commissaire Marie-Dominique Pantin,' he read aloud from her card, the phone still to his ear.

'I'm head of security at Domme, and we are here to secure the home of our colleague, Directeur-Adjoint Kerquelin,' she said.

'Let me speak to her,' came Lannes's voice in Bruno's ear. He handed her the phone, saying, 'General Lannes, Madame Pantin.'

'Mademoiselle,' she corrected him, putting the phone to her ear.

He could only hear her side of the conversation, which was mainly monosyllabic, except for one '*Bien entendu*' and a final '*D'accord, mon général*', before she handed Bruno back his phone.

'Your orders are unchanged, Bruno,' said the General. 'You stay there and allow nobody in until Jules Rossigny gets there from Bordeaux with his team. You know him, I believe. Commissaire Pantin and her team will await their arrival and she's contacting La Piscine for further orders. I've already spoken with them so you won't have any trouble. She will accompany Rossigny as he makes his inventory and I presume she'll make her own. Please call me when Rossigny arrives.'

Bruno tapped his phone off and apologized to Commissaire Pantin. She nodded and said, 'You're friends with Isabelle Perrault, aren't you?'

'Yes,' he replied cautiously. He and Isabelle were much more than friends, with a complicated history that had included a passionate summer affair, an abortion that he'd only learned of after the event, some happy reunions, depressing partings and a shared basset hound. 'Do you know her from Paris or when she was with the police here in Périgueux?'

'In Paris, where we have a group of women in this business who get together every week or so for dinners, mutual support and commiserations about the men we have to work with.' Her eyes sparkled with humour as she spoke the last phrase. 'She says you're an exception and that you're a good cook.'

Bruno replied, 'Did she tell you about Balzac, the dog we share?'

'Yes, she had us all in fits of laughter about that weekend when you took him to his first mating. She even gave a fine rendition of his amorous howl. Now that I'm based down here, I'd like to be put on the list for one of his next litter of puppies.'

'Done,' he replied, then changed the subject. 'You must have known Kerquelin.'

'A little. I've only had this job for a couple of months. I

thought you were based in St Denis – you're a bit out of your territory.'

'Along with hundreds of other spectators I was in Sarlat at the event when Kerquelin was injured. I got roped in to keep order and then to help collect evidence in that golden hour immediately after the event that they lectured us about at the police academy. Then General Lannes told me to come here and hold the fort.'

'Isabelle tells me he's always trying to get you out of here and up to his team in Paris, but you won't leave the Périgord.'

He shrugged. 'I couldn't keep my dog in Paris, it wouldn't be fair. And I couldn't keep my horse, my geese and chickens, let alone my truffle trees and my garden and I'd miss all my friends. For me Paris holds few attractions compared to all that. Maybe you'll feel the same way. Domme is a great place to be, one of the greatest views in France, with Sarlat just up the road.'

'I'm still settling into the job so I haven't had much time for tourism yet and I don't really know anybody local except for colleagues, so I'm pleased to meet you. Isabelle says you know everybody.'

'Hardly, but when this business is over I hope you'll come to dinner and meet some colleagues and friends, policewomen, magistrates and so on.'

'Thank you, I'd like that. In the meantime we have this emergency. All I know is that Kerquelin was stabbed at some battle re-enactment in Sarlat and it looks like foul play. So I was sent to babysit his house until colleagues come down from Paris to help look through his archives and make sure there's nothing troubling. I imagine the General's people will be doing the same thing.'

Bruno nodded, pulled out his wallet and handed her a card with his numbers and email address. 'I don't think there's any need for me to stay once Rossigny gets here but let me know how to reach you and hopefully we'll get together soon.'

'My friends call me Marie-Do,' she replied, handing him a card of her own, which carried only a mobile phone number and an email address, with no hint of her affiliation to French intelligence. 'In the meantime, Bruno, what can you tell me about what happened?'

'It's not really clear,' he said. 'He was stabbed through a gap in his armour in the course of a scuffle which did not go according to the stage director's well-rehearsed plan. The problem was that Kerquelin's horse slipped and fell, he got off, and instead of riding around waving his sword heroically, he pushed his way into a sword fight on some steps and you could see people stumbling and slipping. So it may have been an accident, or maybe someone seized the opportunity to try to kill him. At this stage I don't think we can call it a planned attack. Apparently one of your doctors, named Barrat, was with him when he left in the ambulance, trying to keep him alive with a transfusion and oxygen.'

'I know Barrat,' she said. 'He's one of ours. Who's running the investigation?'

'Commissaire Jalipeau, head of detectives, is in charge of the investigation. He's a good man, if old-school in his ways, but don't let that crumpled look mislead you. Once he hears you're a friend of Isabelle, he'll be very helpful. She was his favourite detective and he's always hoped that she'd come back to succeed him some day.'

Marie-Do laughed and rolled her eyes. 'Fat chance. Isabelle has her eyes set a lot higher than that. She loves being in Paris and it suits her, and she's good at what she does, even the international diplomacy part of it. That's something that would drive me crazy.'

'Kerquelin was into some of that,' Bruno said. 'He did some year-long exchanges with the NSA in the States, GCHQ in Britain and with the Germans, almost like being a kind of diplomat. In the UK and US he got involved with local re-enactors of battles. It seems to have been a long-time hobby.'

'I've heard about that,' Marie-Do replied, nodding. 'I know that a couple of colleagues from Domme signed up to join him at this Sarlat event, so we'd better look into that.'

'Is there anything about Kerquelin's work here that you feel able to share that might shed some light onto his wounding?' Bruno assumed that the wound had been fatal but did not want to tempt fate.

'Too soon to say, but let's keep in touch,' she replied, as Rossigny's car rolled up and he came out to wave at Bruno. 'I'll tell you what I can and trust you'll do the same.'

'Yes, but you have an institution to protect and I don't,' Bruno replied.

Marie-Do threw him an amused glance and almost laughed as she said, 'It's so refreshing to encounter such innocence in this world. You might want to think about why Lannes has the reputation of being the most assiduous empire-builder since Genghis Khan.'

'I think he'd probably be flattered to hear that, but in the meantime, while you're searching here, you might want to start with the locked room in the attic, which seemed like the only secured space in the house.'

'How long were you here, Bruno, before we turned up?' Marie-Do asked as Rossigny joined them, shaking hands politely.

'I was here for forty minutes or so before you got here,' he told them. 'General Lannes asked me to look around for any signs of a break-in. I saw nothing obvious but the latch on the French windows was easily lifted. By the way, Kerquelin's daughter, Nadia, knows of his injury and is staying tonight with a friend, Fabiola, a doctor in St Denis. You may be able to track down his ex-wife and his son who is on vacation somewhere. They should be informed.'

'Suzanne, his ex-wife, is a colleague and friend of mine and of Isabelle,' Marie-Do said. 'She has already been informed and she's trying to track down her son while getting down here as fast as she can. I think you can leave this to us now, Bruno, while Rossigny and I get to work.'

Chapter 4

The next morning, Bruno rose at six, took Balzac for the usual morning run, showered, shaved and left some fresh eggs and a note for Alain and Rosalie who were still asleep. They were staying with him for the weekend while house-hunting. He drove to the Moulin to buy croissants and a *pain*, the largest size of baguette, for breakfast with Fabiola and Gilles at their house. It was a place he knew well since Pamela had lived there in the days of their affair, before she bought the riding school. Like Pamela before them, Fabiola and Gilles rented out the other small houses in the grounds as *gîtes* for tourists. Two of them were playing on the grass tennis court where Bruno had first become friendly with Pamela. Houses, he reflected, could be potent triggers of memory.

He knocked at the kitchen door and heard Gilles's voice telling him to come in. Gilles was in a dressing gown and making coffee. Fabiola, dressed for work, was squeezing oranges in a hand press and Nadia was seated at the table, wearing a tracksuit he recognized as Fabiola's. Of course she would have needed a change of clothes; on the previous evening she had been wearing a costume. She had a copy of that day's *Sud Ouest* open before her, a double-page spread on what it called

50

'The Tragedy of Sarlat'. She lifted her head just as a beam of sunshine crept through the kitchen window and lit her red hair into glorious colour.

'Croissants,' exclaimed Fabiola as he put the paper bag on the table. 'Bruno, you're a hero. I was about to grill the last of yesterday's bread.' She bent to greet his dog. '*Bonjour*, Balzac. Toasted baguette for you and a corner of my croissant. Oh, and Bruno, I called the hospital in Sarlat when I got back last night. They know the doctor who took in the wounded man, Jean-Paul Barrat. He picked up some extra plasma there and took him to Bergerac still alive, so there's hope. They will call me with any news.'

She broke off and glanced at Nadia, who was focused on Balzac. Fabiola shrugged and fell silent, then looked down as Balzac gave her leg an amiable rub of greeting with the side of his head, did the same to Gilles and then advanced on Nadia, the stranger. He stood with one front paw raised, his head in the air, sniffing delicately at the hand she stretched out and then giving it a brief lick before curling up at her feet as if he'd known her for years.

'What a lovely dog,' said Nadia as Bruno set out plates and knives and handed Fabiola a jar of his own apricot jam that he'd brought from home. Nadia then looked a little nervously at Bruno, who was in uniform, and asked, 'Is this an official visit?'

'No, not really,' he replied, trying to give her a reassuring smile. 'It's what I wear to save money on my own clothes.' There were dark shadows beneath her eyes, standing out against the pearl-white skin that she would need to protect against even the weakest sun. 'I came to see how you were and to offer my sympathies. And your godfather, General Lannes, sends his best wishes. I gather he and your father are close friends.'

'Uncle Vincent,' she said, nodding. 'I've known him since I was a baby. He used to take me to Les Trois Vallées every year to teach me how to ski until I started at university. Is he coming down here?'

'I don't know,' said Bruno, concealing his surprise at this unexpected side of the powerful and intimidating General Lannes. 'I got the impression that your father's injury is making a stir in Paris that might keep him up there for the time being.'

Nadia nodded, her face darkening as though a cloud had passed across it, damping down the resilience of youth.

'Yes, Paris and its politics and security always seemed to have an extra place at our dinner table, and breakfast, too,' she said. 'Do you have any news of my father's condition or is that a state secret?' She gave a half-smile to take any sting from the words.

'I know no more than Fabiola,' Bruno replied, trying to give her a sympathetic smile and understanding that she would be accustomed to the security blanket around her father. 'Naturally I'd like to know whether you can tell us anything about what happened, but there's no hurry. Your mother has been told and I think she'll be here later today. And if you have any idea where we might find your brother . . .' His voice trailed off.

'I emailed him so I should get a reply sometime today, but he might well be at sea. He's a competitive yachtsman, obsessed with it and always has been since he was a little boy. He'd rather be out on the ocean than do anything else,' she said. She drank deeply of the glass of orange juice Fabiola passed to her and then reached for one of the croissants Bruno had brought.

'Thank you for this, I was starving. Do you know when we might be able to go back to the house? Even if I can't stay there I'll need clothes and things. Oh, yes, and I also emailed Claire, my half-sister,' Nadia went on. 'Papa is her father, too, from when he was in California. That's where she lives. She texted me that she was getting a direct overnight flight to Paris. We're close because she came to live with us when Papa was assigned over there and Suzanne decided to stay in Paris for her career. Claire is ten years older than me and so she became part-*maman* and part-big-sister. She should arrive in Bordeaux just before noon today and she'll probably hire a car.'

'Is she an American?' Gilles asked.

'Dual nationality,' Nadia replied. 'Her French is just like Papa's. She even uses his old eighties slang.'

'Your father has some photos of himself, much younger, in Silicon Valley with some of the big names of the internet,' said Bruno. 'Was that when Claire was born?'

'Yes, but he and Claire's mother never married,' Nadia said. 'Papa was doing a graduate degree in computing at Stanford and got involved in the Mozilla team that became Netscape. He persuaded his parents to invest. Then he was in at the launch of Google. That was when Suzanne turned up to check him out after a computing magazine did a piece about this young French guy who was suddenly a serious player in Silicon Valley. She saw how much money he'd made and got pregnant with my brother as the dot-com boom turned into a bust. That was just before the Millennium and they came home to France, got married and Uncle Vincent got Chirac to persuade Papa that it was his patriotic duty to haul French intelligence into the twenty-first century.'

'Should you be telling us all this?' Bruno asked.

'It will probably all be in the papers soon, except maybe for Suzanne's role,' said Nadia. She finished off the croissant, swallowed as she washed it down with coffee, and then asked, 'Do you want to question me here or do we have to go somewhere formal? And when might I be able to see Papa?'

'That's up to the medics,' said Bruno. 'Did you have a clear view of the scuffle when your father was stabbed?'

'No, I only heard about the accident when someone called for a doctor,' she replied. 'What do you know so far?'

'Not much,' Bruno replied. 'I'm going to the *commissariat* in Périgueux later this morning where we'll be reviewing all the videos that the police have managed to collect so far. We're still trying to work out what happened. Some of the experts who planned the re-enactment said it might have been an accident when your father had to adapt after his horse went down.'

'I didn't see any of that. I was over on the other side, outside the tavern, in my role of helping to get the English soldiers too drunk to fight. I didn't know anything had happened until I heard somebody shouting for people to stand back and even then I didn't know it was Papa ...' She broke off and then added, 'You know that the tourist board had a couple of cameras filming the whole thing?'

'No, but I'm sure the detectives will have them, and there was an appeal on the radio this morning for people with video on their phones to come forward.' Bruno turned to Gilles, who was making another pot of coffee. 'How about you, Gilles? Did you get anything useful on your phone?'

Gilles shook his head. 'I doubt it. All I filmed was a confused scuffle in the distance. But I already emailed what I had to that address J-J announced last night.'

'I gather your father has a lot of experience in these re-enactments,' Bruno said to Nadia.

'Yes, he loves doing them. He's taken part in seventeenth-century battles in England and American Civil War ones when we lived over there. He wanted to take part in the two-hundredth anniversary of Waterloo but couldn't get enough time off for all the rehearsals they wanted.'

'Really?' said Gilles, a glint in his eye that Bruno recognized as a reporter's instinct. 'Would you have any photos of him at those other battles?'

'Dad has whole albums of them at home,' Nadia replied. 'He keeps them in what he calls his war room up in the attic, a big table where he re-creates battle scenes.' She smiled fondly. 'The one time I saw him really angry was when my brother and I got into his war room, this was in America, and began playing with the toy soldiers. He wasn't angry with us for moving them out of place, more with himself for leaving the door unlocked. And the three of us then had a great afternoon with his books about the battle and putting the soldiers back in their right place. I remember it well; he had set up Chancellorsville, Stonewall Jackson's finest battle, and he died after it by accident, shot in the night by his own men.'

She was animated, almost lively as she remembered moments shared with her father. Bruno warmed to her, looked again at her face and saw it light up as she smiled to enjoy her memories. It was a moment when she became striking, individual and lovely in her way. Wonderful, he thought, the many ways women could soar through every first impression and become intriguing.

Nadia was still smiling but a tear had formed in her eye, poised to trickle down her cheek. 'He took us to Civil War battlefields – Manassas and Gettysburg, Fredericksburg, Antietam.' She raised her hand to brush the tear away. 'It was a strange childhood but I enjoyed it, more than my brother did. I think it was Dad's way of getting us to share his passion for history, urging us to read books and maps, learning how long it took to walk from one part of a battlefield to another, how tired and thirsty you could get, and how easy it was to get lost.'

'He sounds like an interesting man,' said Fabiola. She stood up, explaining that she had to get to the clinic by the time it opened at eight.

'Nadia may have to stay here another night or so, if that's possible,' Bruno said. 'Given her father's job, there's a security flap at the house, checking that there's no secret material.'

'Domme,' murmured Gilles, that glint in his eyes again. 'That means Frenchelon, our secret listening post we humble citizens are not meant to know about. People in Paris must be getting nervous.'

Fabiola gave him a brisk kiss on the cheek and a fond look as she grabbed her bag and car keys and headed for the door. 'Nadia, you are very welcome to stay here as long as you like, your sister too, if you don't mind sharing a room. And don't let

Gilles interrogate you. There's nothing that man won't do for a double-page spread in *Paris Match*. Consider yourself warned,' she said, about to close the door behind her. 'Bruno, can I talk to you for a minute?'

'Do you really write for *Paris Match*?' Nadia asked Gilles as Bruno and Fabiola left. 'I virtually learned to read from it. My mother got it every week, wherever we were in the world. Even before I could read I was fascinated by the photos.'

Fabiola was leaning against the door of her car, arms crossed beneath her breasts and looking fierce.

'What is all this bullshit, Bruno?' she said in a quiet but angry voice. 'I didn't want to upset Nadia but the ambulance didn't go to the hospital in Bergerac after picking up the plasma. It went to that secret place at Domme. They seem to have some kind of clinic where that doctor, Barrat, is apparently in charge. Nor did they go to the hospital in Périgueux, even though Sarlat had called them to set up the intensive care unit. My friends at Périgueux tell me they heard there was a special helicopter laid on but it took him instead to the secure wing at the Piqué military hospital outside Bordeaux.'

'That's news to me,' Bruno said, his eyes widening as he heard this. 'All I know is that Kerquelin is a high-up in French intelligence, a top-level computer expert, and by the time I got to his house the Interior Ministry was taking charge of things. The important thing is that he seems to still be alive.'

'That's what I find very hard to believe,' Fabiola snapped. 'From the amount of blood he lost, a major artery, probably the aorta, had been punctured. Repairing that probably means open heart surgery and an artificial pump to maintain blood flow. Putting such a patient on an hour-long helicopter flight would be unforgivable. I don't care how important he is to our so-called security services.'

Stunned by this tirade which seemed directed more at herself than at him, Bruno had no idea what to say.

'Do you have medical contacts in Bordeaux who might—' he began hesitantly.

'I blame myself,' she went on, ignoring his remark. 'I should never have let Barrat take charge like that, even though he said Kerquelin was his patient.'

'I'm sorry you're so upset by this,' he said. 'Perhaps I should have stepped in, but between two doctors . . .' His voice trailed off.

'It's not just that,' she said grimly. 'It's Gilles. He wants to go off to Ukraine again. Ever since he did that interview with the TV star who was running for the presidency, he thinks he owns that story, and the Ukrainians want him back again for something. I hate it.'

'Well, Gilles has made that story his own, ever since his reporting on the battle in Maidan Square where this all began, back in 2014.'

'You mean that terrible two days when I didn't know if he was alive or dead or if I'd ever learn what happened to him?' she demanded, her voice rising.

'None of us will forget that,' Bruno said. 'But that's Gilles. He's a journalist, it's what he does. And that's part of what makes him the man you love.'

She rolled her eyes at him, jerked open the car door, installed herself, slammed the car door and drove off, the electric motor

58

of her Renault Zoe unable to relieve her feelings with the roar of a conventional engine – but gravel flew as she raced off up the drive.

Back in the kitchen, Bruno found Gilles talking of his time at *Paris Match*, happily unaware of Fabiola's outburst.

'I'm freelance now, but I still write for them from time to time,' he was saying. 'I was with *Libération* before that, which was how I first met Bruno, in Sarajevo.'

'How did you come to settle down here?' Nadia asked.

'I came down for *Paris Match* to cover some Satanist goings-on around the death of a young heiress, and found myself re-united with Bruno. Then I met the beautiful Dr Fabiola and lost my heart to her and to this region. By good luck I then got a contract to write a book and here we are. The best decision I ever made. How about you, Nadia? Are you entranced by our glorious Périgord?'

'Domme is certainly the loveliest place we've ever lived and I'm fascinated by the valley and all the history and the pre-history, but it's very quiet out of season and crammed with tourists in summer. I'm only there during vacations. Most of the time I'm at university in Bordeaux.'

'What are you studying?'

'Philosophy, history and literature, and don't say that I'll never get a job with that or you'll sound just like my mother.'

'That's what I studied and it served me well,' said Gilles.

'I gather you'll be seeing your mother today,' Bruno said. 'That should be a comfort.'

'You think?' Nadia replied drily, rolling her eyes and leaving little doubt that her relations with her mother were not close.

'Have you not seen much of her since the divorce?' Bruno asked.

'About as much as I could stand. We weren't a happy family and she wasn't exactly cut out to be a mother. I always had to call her Suzanne, never Maman. I was never sure whether she really wanted to have been born a man or whether it was just part of her need to compete with my father. She wants to be the queen bee of French intelligence and couldn't bear the thought of Dad beating her to it.'

Gilles glanced across at Bruno, his eyes wide in surprise. Bruno was at a loss for a reply to Nadia, so he simply raised his eyebrows.

'They even competed for us,' Nadia went on, a chill in her tone. 'So I became Papa's girl and Richard became Mama's boy. My father and I always called him Richard, but she tried to insist on Ricky. Anyway, Richard and I aren't that close and my relations with Suzanne are no more than correct, sometimes not even that.'

She looked up at Bruno defiantly. 'So, I'm not looking forward to seeing her again and dealing with her obsessive need to take charge of everything. Many of my happy memories are in that house with Papa. He's a big man with a wonderful deep laugh and sometimes I thought the whole house would shake with it. My best memory of childhood is being held in his arms against that enormous chest while he laughed. I called it a Papa-quake, like an earthquake only comforting.'

This time, more than a single tear seemed to come to her eyes and she took a paper napkin from her plate and blew her nose loudly and thoroughly, not discreet feminine dabs at her nostrils but in an almost boyish way that made Bruno want to smile. It made him think of the girls he'd trained on the local rugby team.

'Do you know what you want to do after you graduate from university?' Bruno asked. 'From what I saw in the pageant yesterday, I think you could do very well as an actress.'

'Oh no, not that. I want to teach, research, spend a lot of time in libraries, have lots of dogs and raise my children like my dad did. Suzanne wants me to join the family business, as she calls La Piscine, and follow in her careerist footsteps.' Nadia shook her head. 'No way.'

'Well, if you've been raised to be so clear about fulfilling your own goals, maybe your parents didn't do a bad job,' said Gilles. 'It's the fate of being a parent to give the kids something to rebel against.'

Nadia shrugged and muttered, 'Suzanne certainly succeeded in that.'

'Does your brother feel the same way,' Gilles asked, 'or does he go along with her ambitions for him?'

'It's too soon to tell but I get the impression that Richard is breaking away, spending less and less time at her place in Paris,' she said. 'He's always been into sailing and he's been crewing on an ocean racer out of Brest, dreaming of competing in the America's Cup. So he's moving out of her clutches and more recently when we see each other we get along fine.'

'Did you ever go along with your father, re-enacting the various battles?' Gilles asked.

'Not to go camping with him under canvas with the other soldiers,' she replied. 'Suzanne wouldn't have that – not at all the right thing for a well brought up young girl. We'd go out for the day and watch – what little we could see with all the gunpowder smoke. The parades were fun, and when the soldiers were lining up for battle, and going around the camps where a lot of the wives and girlfriends of the volunteers were dressed up in period costume. They had drummers and bands. In England, one of the battles was the siege of a stately home, which was more Suzanne's idea of a good day out. She pulled some strings to get a letter of introduction to the milord who owned the place and got herself invited to lunch, so I was able to have a picnic with Papa. We were on a rug in the camp and he was dressed like one of Oliver Cromwell's Puritan soldiers.'

She smiled fondly at the memory. 'That was a lovely day.'

'What would you think of my writing a piece about your father's re-enactments for *Paris Match*?' Gilles asked her. 'With some of your photos. It could make a great spread, this guy at the heart of France's secrets but his hobby is the ancient battlefields. I'd need your help but it may have to wait a bit because I'm flying to Ukraine tomorrow.'

'Let's see what happens with Papa,' she replied. 'But don't say a word to Suzanne, if you meet her. What's happening in Ukraine? I thought that war had died down.'

'I'm not sure, but I got a call from a guy I know on the president's staff in Kyiv. He was being very cagey but he said it would be worth my while.'

'Did you write the piece about the guy who became president after playing one on TV, like a Slavic version of *West Wing*? I remember it.'

'Yes, that was me,' Gilles began, and Bruno took his leave, saying he was expected at police headquarters in Périgueux, and left Gilles, Nadia and Balzac to their breakfast.

Chapter 5

J-J had taken over the big conference room at the police *commissariat* and three male and three female officers in uniform were sitting in front of separate screens, scanning videos. J-J had an even bigger screen to himself, or rather to himself and Guyon, the stage-fight consultant Bruno had met the previous day. On the whiteboard that covered an entire wall, someone had drawn a map of the Sarlat main square, showing the location of the benches for the audience. To their right were the steps where Kerquelin had fallen and to the left stood the church Sainte-Marie with the sheepfold and market stalls. Beyond them was a smaller square flanked by a fifteenth-century building known as the Hôtel de Plamon, and another, of later vintage, called Hôtel du Mirandol. At the time, Bruno's attention had been fixed on this smaller square where the townsfolk were attacking the men dressed as the drunken English soldiers. From his place high on the left side benches, the action on the steps in front of the Hôtel de Ville to the right had been hard to see.

'*Bonjour*, Bruno,' said J-J, shaking hands. 'The good news is that Kerquelin is still alive but in intensive care. The prognosis is barely fifty–fifty and he might need a heart transplant. And no visitors allowed. At least that gives us something new to tell the press conference that we'll have to face this afternoon. And Guyon has identified two extra armed men dressed as townsfolk at the place where Kerquelin was stabbed – he wasn't supposed to be on those steps anyway.'

'That's why there was such a confused scuffle,' said Guyon. 'I'd choreographed the whole attack for six knights in a wedge in the centre, and having three more threw off all my spatial planning.'

'Could the pageant director have approved that without your knowledge?' Bruno asked.

Guyon shook his head. 'He says he didn't and I believe him. It would invalidate all the insurance.'

'We just called him,' said J-J. 'He's at the incident room in Sarlat. We came up here because we have the facilities to go through the videos. We've got hours of footage from the phones of people in the crowd but the TV crew missed the battle on the steps altogether. They were shooting the action in that small square right in front of the benches. The best sequences we've seen so far are the two placed at either side of the square by the director. The problem is that each camera was mounted on a tripod in balconies and quite high, so the one that should have got a frontal view of the charge by the knights was shooting over their heads – the action on the far side of the square by the Sainte-Marie church. That was where the townsfolk were attacking the English archers. So we have a rear view of the knights from that other camera.'

J-J sat down, rewound the tape and started it again just as the tall knight in the black surcoat appeared on the screen. He was on foot and waving his sword while apparently calling to the other knights to join him as he headed to the steps where the English soldiers were forming a defensive line.

'That's Kerquelin,' said J-J.

'My plan called for three knights in white surcoats and three in red to attack the English on the steps,' said Guyon. 'Behind the knights I had planned four townsmen with a couple of townswomen and two more men on each flank. But when du Guesclin's horse fell, the damn fool decided to join them on the steps rather than ride around them brandishing his sword, as I had planned.'

'That's the first problem. Now look, because here come two more guys dressed like the other Sarlat townsmen, carrying clubs and war hammers. They push their way in right behind Kerquelin, just as he has his sword raised over his head to attack the English line. And that was when the steps were so crowded that people began stumbling and falling over each other.'

J-J set the tape to inch forward, frame by frame, showing the impact of the extra townsmen was dramatic, toppling two other knights to their knees on the steps, where they tripped over some of the armed townsfolk joining the charge.

'All of the footage we've seen so far is from the same angle, behind the charging knights,' said J-J. 'We don't seem to have any footage taken from behind the English soldiers so we could see the knights' charge from the front. We have one piece of footage from a mobile phone in the audience that gives a partial side view which shows Kerquelin falling. We think we have five, maybe six possible suspects who were close enough to inflict the knife wound, and one of them is a woman.'

J-J handed Bruno some printouts of individual frames from

the video. The first showed one of the washerwomen, arms bared to the elbows and wielding a sturdy pole like a lance. She was falling over a sprawled townsman who was down on one knee, one hand on the floor to keep his balance, the other raised and holding a knife. The next frame showed him trying to get to his feet while trying to help the washerwoman keep her own balance. The hand bearing the knife was obscured by one of the knights.

'That seems to be the nearest knife to Kerquelin that we have seen so far,' Guyon said. 'But then look at these two images.'

The first frame showed Kerquelin on foot and on the way to the steps, half-turning to wave on the townsfolk.

'Look at the dagger in his belt,' Guyon went on, 'and now look at this.'

This new frame showed Kerquelin heaving himself to his feet from the tumbled sprawl of people on the steps, just as a woman dressed as a milkmaid seemed to threaten one of the English soldiers with a wooden bucket.

'Look at him again, the surcoat flapping loose because he's lost his belt,' said Guyon. 'Not just no belt, but also no dagger this time. The presence of Kerquelin on those steps was not authorized by me which raises a serious insurance problem. But since nobody expected him to be on those steps, this looks to me more like an accident than a premeditated attack.'

Guyon explained that as an experienced film and stage-fight director with a special licence from the actors' union, his approval of the choreography was required by the insurers of the whole event. The Mayor of Sarlat and Muselier, the overall director, had each signed the insurance contract that gave Guyon complete authority over the fight scenes. That contract included a copy of Guyon's own plan with a precise time frame, number of characters, weapons involved and sequences of the various movements. Each of the participants in the pageant had to sign a letter of indemnity, drafted by the insurers, which said they agreed to abide by the rules of the choreography.

'Muselier wanted more knights in the attack up the steps and I said no,' Guyon said. 'I insisted on no more than six, maximum. There wasn't really room for more. We compromised by letting him have more knights on horseback riding into the square, but these others had to stay on horseback, riding around and cheering the other knights on. And it was in the insurance contract that only one man was to wear the black surcoat, Kerquelin, and he was to stay on his horse.'

'So three people disobeyed the instructions. The two joining in the charge, dressed as townsmen, is that right?' asked Bruno. 'And Kerquelin also broke his orders when his horse fell, and he decided to join the fray, but nobody knew the horse was going to fall so nobody could have planned all this in advance.'

'Yes, that's right, and that invalidated the insurance contract, and may have ended my career in this business,' Guyon said, the bitterness clear in his voice. 'So Kerquelin's family can sue the pants off them, as can the town of Sarlat, and all the spectators can claim their money back because the show was stopped prematurely. This is likely to get expensive.'

'Kerquelin's horse slipped and fell on a patch of manure from one of the cows,' said J-J. 'Whose idea was it to have the cows?'

'Good question,' Guyon replied. 'It wasn't mine. That was part of the scene arranged by Muselier. But Kerquelin should never have ridden that far forward to where the cows had been. We had taken precautions. If you look at the horse, it's wearing a manure bag, that leather bag under the tail that's strapped to the saddle, like the horses that drive carriages around the Bois de Boulogne in Paris. All my horses were fitted with them.'

'Can you identify who these extra townsmen might be?' Bruno asked.

Guyon shook his head, pointing to one of the photos that showed a side view of a man dressed in a rough leather jacket and leather cap over a kind of chain mail balaclava that came down to his eyebrows and covered his chin and cheeks.

'His own mother wouldn't know him under all that,' said Guyon. 'There is just one thing.' He froze the video when the man in the strange helmet was turning his head, to reveal some mark on the man's neck. 'We need that frame blown up because I think that might be a tattoo. It might help you identify him.'

'So whoever dressed them up, or if they did it themselves, these two extras got hold of the same leather jerkins as the real townsfolk,' said J-J. 'But one of them had that chain mail covering his face. That makes it less likely that this was an accident. It seems these guys turned up of their own accord.'

'I'm not sure,' said Guyon. 'For this event we had lots of volunteers and every man wanted to be a French knight in armour. We had trouble getting enough people to play the English archers. Some of the volunteers said if they couldn't be French knights they didn't want to take part. It's like kids playing good guys and bad guys. So I wouldn't rule out an accident – a couple of frustrated volunteers might have got some makeshift armour together and joined in anyway. I've seen it happen before, which is why I always try to secure the scene. You can do that on stage or on a film set but it's almost impossible in a town where there are so many ways in and fire regulations mean we can only put up temporary barriers.'

'Do we know how these two newcomers arrived?' asked Bruno. 'If they had horses, could we see if some local vets might recognize them?'

'So far we don't know how they arrived, nor where they came from,' said J-J, advancing to stand before the big map and using a fat finger to point as he spoke. 'Kerquelin and the horsemen came in from the south, past the cathedral and then into the main square to ride past the audience on the benches, and that was where Kerquelin's horse fell. We think the two extras may have come in from the rue Montaigne, to the east, but there are some alleys that could have brought them out to the side of the steps in front of the Hôtel de Ville. Or they might have come in from the west, coming downhill from the rue de la République and then through this alley by the Hôtel de Vienne. If they used those alleys, they probably came on foot. And they made their escape in the confusion after the alarm was sounded. We had some French infantry who were to march in later and because we couldn't afford proper armour, we had them dressed in trousers and jackets of sacking painted in metallic grey, with white surcoats on top.'

'I was in the audience and I didn't see any French infantry,' said Bruno. 'Only the knights in armour and the townsfolk, and the guy with one leg.'

'No, the infantry were marching in from the gate just beyond the cathedral when the alarm was sounded by that young squire asking if there was a doctor in the audience,' said Guyon. 'I was wondering if two of them might have slipped away earlier to join in the main fight on the steps.'

'We'll have them all interviewed,' said J-J. 'And we have the names of all the knights and would-be knights and the people the cameras show to have been on the steps; they'll be interviewed today, if you want to sit in. And we got nothing from the dagger that was left in the ambulance – no prints were on the handle and it was one of several provided by the town of Sarlat.'

'Could it have been Kerquelin's dagger, the one from the missing belt?' Bruno asked. 'There were probably no fingerprints because of his gauntlets.'

'Maybe, but we used those knives over my objections,' Guyon broke in. 'When I can, I prefer to use one made for the stage. They have an extra-long and hollow handle so the blade can retract when it meets resistance. We used it in some of the rehearsals but Kerquelin said he'd rather use the same one as the others.'

'Don't you have the last word on safety concerns?' asked Bruno.

'Yes, but you can't win every battle, and there is a limit to the number of times you can say no and still expect to get hired in this business,' Guyon said, the weariness of experience in his tone. 'There's always a tussle between me and the director but he has to fight on another front, with the people who put up the money. In this case that means the town of Sarlat, which has a conservative mayor and is under the control of the tourist board of the *département*, which is controlled by the socialists. Those two fight all the time, except when it comes to fighting against us to lower the budget.'

'Sounds a bit like our budget battles,' said J-J. 'How do you get along with your director?'

'As well as can be expected, probably better than most. We've worked together before and probably will again unless this disaster makes us both unemployable,' Guyon said. 'I just hope the actors' union can help pay the legal fees I think I'm going to be facing. Sarlat may have ended my career.'

'All the more reason for you to keep on looking at those films,' said Bruno, his voice as sympathetic as he could make it. 'As far as I can see, you've been the most helpful and useful witness we've found. So thank you for that, and if you can help us find these two strangers, that could get you off the hook with the town and the insurers – they may well be the ones who are responsible.'

Guyon raised his head as if to say something but shrugged as J-J interrupted and said, 'I've asked for some digitally enhanced pictures of the mystery men. They should be ready any minute now. Can you look at them as well? And we're getting film from the surveillance cameras of some local business premises. They might show us how these two guys came into the square and maybe also how and when they left.'

'So I'm going to be here all day?' Guyon asked with a sigh. 'I should be talking to my agent and his lawyer but I don't suppose I have much choice in the matter. All this and my retractable knife has disappeared from my locker, must have been in last night's confusion.'

'Think of it as trying to save your career,' Bruno said. 'And in the meantime, the coffee's good here.'

The enhanced images arrived and the neck tattoo seemed to be part of a spider's web, distinctive enough to be useful, except that more and more criminals found that a fake tattoo was a simple way to confuse witnesses. Far more interesting were images from a bank's surveillance camera on the rue de la République. It showed two men wearing what seemed to be silver-coloured trousers and knee-high boots, their faces almost hidden by their hooded jackets and large backpacks. They turned down an alley and disappeared. The date and time stamp on the video footage showed that their image had been caught on camera just fifteen minutes before du Guesclin's horsemen launched their attack.

J-J's phone rang with a call from the Bergerac police. A woman presenting DGSE papers identifying her as Madame Suzanne Kerquelin had arrived and demanded to be escorted to the hospital to see her husband and then to the Sarlat police station.

'She's his ex-wife,' Bruno said.

'As a divorced wife she would be welcome to perform the formal identification of her husband but he isn't dead yet, and I don't think the surgeons would want her in the intensive care unit,' J-J said into his phone. 'Inform her with my compliments that we are currently overwhelmed running a complicated investigation, so the Sarlat station is off-limits to all non-essential personnel. I assume the DGSE can arrange its own transportation. And she's not to be allowed into her husband's house at Domme unless escorted by one of the team sent by General Lannes.'

J-J ended the call, rolled his eyes at Bruno and grunted, 'Prima donnas from La Piscine. Always the same, expecting us lesser mortals to fetch and carry for them.'

'I could go,' said Bruno. 'I don't think I'm contributing anything here that your own people aren't doing.'

'Feel free,' J-J replied. 'But I still don't want her in the house at Domme until I'm sure it's been gone through properly for possible evidence. I have to assume we're dealing with a deliberate attempt at murder here, not an accident, and although we've established the means and the opportunity we don't have the slightest clue about motive. An estranged ex-wife might just be relevant. We'll have to talk with her.'

'By the way,' Bruno asked, 'what happened to Kerquelin's horse?'

'The word was it had a broken fetlock,' Guyon replied. 'The vet says he'll see how bad it is on an X-ray. He may have to have the horse put down.'

Bruno grimaced and asked for the name of the vet. It was a man he knew, called Caillevent. He put away his pen and notebook, picked up his cap and shook Guyon's hand, thanking him for his help. Suddenly the door opened and Prunier, J-J's boss as Contrôleur-Général and head of the Police Nationale in the *département*, burst into the room.

'The Sarlat Mayor is going ahead with the re-enactment for the rest of the week as a tribute to Kerquelin,' Prunier announced in shocked tones. 'He's going to ask Kerquelin's daughter to take her father's place as du Guesclin. Can you believe it?'

J-J rolled his eyes and sighed. 'Isn't he confusing du Guesclin with Joan of Arc?'

'He's a mayor, taking advantage of all the publicity to try and get some of the town's money back,' said Guyon. 'The people of Sarlat have invested a lot of taxpayers' money into this pageant and if I was in the Mayor's shoes I might do the same. And if you were facing a new election next year, so might you.'

Chapter 6

Once Bruno was clear of city traffic and heading for Bergerac on the Route Nationale, he put in his earplugs, already connected to his phone, and called Isabelle on the secure number to ask what she could tell him about Suzanne. After the shortest of greetings, Isabelle said, 'You know the Elysée was going to put Kerquelin in charge of La Piscine starting next year? So if he's too ill to do it this is Suzanne's opportunity to get the top job. She's already been calling around saying it's time for a woman to run the place. In general, I'd agree with that except I'm not sure about this particular woman, and I'm not the only one who feels that way. She's harder than nails, doesn't work well with others and some of her Arab links are a bit too close for comfort. I'm also not alone in thinking that.'

Suzanne's maiden name was Rouelle. She was the only child of a distinguished French Arabist, Isabelle explained. He had written the standard work on the Arab astronomers of the Middle Ages and was one of the founders of the Institut française du Proche-Orient. He had spent much of his life in Damascus, Cairo and Fez, and Suzanne had been brought up like her father to speak classical Arabic. Her mother, from an aristocratic Moroccan family that was close to the monarchy, had died in a car accident when Suzanne was very young. She could pass for a local in much of the Arab world and she was widely credited, not least by herself, with the special relationship developed under Presidents Chirac and Sarkozy with the United Arab Emirates. The links were especially close with Abu Dhabi, where France now had a military base, naval facilities and had signed a twenty-billion-euro arms deal to sell Rafale jets and military helicopters to the country. Branches of the Sorbonne and the Louvre had been established there. Of special interest to DGSE, France had an electronic intelligence post at the Al-Dhafra air base, operated in partnership with their German equivalent, the Bundesnachrichtendienst, or Federal Intelligence Service.

'It was one thing to have this close relationship with Arab states when we needed their oil and gas,' Isabelle went on, 'but they could soon find themselves sitting on massive reservoirs of fossil fuels that fewer customers want to buy. And when that happens, not many people in Paris think the monarchies and sheikhdoms are going to remain in charge of the Arab world. So Suzanne's particular Arab connections may look a little less useful.'

'I think we'll depend on oil for some years yet,' Bruno said. 'To be fair, who really knows what will happen in the Arab world when fossil fuels are abandoned, if they ever fully are? And there is huge respect across the Arab world for Western scholars like Suzanne's father who always took them and their heritage seriously. The key fact is that Suzanne was the translator at so many meetings with Arab leaders; most Arab leaders and every French president has known her personally. And you know what they said about the way Jacques Chirac used to treat the women on his staff.'

'*Dix minutes, douche comprise*,' Bruno said, laughing. Ten minutes, including the shower afterwards. 'Apart from her, are there other candidates?'

'The reason Kerquelin was next in line was that he modernized the whole foreign intelligence system by bringing artificial intelligence into electronic systems, communications, ciphers and satellites,' she said.

Kerquelin had been the expert who warned France's security services that satellite communications were giving way to optical fibre, she went on, and had persuaded the navy it was in their interest to provide submarines with equipment to tap into undersea cables. He also dramatically improved relations with the Americans, English and Germans and had started forging closer links with the intellectual and academic world with his system of 'Axioms'; conferences where bright outsiders were brought in to debate policy and priorities.

'Suzanne understands the politics of that, which is why she has steadily been taking over the Axioms network her ex-husband began,' Isabelle went on. 'Now that his life's in danger, everyone will be speculating about who will run La Piscine. Some people in the defence and interior establishments will want General Lannes, but DGSE cherishes its independence and the Elysée has its own reasons to limit the powers of those two ministries. So I don't think Lannes will get it. They may bring in someone from outside, maybe from the military or the Quai d'Orsay.'

'What about you?' he asked, not entirely in jest.

'Too young,' she said, laughing. 'Maybe in ten, fifteen years. I'll let you know if I hear something. Why are you so interested?'

'I'm about to meet Suzanne, having heard about her failure as a mother from her daughter, Nadia. They don't get on. By the way, I ran into a friend of yours last night when Lannes sent me to babysit Kerquelin's house – a woman named Pantin, the new head of security at Domme.'

'Ah, yes, Marie-Do, be careful around her. She has a reputation as something of a heart-breaker.'

'And you aren't?'

'Ah, Bruno, you above all people must know that my heart belongs only to the most attractive model of masculinity in the Périgord, the one and only Balzac. Is our dog well and is he missing me?'

'He howls himself to sleep each night as he gazes at the photo you left in his kennel. You must have known I'd find it.'

'I know you found the one I left under your pillow. *Bisous*, Bruno. Please keep me informed.'

The former Madame Kerquelin was waiting for him in the Commissaire's otherwise empty office at Bergerac, concentrating on her phone. The speedy play of her thumbs as she texted was impressive, even as she raised her eyes to his, rose and gave a smile so fleeting that it didn't even try to be convincing.

'You must be the local chief of police I was told to expect,' she said, putting out a languid hand almost as if she expected him to kiss it. Instead, he shook it cheerfully and welcomed her to the Périgord, taking in her trim figure in a tailored blue suit. He had learned enough of fashion to recognize a

Chanel. Her glossy dark hair reminded him of her Moroccan ancestry although her eyes were a blue so startling that he wondered if she might be wearing contact lenses. He knew she was in her early fifties but from her looks he'd have thought her to be ten years younger. Her throat was smooth as a girl's and only the skin on the backs of her hands suggested an older woman.

'I gather you've been looking after my daughter, which I know can be a challenge,' she said, gathering a Hermès handbag from the desk and pointing to a Louis Vuitton suitcase. 'And I believe you're to be my transport to Domme, now that I'm not allowed to see my husband.'

'Actually, it was a pleasure to meet Nadia, and please accept my sympathies on the injury to your former husband,' Bruno said politely. 'He's evidently a remarkable and talented man. Do you have any more luggage or should we go to Domme?'

'Only that suitcase. I thought I'd stay at Brice's house with Nadia. I presume the security team has finished their search.'

'I'm afraid not,' he said. 'I called Mademoiselle Pantin, the security chief at Domme, while driving here and her team is still there and will be there tomorrow too. But she's arranged accommodation for you at Domme.'

'And where is Nadia? She's not answering her phone.'

'She's staying with friends in St Denis and I'm sure she'll be in touch as soon as she can. She knows you were coming down but she wasn't clear what time you'd arrive. I'll call the friends where she's staying.'

He phoned Gilles who told him that Nadia had gone for a walk more than an hour ago. Gilles had lent her a map of the local *randonnées*, the well-signposted walking trails. He'd get her to call her mother once she got back.

'Any idea where she's headed?' Bruno asked.

'She said she might head for Les Eyzies, so about two hours.'

He thanked Gilles, ended the call and passed on the information to Nadia's mother, who tightened her lips and made no secret of her irritation.

'I'm afraid Nadia can be a thoughtless girl with little consideration for others,' she said. 'I sent emails and left messages on her phone. As usual, no response.'

'She's had quite a shock, being in the pageant when her father was injured,' Bruno said. 'And I gather she's very close to him.'

He picked up Suzanne's suitcase and led her outside to his modest police van. He noticed her eyebrows lift as he put her case in the back, beside his sports bag and muddy rugby boots and beneath a sweatshirt that he'd hung up to dry. There was a distinct aroma of dog from Balzac's cushion, tucked in beside a wicker basket containing some cherry tomatoes and radishes from his garden and some of that morning's eggs from his chickens – he would deliver to colleagues in the Mairie when he got back to St Denis.

'Would you like a fresh cherry tomato, just plucked from my garden this morning?' he asked, ignoring her raised eyebrow. He picked out two, popping one into his mouth and offering her the other.

'No thank you,' she said coldly, as she stood beside the passenger door of his car, clearly waiting for him to open it for her. He ate the second tomato, closed the rear of the van and went to open her door. Bruno extended an arm to help her clamber in, which was evidently not easy with her tight skirt and high heels.

'How long will this trip take?' she asked.

'To Domme, usually about forty minutes,' he replied. 'But with the tourist traffic today, maybe an hour.'

'Don't you have a police siren on this van?' she asked. 'That would get us through the traffic.'

'Of course, but I only use it in emergencies,' he replied, ignoring the irritated glance she threw his way.

By the time Bruno was in the driver's seat, her attention was fixed on her mobile phone and they drove off in silence. From Bergerac he took the back road through Sainte Alvère and Meyrals where there would be less traffic, but just after the hilltop village of Audrix he saw a line of pony-riders led by Miranda approaching the road. He stopped, put on the flashing lights, and fetched a big radish from the back of his car, and went to stop other cars while the riders crossed the road. As Miranda approached, Bruno gave her pony his radish. She blew him a kiss and waved in thanks. He blew one back and returned to his car, where Suzanne looked pointedly at her watch and said, 'I need to reach Domme in time for lunch with a colleague.'

'And we need to look after our tourist trade and our small businesses,' he replied. 'Their taxes pay my wages, and yours too, *madame*.'

Well, Bruno thought, at least a conversation has begun, and he asked where she was having lunch. The Esplanade in Domme, she replied.

82

'That's very good and it's got one of the finest views in France. I'll drop you there and they'll take care of your suitcase. And I'll try to get Nadia to call you.'

In response, she flashed him a brief smile, which seemed like progress.

'I know you're with La Piscine,' he said.

'I have an office there,' she replied. 'But I also have a desk in the Elysée since much of my work involves liaison with the presidential staff. You may have heard we're moving soon to a larger new place in Vincennes, better protected against cyber threats.'

'I heard about it on France Culture,' Bruno said.

'There are no secrets in France these days,' she said drily. 'Anyway, I know of your connection to General Lannes; he's an old family friend.'

'I know he's your daughter's godfather.'

'He's the one who helped recruit my husband into the service when he was making his fortune in Silicon Valley.'

Bruno managed to keep a reasonably civil conversation going until they reached the crossing over the crowded main road. Then he crossed the bridge at Castelnaud before heading for Domme. With the sweep of the river dominated by the great medieval fortresses of Beynac and Castelnaud, Suzanne condescended to admire the view.

'Haven't you been here before?' Bruno asked.

'Only on office business and we came in by helicopter,' she replied. 'My contact with Brice naturally ended with our divorce.' She turned in her seat to examine him, and asked, 'Are you directly involved in the police investigation into this attack?'

He nodded. 'Yes, and I was there when it happened, but without a direct view. I went down to the scene with a doctor where we found the knife between his ribs. Commissaire Jalipeau is still examining hundreds of videos of the pageant, trying to establish whether this was an accident or something more sinister.'

Bruno explained Kerquelin's decision to ignore the script and pile into the mêlée on the steps, throwing off the careful planning of the mock fight.

He drove up the hill to Domme, turned through the imposing stone towers that flanked the ancient gate, and told her about the Knights Templar who had been imprisoned there. He avoided the main street that was filled with food and souvenir shops and thronged with visitors. He parked in front of the church, left his police lights flashing, and took her to the main viewpoint on the point of the cliff that overlooked the Dordogne valley with the picturesque arches of the bridge. Brightly coloured kayaks were passing beneath the arches. It was too late in the day for the hot-air balloons that took passengers along the valley in the early mornings, swooping down almost to the river before the gas burners were lit, sending them soaring high again.

'One of the great views of France,' he said. 'The two great fortresses that glowered at each other across the river in the Hundred Years War – Chateau Beynac, which was held by the French, over there, and Castelnaud, held by the English, to your left. The gardens of Marqueyssac are over to the right.'

'Wasn't Beynac the chateau used in that Luc Besson film of Joan of Arc?' she asked. 'With Malkovich playing the King and

Dustin Hoffman as the Conscience? I remember seeing that with Brice, it must have been twenty years ago.'

'I believe it was. Did you do much travelling together when you were stationed abroad?' he asked.

'Of course,' she said curtly. 'All to do with our work.'

'What about Taiwan?' he asked, thinking of the guidebook in Kerquelin's bedroom.

The question evidently startled her. 'What on earth makes you ask that?' She suddenly sounded aggressive, almost fierce.

'A guidebook in his house,' he replied. 'It looked well used.'

She shook her head dismissively and headed for the restaurant. Bruno followed with her suitcase. An older man with carefully coiffed grey hair and a trimmed white beard rose with the help of a stick from his seat at a table on the terrace and called out, 'Suzanne.'

She waved airily at the man and handed Bruno a card with her name and numbers. 'Make sure you call me as soon as you hear from Nadia and make sure that she calls me. You can leave my suitcase at the front desk.'

'Dominic, *j'arrive*,' she called out to the waiting man, leaving Bruno to his task, and to wonder whatever had happened to make Parisians assume they could ignore the usual French courtesies. And what had irritated her about Taiwan?

Chapter 7

Bruno climbed back into his van and returned to St Denis, thinking about the folder that contained Kerquelin's will, the names of lawyers and the investment trusts in different countries and various American states. All that Bruno knew of South Dakota was that it was home to Mount Rushmore, where the heads of various presidents had been carved, and that many American Indian tribes, for whom he'd enjoyed a boyhood fascination, had roamed and hunted there. Delaware was familiar only in a song that Pamela sometimes sang: 'What did Delaware, boys? She wore a brand New Jersey.' Suzanne had said something about her ex-husband making a fortune in Silicon Valley before General Lannes had persuaded him to return home to serve France. Perhaps Kerquelin's wealth somehow suggested a motive for his stabbing.

Bruno remembered a lunch in Périgueux with J-J and an intriguing and ferociously intelligent friend of his, Aristide Goirau, head of the *fisc* – the financial police – in Bordeaux. The topic had been the French and European operations of a Russian oligarch, and the political and security complications in the case had inspired General Lannes of the Ministry of the Interior to assume control. During the lunch Bruno had asked for Goirau's card and had scanned it into his phone. Now he put the phone into its cradle on the dashboard, inserted his earpods and called Goirau.

'Bruno, good to hear from you. I fondly remember that lunch with J-J, when we talked about that intriguing affair that ended up far beyond our humble station,' Goirau said, in the sharp, clipped voice Bruno recalled. 'What can I do for you?'

'Why are South Dakota and Delaware significant in finance?' Bruno asked, and explained his findings at Kerquelin's house, without mentioning Kerquelin's name.

'Delaware is known to be remarkably friendly to corporations and doesn't require companies to list their owners when formed,' Goirau replied. 'Almost two-thirds of the Fortune 500 corporations have their legal home there. Altogether there are more than a million corporations in a state with about 900,000 residents. The taxes are low, the supervision lenient, and taxable profits earned elsewhere can be transformed into non-taxable earnings in what is known as the Delaware loophole.'

'And South Dakota?' Bruno asked.

'That is capable of providing rich people with even more miraculous benefits,' Goirau said. 'South Dakota invites you to set up a perpetual trust for your heirs which will be tax-free, completely secret and protected from outside lawsuits, including divorce and alimony actions. At last count it had close to half a trillion dollars in assets based there.'

South Dakota had traditionally been a poor and under-populated prairie state, Goirau explained. But in 1981 it had a remarkable governor, an ex-Marine named Jankelow who became famous for taking his own rifle along to a hostage crisis. When an American financial crisis sent inflation soaring, Jankelow saw an opportunity. President Franklin Roosevelt's New Deal in the 1930s had given the United States an anti-usury law that limited the interest rates banks could charge. As inflation went into double figures, the usury limit meant that the new credit card companies were losing money fast. Governor Jankelow persuaded Citibank to move its entire credit card operation to South Dakota, welcoming the company with a new state law that allowed them to charge an interest rate at which they could remain profitable.

'Jankelow then began looking for more opportunities and he found one in these perpetual trusts,' Goirau went on. He explained that along with Switzerland, South Dakota was now the world's leading location for money that people wished to be both safe and discreet. After the Swiss banking scandals of 2009 and 2010, most countries wanted to clamp down on money-laundering and tax evasion. They agreed upon the Common Reporting Standard, which required countries to exchange information on the assets of each other's citizens kept in each other's banks. Overnight, places like the Bahamas, Jersey and Liechtenstein lost much of their appeal as places to avoid tax. But the United States never signed on to the CRS.

'The Americans require other countries to send data on foreign nationals to the USA, but do not return the compliment. As a result, the United States is becoming the tax-avoidance capital of the world and a lot of that money is going to South Dakota. I remember one of the few cases that became public,' Goirau added. 'When China imposed new tax rules on its citizens, the billionaire Sun Hongbin quietly transferred almost $5 billion worth of shares in his Chinese property company to a South Dakota trust. And think about what the perpetuity trusts really mean.'

'You mean they go on for ever ?' Bruno suggested.

'Exactly. Now assume that you put a million dollars into such a trust, invest it and it gets an annual return of six per cent,' Goirau went on. 'Remember this is tax-free. So after two hundred years, it will have grown to $136 billion. After three hundred years it will be more than $50 trillion – twice the size of the current US economy. We will have dynasties that make the Medicis of Renaissance Italy and the Rothschilds look like financial pygmies.'

'And this is legal?' Bruno asked in wonderment.

'Alas, yes. The United States has apparently decided that dirty money is better than no money at all. I have no objection to people using their savings and their brains to invest and become rich, so long as they pay the proper taxes to the community that is the ultimate source of their wealth. There are few things that tempt me to become a revolutionary, Bruno, but you've touched on one of them.'

'I'm very pleased to hear it, Aristide,' Bruno replied.

'I may be leaping to a conclusion, but I suspect your investigation is linked to the news about the tragedy at Sarlat,' Goirau said. 'Kerquelin would be one of the few Frenchmen in a position to benefit from such trusts.'

'Is he really that rich?' Bruno asked.

'Hard to say, but since he helped write the source code and the basic algorithms for Google, and he was paid in shares rather than the cash the infant new company did not yet have, we assume he must now be a very rich Frenchman.'

'And this Dakota trust cannot be taxed, right?'

'Right. When Kerquelin agreed to the patriotic appeal that he come home and apply his skills to French security, he struck a deal for himself and his heirs. Whatever assets he held outside France would not be subject to French tax. We tax only his salary and various earnings from his other, wholly legal, investments and they on their own make him a wealthy man by French standards. But whatever he owned when he was persuaded to return to France, he has kept, and it grows tax-free out on the South Dakota prairie. And his heirs will enjoy that money as well – for ever and ever. Of course, when the deal was signed Google was barely known in France and the explosion in value of its shares was far in the future. I suspect even Kerquelin had no idea just how rich he would become.'

'Thank you for this, Aristide. You've been a great help.'

'Just one public servant helping another. By the way, J-J said that if I ever had the opportunity to dine at your own table, I should seize it with alacrity.'

'It would be a pleasure,' said Bruno. 'Let me know when you're coming this way and I'll arrange a dinner. And you can stay overnight, if you like.'

'Thanks so much. Keep me posted on the Kerquelin affair and those wealthy heirs of his. A young man and a daughter, I believe?'

'Two daughters, half-sisters,' Bruno replied. 'And a son who seems more interested in sailing.'

'In that case he might need the money. I once heard that

sport described as standing in your clothes under an ice-cold shower while ripping up hundred-dollar bills.'

When Goirau ended the call Bruno wondered whether Nadia had any idea just how rich she was going to be. In some ways, he thought, it was a problematic inheritance to leave to one's children. It was a temptation to idleness and extravagance, and it would take a strong character not to start thinking of the rest of the human race as not only poor but as somehow less deserving. He remembered some wealthy American woman being quoted as saying that 'only the little people pay taxes'. It would be sad if that attitude afflicted Nadia, though she seemed to be a level-headed young woman.

He was approaching Meyrals when his phone vibrated. Nadia was phoning from Les Eyzies to say that her half-sister, Claire, was on the way from Bordeaux and should arrive in the Périgord that afternoon. He suggested meeting her at the café in front of the museum in ten minutes. There he found her nursing a coffee and still wearing Fabiola's tracksuit.

'I spent the last hour or so driving your mother from Bergerac to Domme,' he said, after ordering an espresso. 'She says she needs to talk to you, in case you may have to arrange a funeral.'

'I refuse to believe he won't survive. And in any event, neither Claire nor I would want my mother involved,' Nadia said firmly. 'She was divorced from my father. She has no say in the matter.'

'Have you heard from your brother?' he asked.

'He didn't respond to my email, so I suppose he's at sea,' she replied. 'I'll try to track down a number for his sailing club. They might know. I'm not sure he'd want to come here, anyway. He only socializes with his crew members. He's got

Asperger's Syndrome.' She paused, took a sip of her coffee, looked at him almost defiantly, and said, 'I suppose we're a pretty screwed-up family.'

'Not by local standards,' Bruno replied, smiling. 'Around here most people stayed in their little villages over the centuries, intermarried and interbred. If it hadn't been for all the marauding soldiers, wandering pilgrims and naughty priests mixing up the gene pool we might all be gaga. Anyway, you and your brother's genes are pretty well mixed – French, Breton and some Moroccan through your mother. You have her eyes, that striking blue. Does your brother look like you?'

'No, not much. But then I don't look like Claire, my half-sister, as you will see when you meet her. She's lovely, with sultry Latin looks.'

'I look forward to it,' he said, politely. 'And I think you and your sister should talk to a lawyer and to General Lannes about your father's will,' he added. 'You are all trustees of your father's estate, according to a document that I saw on his desk when I had to go and secure the place.'

'I know,' she said. 'My father told me about that. There's another trustee, an old college friend of his in California whom we called Uncle Angus, my other godfather. He's on his way over here now, coming with Claire.'

'Angus McDermott,' Bruno said. 'Yes, I remember seeing his name. Did you tell him your father's in hospital?'

'Yes. Uncle Angus was coming anyway. It was my father's turn to host our annual reunion and he wanted everyone to see the re-enactment, so he rented a chateau for the week.' Nadia's eyes filled with tears as she spoke.

'Will you have to cancel?'

'No, everyone is still coming, to support us and Papa. They'll get here tomorrow when the rental starts.'

'Which chateau is it?' asked Bruno.

'Château de Rouffillac, overlooking the river near Carlux, wonderfully restored.'

Bruno knew the place, a twelfth-century fortress that dominated the cliff rising from the north bank of the Dordogne river, almost due south of Sarlat. It had been heavily restored in the nineteenth century and more recently bought by a wealthy couple from Silicon Valley, an Englishman and his American wife. No expense had been spared, he'd heard, to re-create a medieval chateau with modern plumbing in several luxurious suites. There was even a nearby landing pad for helicopters.

'When you say "everyone" is coming, who are you referring to?'

'It's mostly old friends,' Nadia replied. 'They were all at Stanford, studying computers, and they all began working together at the birth of the internet, whether with Mosaic or Netscape or helping with JavaScript or alongside Scott Hassan at what became Google. It must have been amazing, like going from clubs to bows and arrows and then to tanks and missiles in just ten years.'

'Your dad must have had quite a life – California, computers, Google and then back to France, along with family and travel and those re-enactments he enjoys.'

'Do you know yet what happened, exactly? Suzanne always said she and my father were assassination targets.'

93

'The police are still working through hundreds of videos to establish the exact sequence of events. It may well have been an accident.'

'I thought you said this morning that you were going to Périgueux to look at the videos people had sent in.'

'I did, and it's still confusing; there are so many images, all of them at slightly different moments. Apparently your dad was supposed to stay on his horse and not join the tussle on the steps. But his horse slipped in manure so he clambered off and charged in. The choreographer was very upset about it.'

'That's classic Papa,' she said, an affectionate smile on her lips that did not reach her eyes. 'He was always determined to be at the heart of the action. Will the horse be okay?'

'I haven't heard, but I'll ask,' Bruno replied. 'Did you know the Mayor of Sarlat wants to go ahead with the event for the rest of the week, and wonders if you might take the part of du Guesclin?'

'I'd rather just keep my role as the young maiden,' she said.

'It would be possible to do both,' Bruno said.

'I suppose you're right,' Nadia said, suddenly grinning at him, almost defiantly. 'I think Papa would be pleased, so why not?'

'In that case you'd better get in touch with the Mayor of Sarlat and contact Guyon, the choreographer. I could drive you to Sarlat now and Claire could join you there.'

'I think we both want to go to the hospital first and see Papa,' she replied. 'Is he at Bergerac?'

Bruno shrugged. 'I think he's been moved to some secure military hospital near Bordeaux, but I don't know for sure. General Lannes would be able to tell you, if you can reach him.

I'm told there's talk of surgery so you probably wouldn't be allowed in to see him.'

'Let me call Claire first about meeting in Sarlat,' she said. 'Then I'll call Uncle Vincent to find out about Papa.'

As she began to dial, Bruno called J-J to see if there were any developments. J-J said he had held a press conference at noon at which he said that the police wanted to trace two men dressed as townsfolk who had unexpectedly appeared on the steps where Kerquelin had been injured. One man had immediately come forward, calling the police hotline that J-J had arranged. He said that he had been turned down for a role as a knight and, at almost the last minute, not wanting to be left out, he and a friend had decided to join in anyway, wearing old leather jerkins and carrying clubs but no knives. J-J had asked him if he had any way to identify himself on the photos they were examining and the man said he had been wearing an old chain mail helmet and had a spider web tattoo on his neck.

'The guy gave me a name and address, and his phone number checks out,' J-J went on. 'He's promised to give a statement in Sarlat later today when he gets off work and he'll try to bring his friend. So it looks like we're back to square one.'

Bruno told J-J that Nadia would agree to take her father's place in the re-enactment and that her half-sister and a family trustee would be meeting Bruno in Sarlat in about an hour, before installing themselves at the Château de Rouffillac for the following week.

'Are you still going through all the phone videos from the public?' Bruno asked.

'Yes, but they aren't helping us that much. We have more

95

than five hundred videos and we still can't get a smoking gun, or at least, the flash of a knife.'

Bruno murmured something sympathetic and closed his phone. Nadia leaned forward and handed him her own, saying, 'It's Uncle Vincent, for you.'

'*Bonjour*, Bruno,' General Lannes said. 'Thank you for taking care of Nadia and her mother. I've told Nadia that her father is at the Piqué hospital for security reasons and the medics say no visitors. The good news is that Brice's heart was untouched and although he's very weak they're hopeful he can make a full recovery, but he'll be staying in intensive care for a few days. Any word on the videos the police are reviewing?'

'I just spoke to Commissaire Jalipeau, who's leading the investigation. The one possible suspect has come forward and cleared himself, so there has been no progress. By the way, did Nadia tell you she'll be taking over her father's role for the rest of the week?'

'Yes, and I'm not at all surprised. She's an impressive young woman and so is her half-sister, Claire.'

'So Kerquelin may take over La Piscine yet?' Bruno asked.

Lannes gave a bark that might have been laughter, or just surprise. 'For now, Bruno, but let's just focus on getting him healthy.'

'Amen to that,' said Bruno, then ended the call. His phone almost immediately started vibrating, and he saw that the caller was Father Sentout, the parish priest of St Denis. Bruno was not a regular churchgoer, but he was fond of the elderly man, endeared by the priest's devotion to the pleasure of the table and to the fortunes of the St Denis rugby team. It was known to the faithful of the town that a confession on Sunday morning was likely to be a brief affair, since the good Father hated to be late for the pre-game lunch of the club veterans.

'Bruno, I'm with our mutual friend Florence and I'd like to ask a favour. I don't know if you are aware that since I was saddened by the rift between Florence and her parents over her divorce I wrote to their parish priest. I asked if we could help them and Florence to be reconciled when her husband was sent back to prison after violating parole.'

'Not just for violating parole but also for attacking a police officer, namely me, and hitting Florence in public while their children were watching,' Bruno said coldly. 'The guy should never have been given conditional release.'

'I'm not disputing that, Bruno, but this is about Florence and her parents. I think I've convinced them to visit St Denis, to meet their grandchildren for the first time. I'm trying to unify a family that has been at odds for too long.'

'If Florence is willing to try I'll be glad to help if I can,' Bruno replied. 'What do you want me to do?'

'Could they stay with you next weekend? They propose driving down on Friday, having dinner with Florence and the children, spending Saturday with them and then driving back after church on Sunday. It would be a great kindness if you could extend your hospitality.'

'Of course, so long as my cousin Alain and his fiancée don't plan another weekend house-hunting. They're staying with me now so they probably won't get another leave. I'll check with them and call you back. Could I have a word with Florence, please?'

'I knew I could count on you, Bruno,' Florence began. 'I'm not at all sure how this family reunion will go but I think we owe it to the children to try. And my old-fashioned parents will be reassured to think that the priest and the village policeman are my friends.'

'You have a lot more friends than that, Florence, and I think we should get your parents to meet the Mayor, who is far more skilful at singing your praises, and maybe get them to a session with the kids in your computer club, and with your headmaster. If they stay over on Monday we could invite them to our regular dinner at Pamela's with the Baron and Fabiola. I think it's important to show them how you've become a pillar of the community with the life you've built for yourself and the twins here.'

'I don't want to try your patience, Bruno,' she said. 'They're not the easiest of people to get along with. And you'll have laundry to do and breakfasts to make, so I'd like to pay you for—'

'Florence, stop it,' he interrupted her. 'We're friends. If you want to put an extra few euros in Father Sentout's collection box on Sunday, I'm sure he'd be delighted. And make sure he gets the choir to put on a special concert so your parents can see you shine as a soloist.'

'Maybe you're right, they always loved church music.'

'For their sake,' said Bruno, 'let's all make sure this works.'

As he put his phone away again, Nadia gave him an amused look and said, 'Police work in the Périgord sounds interestingly varied.'

'It can be,' he replied, grinning at her. 'Should we head for Sarlat?'

'We'd better stop on the way at Fabiola's place to pick up my costume, and I should ask if I can stay another night, perhaps with Claire as my room-mate.'

Chapter 8

Nadia had arranged for them all to meet at the Sarlat tourist office, close to the house of Etienne de la Boétie, the sixteenth-century legal theorist known as the father of human rights who was the town's most famous son. She was eager to show Claire this birthplace of the subject of her university thesis. It stood on the main square of old Sarlat, a classic building of the Renaissance that seemed to be two townhouses squeezed together under tall and pointed gables that were topped with fine chimney pots. Bruno waited outside as Nadia darted inside to see if Claire had arrived. Off to his right, the great square was dominated by the tall rows of benches where he had sat the previous evening to watch the re-enactment. Almost directly ahead was the house where de la Boétie had been born in 1530 when the building was just ten years old.

Bruno never tired of admiring the proportions of the house, its windows and the façade of the region's honey-coloured stone. Some years earlier, he had read Etienne's masterpiece, his essay on voluntary servitude, or how it was that human beings everywhere seemed to have allowed themselves to be ruled when all they had to do to be free was to refuse to obey. After ten years in the French army, Bruno had not been persuaded that freedom was so easily come by. And while he knew that Etienne was widely hailed as the father of non-violent resistance, Bruno's own interest in the French Resistance had convinced him that some vicious rulers were only to be overthrown by force of arms.

'Here she is,' announced Nadia, arm-in-arm with a young woman with glossy black hair, deep brown eyes and a cheerful air, as though the world had always treated her well and she was confident it would continue to do so. Bruno was a little surprised, assuming that she be in something close to mourning, or at least visibly worried about her father. She was wearing a cream silk T-shirt and a black cotton trouser suit and was smiling politely, while a middle-aged man in a dark suit with greying red hair and an amiable face brought up the rear.

'Claire, meet Bruno, chief of police for the Vézère. He's been a great help in this trouble. And Bruno, this is my sister, and my godfather Angus McDermott. He's one of my father's oldest friends from his California days. I'm afraid he speaks very little French. He's a Scot.'

'*Mademoiselle, monsieur*,' said Bruno, shaking hands and pushing to the back of his mind the thought that as trustees of Kerquelin's will each of these three people, or perhaps all three working together, might have a serious financial motive for Kerquelin's murder. 'I'm delighted to welcome you here to the Périgord despite the sad occasion that brings you here.'

'I told them the news about Papa,' Nadia said. 'Remind me, where exactly is that military hospital he's in?'

'Near Bordeaux,' Bruno said.

'*Merde*, we were just there. We could have called in to see him,' said Claire, in excellent French.

'No visitors allowed, as yet,' Bruno said. 'As soon as I hear anything more, I'll let you know.'

'And this is still thought to have been an accident?' asked Claire, evidently sceptical.

'It seems that way, but the Police Nationale are still investigating. They have assigned their chief detective and a large team to the case and the Elysée is taking an active interest,' he said.

'The Elysée is the office of the French president,' Nadia interjected, for Angus's benefit.

Claire briskly translated for McDermott and then said, 'Our booking at the chateau starts tomorrow. Can we go to Papa's house or do we have to get a hotel?'

'The house is still off limits and it's high season so the hotels are all full,' said Nadia. 'I'm staying at a friend's place and there's a second bed.'

'Monsieur McDermott would be welcome to my spare room,' Bruno said in his imperfect English, 'but you would have to share a bathroom with my cousin and his fiancée. My house is in the same village where Nadia is staying.'

'You're very kind,' said McDermott, and then pointed to the square. 'Is this where the re-enactment happened, where all those benches are?'

'Yes, and the show goes on again tonight,' said Nadia, in English. 'I've been asked to take Papa's role, but this time du Guesclin will stay on his horse. I'm sure it's what Papa would want. It's supposed to be sold out but I think we can get you seats. I have to go and see the Mayor about taking the role this evening.'

'And I have to get to the local police station, but would you like to have a rather late lunch first?' asked Bruno.

'Or somewhere to shower and change,' added Nadia.

'A quick lunch would be good,' Claire replied. 'Just something light, my treat.'

Bruno led them to Le Bistrot, at the foot of the rue Montaigne, a reliable place that served good salads and fish, along with the usual Périgord cuisine, until late afternoon. Once he and Nadia had related in detail the events of the previous evening, Bruno asked whether Kerquelin's friends had plans for the coming week.

'Good food and tourism, a lot of talk among old friends and a bit of business,' said Angus, with a touch of a Scottish accent that Bruno recognized from Pamela's speech. 'Ever since we were at college together we've had an investment group, and we'll be reviewing our finances and hope that Brice will be well enough to join us. He'd also planned to take us on a tour of the local vineyards that he likes, to see if we can put together a deal to build an export market in the States.'

Bruno tried to keep his eyebrows from rising in disbelief. The idea that Kerquelin could join them later that week was absurd.

'I know the wines he likes so I can arrange the vineyard tour,' said Nadia. 'Tiregand, Jaubertie, Les Verdots, Bélingard, Le Raz, Moulin Caresse, Feely, Tirecul . . .' She beamed as Bruno nodded approval. These were his favourite wines.

'And Papa and I exchanged emails about the tourism part that he planned,' said Claire. 'A morning at Lascaux, afternoon at Hautefort, a day at the *bastides* followed by the night market in Beaumont. He'd booked a helicopter for us to spend the morning in Périgueux with the afternoon at Brantôme and Bourdeilles, and on to dinner at the truffle restaurant in Sorges. Another day starts with a balloon ride, followed by a truffle hunt and lunch at La Belle Etoile in Roque-Gageac, and then Josephine Baker's chateau. And a prehistory day at Les Eyzies with visits to the museum, and then the caves of Font de Gaume and La Madeleine, and a castle day with Commarque, Castelnaud and Beynac.' Then she turned to Nadia and added, 'Papa booked a big minivan that can seat all his friends and you and I have his Range Rover.'

'I'd rather stay with all the friends in the minivan,' said Nadia. 'We can take turns. But what about the Vézère valley with Limeuil and the St Denis market? And when do we fit in the vineyards, and won't people want some time just hanging around the pool? And you know Papa will want us to take them to Montaigne's tower and Fénelon's chateau.'

'An embarrassment of riches,' said Angus, smiling. 'Your father has arranged with his friends at Dassault for one of their Falcon private jets to fly the others from Paris to Bergerac and back again a week later.' He turned to Bruno, and asked, 'Do you have any idea when or perhaps if Brice will be able to join us? If not, we'd all like to visit him in the hospital, if that's possible.'

'I don't know, but Nadia can probably find out from her uncle Vincent,' Bruno said, wondering if these people had been told how serious Kerquelin's injury had been. 'I think it may be a longer recovery than you think, a stab wound very close to the heart. I saw that he'd lost a lot of blood.'

'You know Vincent Lannes,' Claire said to Angus, simply

ignoring Bruno's words. 'He came to see us in California two years ago and joined us when Harrison Coerver took us on that trip to the Napa Valley vineyard and Lori laid on that gourmet picnic lunch.'

'Ah, yes, the military man,' said Angus. 'He seemed an unusual friend for Brice but they were obviously quite close.'

'Are you all Americans, other than Brice?' asked Bruno.

'Not at all,' Angus replied. 'I'm naturalized but still a Scot at heart, then there's Krishnadev Nalapat, who helped start MindTree in India after he worked with us at Netscape and then helped start the Mozilla free software group. There's Hartmut, who's from Germany and was head-hunted from Netscape by the German software group SAP. And, of course, our dear friend Sonny Lin from Taiwan who is joining us later. He was brought into the chip business by Morris Chang when he was chairman of TSMC, the world's biggest chip-maker. Harrison Coerver is an American who made his money with Apple and moved into venture capital, like me. Last but not least is Phil Gergen from New York who helped build Windows95 and stayed with Microsoft. His wife, Mavis, is part of the group as our lawyer. They're amicably separated, but come as a couple to our reunions.'

'And what do you do in this group?' asked Bruno, still reeling at the thought of the wealth involved in renting helicopters, private jets and a luxury chateau. Maybe that was why they assumed Kerquelin's injury was just a passing inconvenience.

'Uncle Angus is the money man,' said Nadia. 'Finance director, investment manager, genius accountant.'

'And I work for him,' added Claire, smiling at Angus as if he were her favourite uncle. It was a good smile, Bruno thought, from her eyes as much as her generous mouth. And it was in her poise that Bruno saw a resemblance to Nadia. She was an attractive woman and carried herself as if she knew it but without taking herself too seriously, unlike Nadia's prickly mother. Claire's skin was a golden-brown, perhaps from the California sunshine. She was well-built with the broad shoulders of a serious tennis player yet with elegant and manicured hands. Bruno noted with approval the close and relaxed relationship she enjoyed with Nadia. And it was a pleasure to watch the animation in Claire's face as she spoke of her job and her evident affection for McDermott.

'Uncle Angus may look amiable but he's a slave driver. Still, he lets me out of the cage for this annual jaunt,' she said, smiling. 'It's like having lots of godfathers and everyone takes turns to host the event. Last year we were in Taiwan with Sonny and before that Hartmut arranged a luxury cruise ship for us to sail down the canal that goes from the Rhine to the Danube canal and all the way to the Black Sea. Did you know that Charlemagne originally planned to build it twelve hundred years ago? It was only finished in the 1990s.'

'Next year we plan to meet in India with Krishnadev,' Nadia added, as the waitress cleared their plates away and brought coffee and the bill. Angus swiftly picked it up and put down a black AmEx card, waving aside any suggestion that Bruno and Claire might help pay.

'We picked up a map of Sarlat in the tourist office,' Angus added. 'So if you and Bruno have business to deal with, Claire and I will play tourist and we'll all meet up again in front of the cathedral at, shall we say four?' He slid a business card across the table to Bruno. 'Text me if there's any delay.'

'I may have a police meeting at five in Périgueux,' Bruno said. 'But you have your rental car and Nadia knows the route to Fabiola's house and I can meet you there, Angus, and take you to my home.'

They parted, Nadia heading for the Mairie and Bruno for the police station to see if Messager had any news. Some progress had been made, Messager said in his ponderous way, when they were installed in his office.

'We've been able to confirm the identity of the man with the spider web tattoo and taken a statement from him and his friend. I'm satisfied that both are in the clear. We've also taken statements from all the people who were involved in the scrum on the steps. None of them has been able to clarify how Kerquelin was stabbed, and all the knives have been accounted for' – Messager paused for effect – 'except the one Kerquelin was carrying.'

'I hardly think he stabbed himself,' said Bruno, and Messager grunted a reluctant agreement.

'I was against going ahead with the re-enactment this evening with Kerquelin's daughter, but the Mayor insisted,' Messager went on. 'He said the town had invested too much money in this event not to try to earn it back, and that all the publicity would ensure we had a full house. Any news of Kerquelin's condition?'

Bruno explained what he'd heard from General Lannes, without specifying the hospital, and took his leave, telling Messager he'd call him later if anything new emerged from

J-J's briefing. In his car he put the phone into the cradle so he could free both hands for driving and called J-J to say he'd just seen Messager and was on his way to Périgueux if needed.

'Do you have anything new beyond the statements Messager sent me?' J-J asked.

Bruno described his meeting with Nadia, her sister and McDermott, mentioning that they were the three trustees of Kerquelin's will, and that from the next day Château de Rouffillac would be hosting eight members of the global mega-rich.

'Feeling jealous?'

'Not really,' Bruno replied. 'I like my life the way it is. I get the impression that Kerquelin and his friends just happened to be in the right place at the right time with the perfect skills and enthusiasms. They were paid in shares that were almost valueless when they first got them, so it's like winning the lottery. After meeting the former Madame Kerquelin, I certainly don't envy his life with her. Anyway, it sounds as though there's not much point in coming to your evening briefing but call me if you need me.'

Bruno looked in his phone's address book for the number of Caillevent, the vet, to ask about the horse Kerquelin had been riding, expecting to hear that it had been put down. Not at all, he was told. The horse had a badly sprained ankle, but nothing was broken and it was standing easily on three legs in Caillevent's barn. Well, he thought, thank heavens for small mercies.

'Not a pleasant job, I guess, cleaning off the manure the poor horse slipped on,' Bruno said, sounding sympathetic. Caillevent was close to being a friend, sitting with Bruno on the same regional youth sports committee.

'That was the odd thing,'Caillevent said. 'Not a trace of it on the legs or rump or feet. It must have slipped on the cobbles.'

Bruno digested this, or rather chewed over what he'd heard as he headed for St Denis on a back road where there would be less tourist traffic. He was planning to return home to shower and change, perhaps to see Alain and Rosalie, and then go to the riding school to take Hector and Balzac for a run. But he thought he'd better talk to Fabiola about Kerquelin. Although Nadia had been in shock the previous day, she and Claire were less concerned today. And it sounded as if Kerquelin had abandoned his barely hurt horse deliberately, as though he wanted to be at the heart of the action. Maybe he should discuss this with Fabiola. But first he called Alain and learned that they had finished house-hunting for the day and were already at his place and were planning to make dinner.

'We have some news that calls for a celebration,' Alain said excitedly, coming to the police van at the moment Bruno arrived, as if he'd been watching for his return. Rosalie darted out of the kitchen door to join them. 'Remember you and Florence advised us to talk to her headmaster, Rollo, about our hopes for a new career in teaching? When we told him of our plans to go to trade school, he said he was all in favour and he may have come up with a very neat solution that helps both him and us.'

Bruno knew that a new wing was being added to the St Denis *collège* for a gym and several extra classrooms. But now he heard Alain's news that Rollo also had a budget to hire new staff to teach a trade course for apprenticeships in construction, plumbing and electronics, for which Alain and Rosalie were perfectly suited.

'When Rollo asked Rosalie what her tech skills were she showed him her air force qualifications in plumbing and in construction, and those military credentials are recognized by the civilian trade,' Alain said.

'And Alain's diplomain electronics is also recognized,' Rosalie said. 'So Rollo asked us if we'd like to join his staff.'

'That's great, Alain,' said Bruno, forgetting his thought of calling Fabiola, delightedly pumping Alain's hand and giving Rosalie a hug. 'So you'll be based right here in St Denis. Will the air force go for it?'

'I was afraid they wouldn't but Rollo explained to my admin officer that the construction of the new wing was behind schedule and would not be ready until January. Air force regulations say that getting a civilian teaching diploma can be counted as time served so we can do a three-month initial teaching course at Bergerac until Christmas, and then two terms with a day of teacher training each week while we work. By this time next summer, we'll be out of the air force with our pensions and on full salary as qualified teachers.'

'And you haven't heard about what comes with it,' said Rosalie. 'We'll qualify for one of those subsidized apartments at the school, just like Florence. She'll be our neighbour. So we can buy a place of our own at our leisure, fix it up and rent it out until we retire with a house waiting for us.'

'That's amazing,' said Bruno. 'This calls for a celebration. I think I have some Champagne in the fridge—'

'We already bought a bottle,' said Rosalie, interrupting him. 'And I've made us dinner, a *blanquette de veau* with a plum tart for dessert.'

'Better and better,' said Bruno.

Rosalie cheerfully steered him to the table in the sunlight as Alain darted inside to get the Champagne. 'Hubert at the wine store told us about the Monthuys Champagne you like, so we bought a bottle.'

'When do you move into the apartment at the *collège*?' Bruno asked, raising his glass to them before taking his first, refreshing sip.

'It's vacant, so we can start fixing it up this week, give it a thorough cleaning, a paint job. I think we'll need to overhaul the electricity and the plumbing and then think about furniture,' said Alain. 'We'll go back to the airbase until the teaching course starts in September, and that's residential. And then we'll have Christmas here in St Denis and start work in January.'

'And we've set our wedding date for the twenty-first of August,' Rosalie broke in. 'That will give us time for a honeymoon before we start the course, and we'd both like you to be our best man.'

Bruno sat back, beaming, and took another sip. The thought of having family of his own nearby was deeply satisfying. Born an orphan and raised for his first six years in a church orphanage before being taken into his aunt's crowded and chaotic home in Bergerac, Bruno's closest relationship had always been with his cousin Alain. Each of them had sought some discipline in their lives, Bruno in the army and Alain in the air force, and had left home as soon as they could. They had run across one another from time to time. There had been a shared weekend leave in Paris of which Bruno had no memory, except of an empty wallet. During their time in the service, they had crossed paths once in the Ivory Coast, where France maintained a base and a training section, and again in Djibouti for a single evening, and had spent a weekend skiing in Canada together when they had both been on an air-land combat team training for winter warfare. But those brief reunions had riveted them together. And now that Alain's mother, Bruno's aunt, had died, they had each listed the other as next-of-kin.

Bruno took a glass and a half before hugging them, opening a bottle of the Château Tiregand 2011 to go with dinner, and remembered to warn them that the other spare room would be occupied that night by Angus. He left for the riding school, promising to be back in ninety minutes. He was looking forward to Balzac's greeting and the way that Hector quivered with happy expectation when Bruno saddled him. He'd also be able to share the happy news of the impending marriage with Pamela, Gilles and Fabiola. Maybe he'd become Uncle Bruno. And he'd have to thank Florence for the part she had doubtless played in suggesting to Rollo that Bruno's cousin and his new wife could fill the double vacancy at the *collège*. For the first time since the emergency had erupted in the main square of Sarlat the previous evening, Bruno felt himself at ease and content.

It did not last. Fabiola, already in riding clothes, with her Andalusian saddled, was standing at the stable door waiting for him, staring coolly at him with her chin high and her hands on her hips. There was no sign of Pamela, nor of Gilles or Félix, the stable boy. Other than Hector, the stables were empty, and rather than rush to greet him, Balzac seemed to sense the tension in the air and walked gingerly forward to run his muzzle against Bruno's leg before squatting and looking uncertainly from Bruno to Fabiola and back again.

'What the hell is going on with that man who played du Guesclin last night and who has since disappeared?' she began. 'Where exactly is he and who is looking after him, if he's still alive?'

'His name is Brice Kerquelin and you told me this morning that he's in intensive care in the Piqué military hospital,' Bruno replied calmly. 'I'm told he's still in danger but is expected to make a full recovery.'

'From what I saw of his condition last night I find that very hard to believe,' she snapped. 'Barrat won't return my calls. The Piqué hospital refuses to talk to me since I'm a civilian; they say it's a military matter and hang up. There are maybe three surgeons in this region who are qualified for the open-heart surgery that the man evidently needed and not one of them has been called in. The medical council for Nouvelle Aquitaine say the matter is out of their hands.'

'And I know no more than you do,' Bruno replied, deliberately speaking calmly and thinking that with Fabiola in this aggressive mood, it was no time to share his own concerns. 'You know that Domme is one of the most secret intelligence bases in France and that Kerquelin is a senior figure, a cyber-expert who may well be irreplaceable. France has enemies who would probably see him as a highly important target. You can understand why the security services are taking precautions that must seem to you to be medically absurd. Please consider this from their point of view, and bear in mind that they have a sense of duty that matches your own devotion to your profession. Their immediate fear was that this was an attempted assassination of a senior colleague, so the security blanket was immediately applied. And if you ask me, they were right to do it. In their shoes, I'd probably have done the same thing.'

'Do they still think he's in danger?'

Bruno noted gratefully that she had used the word 'they' rather than 'you'.

'Nobody is sure but understandably they don't want to take any chances. All the video and witness evidence so far points to an accident rather than murder, but these are early days. What I can tell you is that Kerquelin himself was probably to blame. He should never have been on those steps. When his horse fell he just blundered in and threw out all the carefully rehearsed choreography of that fight. But at least it turns out the horse is all right.'

Fabiola studied his face for a long moment and then nodded. 'I see. So you're telling me that such a senior and important man was a damn fool who was responsible for that chaos on the steps and somehow got hurt in the process.'

'With his own knife, it seems,' Bruno said. 'All the others have now been accounted for.'

'Does that mean you're thinking he attempted some kind of bizarre and demonstrative public suicide?' This time her voice was more normal, curious rather than aggressive, as though she was trying to understand.

Bruno shook his head. 'Not with his other daughter and his best friends arriving. And not from what I learned of the man from his home, his family and his commitment to his work. By the way, Nadia will be late coming back tonight because she's agreed to play the role of du Guesclin, taking the part of her father in the re-enactment.'

Fabiola rolled her eyes. 'That's crazy. You have to be joking.'

'Not at all; she'll still play the role of the maiden in the first part and then the role of her father at the end. She's vowed to ride slowly and stay on the horse. She wants to do it as a kind of tribute to her father.'

'And from what I know of Nadia from our women's group, she probably feels it's some kind of duty, not least to all the others taking part,' Fabiola said slowly, her voice now almost normal. 'She's an impressive young woman, very level-headed and sensible.'

The women's group was a project that Fabiola had launched with Florence and Pamela. They had brought in the Mayor's partner, Jacqueline, a historian who still taught a semester each year at the Sorbonne. Other successful women involved included a local accountant, a *notaire* and a pharmacist. Groups had also formed in other villages and small towns of the region. The object was to raise the sights of the young girls of the region beyond the usual roles of becoming hairdressers or shop assistants or locked into an early marriage.

Pamela had told Bruno that the idea had been inspired by Félix, who was raised by a drunken, unemployed father and a mother from the Caribbean whose work as a cleaner kept the family together. Félix had been in and out of trouble, a truant on the way to being a delinquent when Bruno had learned that the youngster loved horses. He persuaded Pamela to give the boy a chance as a part-time stable hand, and Bruno had rescued a battered old bicycle from the town's recycling dump so Félix could get to the riding school in the mornings and evenings. Félix now taught others to ride horses and ponies, and was doing very well at the *lycée*, heading for university and determined to make a career as a vet.

If it worked for a boy like Félix, they could do the same for girls, Pamela and her friends had decided. They had started with the girls who played on the St Denis women's rugby team that Bruno coached. Young women like Nadia had been persuaded to offer their own services as mentors and part-time tutors, running reading groups and borrowing the small bus from the retirement home to take the girls to museums and galleries in Les Eyzies, Périgueux and Bordeaux.

'Nadia will be coming back here after tonight's show with her sister, Claire, hoping you'll let them share the room. They should be out of your hair by tomorrow because they've booked rooms at Château de Rouffillac,' Bruno said. 'One of their father's friends is going to stay in my spare room tonight. He and Claire took an overnight flight from San Francisco and I saw them all in Sarlat for lunch today.'

'I still think there's something fishy about all of this,' Fabiola said, 'not that I can put my finger on it. Speaking as a doctor, I find the treatment of Nadia's father to be outrageous, and for the life of me I can't understand it.'

'Welcome to police work, where we usually begin in ignorance, find proof to be elusive, witnesses to contradict one another and suspects to be numerous. Even when we finish our investigation we're left with the nagging guilt that certainty is seldom reliable,' Bruno replied, waved farewell and took Hector off for his ride.

But as he drove back to dine with Alain and Rosalie, he understood Fabiola's outrage. He had been there when she had pointed in disbelief to the flood of blood, had seen the knife plunged in deep and perilously close to the heart. And already the wounded man was supposedly recovering and might even be able to see his family and friends later in the week? Bruno thought that the official version of Kerquelin's wounding was becoming increasingly hard to swallow.

Chapter 9

After a croissant breakfast at Fabiola's the next day, Bruno waved *au revoir* to Nadia, Claire and Angus, who were heading to meet the other chateau guests at Bergerac airport and giving Gilles a lift to Bergerac station to catch a train to Bordeaux for his flight via Paris to Kyiv. Bruno then went to the Mairie to catch up on his paperwork. He'd hardly begun when the Mayor called him in.

'I hear from Rollo that your cousin and his wife-to-be are going to become citizens of St Denis, teaching at the *collège*, and that gives me an idea,' the Mayor said. 'Rollo tells me they'll be teaching apprentices to be electricians and construction workers. And you know, of course, that our town vineyard's plans for a purpose-built visitors' and tasting centre have been delayed by a cash shortage?'

Bruno nodded again, and began to understand where this conversation was heading.

'Rollo and I wondered whether the first project for the apprentices might be to construct the centre, so the labour would be free and we'd only have to pay for the materials, the plumbing and the electrification.'

'We'd still need to pay an architect,' Bruno said.

'Maybe not. I had a word with Jack Crimson, who as you know spends a lot of time visiting the vineyards. I asked him which were the best tasting rooms. He said that Château de Tiregand, Château Belingard, Château de la Jaubertie and Les Verdots were among his favourites. He said that if we wanted to offer visitors a light lunch or other refreshment, which we most certainly do, he thought the facilities and design at Château de Fayolle in Saussignac were outstanding. It is run by an imaginative American couple and he poured me a glass of their Sang du Sanglier red, which I thought was very good. Jack said you knew it, and that you had been to their *terroir* together. Is that right?'

'Yes. Their wines are excellent, particularly that one, and so are the facilities. They're large and airy with a high roof. There's an almost circular tasting bench, with taps and basins at each place, a very good display space and a nice terrace where people can have lunch.'

'Did you know that they designed and built the place themselves?' the Mayor asked. 'Jack thought we might be able to borrow their plans, for a reasonable fee. I asked Michel from our works department to go to the vineyard, and he liked what he saw. He took some photos and came back and estimated that we could get all the materials we needed for around twenty thousand euros. If we have to pay for the labour, he said, we would more than double that price. But as an apprenticeship project, the labour would be free. I think that calls for a drink.'

The Mayor brought out two cognac glasses and an unlabelled green bottle from the cupboard in his desk. 'You remember that magnificent *gnôle* that Driant made, the one that Dr Gelletreau likes so much?'

'The best *eau de vie* in the valley,' said Bruno, eyeing the bottle with respect. 'Not exactly legal, though.'

'Gelletreau had it analysed and, using Driant's old still, which is waiting to be restored so that it can be put on display in our museum, he's been trying to re-create it. This is the result,' said the Mayor, pouring out two glasses and handing one to Bruno.

'*Mon Dieu*,' Bruno exclaimed, clearing his throat after his first, fiery sip. 'That tastes exactly like the real thing. It can't possibly be legal.'

'No, but as chairman of the trustees of the museum, I'm duty-bound to certify that the still we will put on display is the genuine antique. And how can we be satisfied it's the real thing if we didn't taste the product? Your very good health, my dear Bruno.'

'And yours, Monsieur le Maire.'

'I almost forgot to tell you,' the Mayor said as Bruno reached the door. 'General Lannes is expecting your call.'

Once back in his office, Bruno called the familiar number and saw the tiny green light which said their call was encrypted and secure. He asked for General Lannes and was put through at once.

'Ah, Bruno, good to hear from you. Your new assignment begins right now. You're to review the security procedures at Château de Rouffillac alongside the head of security at Domme, Mademoiselle Marie-Dominique Pantin, whom you've met. Once you're both satisfied, she'll return to Domme and you'll remain at the chateau in sole charge, with a small squad of troops under your command who will make their own billeting arrangements. I want round-the-clock patrols and sentries, the usual procedure, but they should remain as far as possible out of sight; I don't want Kerquelin's guests alarmed. But the priority is to keep them safe, just in case whatever happened to Kerquelin was intentional. Understood?'

'Yes, sir. May I know which unit you'll be assigning to my command?' Bruno's mind clicked into that automatic litany of the professional soldier, MM–CC, which stood for Mission and Means, Communications and Command.

'You'll have a squad of parachute dragoons, from the same unit you got on with so well during that troubadour business. Rumour has it that you even cooked the troops omelettes with some eggs from your own chickens. Those new troops should be more than happy to be under your orders.'

'Yes, sir. And the rules of engagement?'

'The usual: shoot to kill if your life or the lives of those civilians under your care are endangered, but be cautious. We've informed your *préfecture* that an army–police liaison exercise is under way in the area. You have your service weapon and the squad will bring some extra gear for you: body armour, night vision glasses, and an FN SCAR weapon for you.'

'Yes, sir. Flares and anti-personnel grenades might be useful if you expect any kind of armed attack. If the threat looks serious, we might need floodlights, mortars and a detailed evacuation. There's a ruined village between Carlux and Rouffillac and some public gardens nearby, Les Jardins de Cadiot, a potential helicopter landing site for possible evacuation or reinforcements.'

'Let's not go over the top, Bruno,' Lannes replied. 'Through

Mademoiselle Pantin, the security team at Domme will be available in an emergency. One more thing: if and when Brice Kerquelin is well enough to join the group, I'll accompany him. Until then, since for security reasons there can be no hospital visits, I'll give Brice's daughters a daily report on his condition.'

'When should I expect a full briefing on potential threats?'

'This is your briefing, Bruno, unless new intelligence comes to my attention. I'll let you know if the situation changes. This assignment will continue until all the guests leave Bergerac. Until then, the security of Brice Kerquelin and his guests and daughters while in the Périgord will continue to be your responsibility. Oh, and Bruno, if I were you, I'd take along some decent clothes in case they invite you to dinner at the chateau.'

'I will. Just one more thing. I gather they have a busy schedule of sightseeing planned: castles, caves and vineyard visits. Am I supposed to accompany them at all times?'

'Yes, with at least your personal weapon. But use your discretion. These people probably won't appreciate you hovering around them all the time. I'll arrange for troops in civilian clothes to follow the guests whenever you leave. Get me a schedule of their plans as soon as you can.'

'What about the former Madame Kerquelin? Should I expect her to make an appearance? After all, she knows all these people.'

'Ah, Suzanne, a dangerous woman,' Lannes said with a sigh. 'It might be hard to exclude her. Play it by ear, Bruno. And watch your step with Mademoiselle Pantin. You'll meet her at the chateau at noon today for the security review. If anything comes up, let me know. Good luck.'

Bruno returned to his office, sat back and realized that was the second time someone had warned him about Marie-Do. He did not understand why. In his own brief encounter with her, she had been correct, collegial and even friendly. She had also spoken favourably of his dog, and about perhaps taking one of his puppies. She would not have been appointed head of security at Domme unless she was seen as a highly capable professional, and that was how he resolved to treat her.

After briefing the Mayor on his new assignment, Bruno drove home to pick up some clothes, toiletries and weapons. He then had to pick up Balzac and some dog food, and warn Pamela he wouldn't be riding Hector for a while. He should also fill up his elderly Land Rover. It wouldn't be wise to leave a police van parked at the chateau. He should call J-J to explain, and he'd have to call a neighbour to arrange for his chickens to be fed and watered. And he'd need to email Fabiola, the Baron and Jack Crimson so they knew where he was and when to expect his return. He should also call Marie-Do to arrange their meeting at Rouffillac. He would also call Nadia, to ask how her performance had gone the previous evening, and to let her know of his presence, under orders, at Rouffillac.

Ninety minutes later, he saw Château de Rouffillac standing alone and magnificent atop the hill that loomed over the Dordogne river, its golden stones seeming to blaze in the sunlight. He drove up the dirt track that snaked up the flank

of the hill and parked to one side of the chateau. To the other side of the main doorway a splendid vintage Jaguar, cream-coloured with sweeping lines and an air of elegant menace, stood as though on guard as much as on display. There was no sign of the minivan that he'd expected, nor of any car belonging to Marie-Do. One of the double doors was open and he rang the big bell that hung to one side. After a moment, a middle-aged woman dressed for housekeeping arrived at the door, looked surprised at the sight of his police uniform and asked what he wanted in a strong local accent.

'*Bonjour, madame*,' he said, touching the brim of his cap. 'I'm Chef de Police Courrèges, under orders to make a security check before your guests arrive. I believe I'm expected, and a colleague from the security team at Domme will be joining me. Are the owners in?'

'I thought I knew your face from TV and the papers, the fire at Castelnaud. That was you, wasn't it?' She glanced down at Balzac. 'Oh, what a handsome dog! Does he hunt?'

'He's getting the hang of it, so I can get the occasional *bécasse* and he's good with truffles. And for security, there's not a better dog in France. I'm glad we could help the *pompiers* save Castelnaud. Please, call me Bruno.'

'I'm Sylvie, one of the housekeepers. Madame is in the kitchen preparing a welcoming lunch. Not a proper Périgord lunch, you understand, just something light.' She gave him a wink, adding, 'You know these Americans. Follow me.'

With Balzac at their heels, she led him through a wide lobby that gave him a glimpse of a formal dining room and a spiral staircase, and a vast sitting room with views over the valley. She turned off through a corridor into a courtyard with a long table set for about a dozen people. To his right, the rear wall of the chateau rose three or maybe four storeys, stretching along to a stone wall with an iron gate and a lawn beyond it, and a low wall guarding the slope down to the river. The south bank of the Dordogne rose perhaps four hundred metres away, and he saw the towers of Fénelon's castle against the skyline.

Looking around, Bruno had a sense of the twelfth-century bones of the castle, overlaid by the nineteenth-century restoration that had sought to give the place the character of the early sixteenth century, the Renaissance creeping in to add gentility to the harsh old fortress. Ahead of him on the far side of the courtyard was a stone bluff that had been made into a kind of fountain, and above it the rise of the hill continued into thick trees. That could be a danger point, Bruno thought, as Balzac trotted around the courtyard, sniffing for any evidence of another dog. To Bruno's left was the other wing of the chateau. Sylvie led him into the ground floor where a huge and very modern kitchen opened before him.

He was startled by the sight of a beautiful young woman, her blonde hair piled into a bun, turning to greet them while tossing a salad. She was wearing shorts that showed off her long, tanned legs, and she could only have been American, featuring that unique combination of corn-fed health, lazy grace and perfect teeth.

'Hi, I'm Cassandra,' she said in good French. 'You must be Capitaine Bruno. We had a call from some general at the Interior Ministry to say we should expect you along with a woman named Marie-Dominique. I guess we've got some real VIPs coming.'

Bruno introduced himself and went to shake her elegant hand, but she waved it so he could see it was still glistening from the oil of the salad dressing. She proffered him a tanned

125

forearm instead, and then her face broke into a wide and almost girlish grin as she caught sight of Balzac.

'A basset,' she exclaimed. 'I just love them, they look so wise, as if they've seen everything. Is he a tracking dog or a hunting hound?'

'A bit of both,' Bruno replied. 'His name is Balzac.'

She wiped her hands clean of the salad oil and bent to pat him. Balzac, who always had a soft spot for women, gave her an appreciative, soft 'Woof' and gazed at her worshipfully as she stroked that special spot behind his ears.

She looked up. 'My husband is down at the pool, doing a last skim for the guests. He can show you around, or you could just stroll around yourself, get familiar with the place. I'm afraid all the main guest rooms are full but we can give you a room with a shower in the staff quarters on the top floor, and I'll set you and Marie-Do a couple of extra places for lunch. It's just quiche and a salad, cheese and strawberries. We'll stay out of your hair but we're just a step away, in that old house on the right you passed as you drove up the lane.'

'I only had eyes for that Jaguar parked outside,' he said.

'You can't miss the place. Why don't you take a look around with Balzac until the others arrive?'

Bruno thanked her and touched his cap, going out to the courtyard and through the gate to the low wall. He looked down at the river. To the left, a little lower, a red-haired man was skimming the swimming pool. That must be Cassandra's husband. Bruno turned right and made a circuit of the chateau. The long wall he had seen from the road below was sixty, maybe seventy metres long. He came back in the front door, looked into the main rooms and then climbed the stairs and found to his left an enormous library that took up much of the wing. The kitchen was below, he realized. On a large desk was a bust of a fine-looking man in eighteenth-century dress, inscribed with the name Thomas Jefferson. Bruno knew Jefferson had been an early American president, and had spent years before the French Revolution as Ambassador for the young United States in Paris, staying there for some months after the fall of the Bastille. From a small plaque on the base of the bust, Bruno learned that in the course of his travels into the French wine regions Jefferson had been in this very room, writing letters, while on his pilgrimage to the nearby castle of the Fénelon family.

Bruno had read somewhere that Jefferson had owned several copies of *Télémachus*, Archbishop Fénelon's treatise on how best to raise and educate a wise and just king. Since Fénelon was tutor to the heir to the throne, Louis XIV had read it with care and been so infuriated by its liberal sentiments that he had exiled Fénelon to the diocese of Cambrai, which was at the time being attacked by a Spanish army. Fénelon had then turned his episcopal home into a hospital. His book had become an international best-seller and a bible to reformers across Europe, who sometimes called Fénelon one of the fathers of the Enlightenment.

With a bow of respect to Jefferson and Fénelon, Bruno moved on to the long corridor that led to a series of grand bedroom suites, each of them grandly furnished but in different styles, and each with the kind of bathroom that would tempt one to linger. One, in a turret, was circular. Bruno felt himself unexpectedly pleased that the place did not seem in the least like a hotel, more like a home that had been in the hands of a fortunate and tasteful family for generations. As he descended to the ground floor, the main door opened and Marie-Do came in, looking anxious and hot in a trouser suit that was too warm for the weather. Behind her was a small Miata convertible with the hood down, parked askew. She must have been hot, driving slowly in the bright sunshine along the busiest tourist road in the region.

'Sorry to be a bit late, Bruno, I had trouble finding the entrance. Is that your dog? He's gorgeous.' She presented her cheeks to be kissed. 'Where's the bathroom? I need to wash.'

'There's one just up there,' he said, pointing. 'It's all right, the guests haven't arrived yet from the airport. Take your time.'

She darted upstairs and Bruno pulled out the small-scale map of the district and his notebook and began making a quick sketch of the chateau and its surroundings, marking the spots where he'd need sentries – at the bend of the track that came up from the road, at the pool to watch the ascent from the road, in the woods above the rocky outcrop. He'd have to walk through all the surroundings, up through the woods to the abandoned village and on to the village of Carlux. He'd also have to check out the approaches from the house where Cassandra and her husband stayed. His map said that one of the small roads coming towards him from Carlux was called the Impasse du Camp Romain, so he'd better look at whatever of those fortifications remained after nearly two thousand years.

'Hello,' said a voice. The red-haired man from the pool was coming towards him wearing shorts and a T-shirt. His face was brick-red from the sun but his features were pleasantly craggy. A bit taller than Bruno, he had the look of a rugby player and an amiable grin as he came forward to shake hands. He had a good grip, firm without trying to show off. Bruno liked him on sight.

'Hi, I'm Kirk. Welcome to Rouffillac.' The accent was English but the French was correct.

'Thank you, I'm Bruno. It's a wonderful place you have here; the study and the upstairs bedrooms and bathrooms took my breath away. And so did the Jaguar that's parked outside.'

'It's a great car, but no air-conditioning, alas. Cassandra gets all the credit for the decor. It took a lot of planning and lots of consultation with our plumbers and electricians but they did a terrific job. Can I offer you a drink? I need a beer.'

'Not just now, thanks, I'm on duty. My colleague, Mademoiselle Pantin, just arrived and is washing.'

'The man from the Interior Ministry said that you were a captain and she's a *commissaire*, but that you were local. Is that right?'

'The highest rank I ever had in the army was *sergent-chef*,' Bruno said. 'These days I'm just a local policeman with the courtesy rank of captain, the equivalent of *commissaire*.'

'That's not what Sylvie just told me. She called you the man who saved Castelnaud from a forest fire.'

'Me and hundreds of others, mainly the *pompiers*. Would you mind showing me around the grounds sometime this afternoon, up to the old Roman fort and the abandoned village? I need to get a good look at the area around here.'

'It will be a pleasure,' Kirk replied, as Marie-Do made her

entrance. Her hair had been brushed and she looked refreshed and much more self-possessed, until there came the sound of a car's horn being repeatedly beeped outside. Kirk and Bruno went to the door to see Claire was leaning out of the minivan window demanding in angry French that someone should move that wretched heap of Japanese tin so that she could park.

Marie-Do's cheeks turned red as she took keys from her bag and went outside to move her convertible.

'That's a good start,' murmured Kirk, with a wink at Bruno, before he turned back to the corridor to call, 'Cassandra, they're here.'

Amid the flurry of greetings and introductions, admiration of the Jaguar, of Balzac, and then of the building, Cassandra made an entrance that imposed a moment of awed silence. Now wearing a wraparound dress in cream silk with matching shoes, her hair down and free, she reminded Bruno of some classical statue from ancient Greece. She smiled and welcomed the new arrivals and suddenly the hallway was noisily busy again with handshakes and greetings. With an elegant gesture, Cassandra stewarded all the guests and Marie-Do into the big living room for a glass of Champagne while Kirk and Bruno were left to unload the luggage from the van.

'Cassandra has already assigned the rooms,' Kirk said. 'I've got a list so if the suitcases have labels we can take them up to their rightful rooms.'

'Sylvie's husband, Louis, usually helps but he's late,' Kirk added as he and Bruno tramped up the stairs with the suitcases. 'He went to Sarlat to do the shopping but he must have been held up by the tourist traffic. Thanks for helping.'

'You're feeding me and putting me up so it's the least I can do,' Bruno said. 'Which reminds me, I need to know where my room is.'

They made three trips with the suitcases and a fourth for Kirk to show Bruno what turned out to be a charming room with a bed, desk, modern bathroom and a magnificent view. Kirk looked uneasily at the shotgun Bruno had slung over his shoulder.

'Is that your usual weapon or are you planning on doing some hunting around here?' he asked, making a joke of it but evidently nervous.

'I should tell you that I'll have a squad of special forces troops under my command nearby. You will probably never see them and they will take care of their own food and shelter, but they'll be patrolling and standing sentry duty while these guests are here. And they will be much more heavily armed than me. I may sometimes be dressed like them.'

'What's going on, exactly, Bruno?' Kirk asked. 'I recognized a couple of the people who came out of the minivan. I made my own money in Silicon Valley but at a much more humble level than these guys. There are some superstars here – Google, Microsoft and venture capital.'

'You heard about the wounding of Monsieur Kerquelin at the re-enactment of the liberation of Sarlat?' Bruno began. 'This is his party, with his daughters, and all your other guests are his old friends. He was involved in the start of Google and now plays a prominent role in French security. So we're taking extraordinary precautions while we work out whether he was hurt by accident or by something more sinister. I rely on you to keep all that to yourself. My view is that it was an accident, and that he'll recover and join his friends and daughters later. The soldiers are just insurance.'

'I hope that's true, but I guess I'd better check my insurance policy,' Kirk said.

Bruno called General Lannes's number and expressed Kirk's concerns to the duty officer who picked up the phone. The officer listened to his request, asked for Kirk's email address, and promised to send a formal letter of indemnity on ministerial notepaper for the insurance broker. Bruno passed on the news to Kirk.

'That's a relief, thank you,' Kirk said. 'Do you really think there's any danger?'

'I've been told officially that there is no known threat at this stage and that the security people are here purely as a precaution because of the prominence of your guests, and because of the unfortunate event at the Sarlat re-enactment.'

'Let's hope they're right,' Kirk said. 'Now, do you want to go downstairs for a glass of champagne and some lunch or would you rather I give you a tour?'

'The tour, please, but let me ask Mademoiselle Pantin if she'd like to join us. You know, I noticed there's a bolt but I don't see a key to the door of this room. Should there be one?'

'No, since this is our private home and not a hotel. Any guest who needs to keep things in a safe just has to ask me.'

'In that case, unless I'm in my room I'd better keep the shotgun locked in my car.'

They went downstairs to find Marie-Do, who had evidently made peace with Claire after the fuss over the parking place and was now enjoying herself and the Champagne. She said she would stay to check the house and the immediate surroundings while Bruno explored the neighbourhood. Kirk led the way through the courtyard and up a path beside the rocky outcrop that led through the trees for perhaps two hundred metres before they came to a ruined church. Balzac immediately began to explore the place and Bruno asked if it had been part of the abandoned village.

'Maybe, or maybe it was a chapel for the castle. The locals say there was a plague here, seventeenth or eighteenth century, which is why the village was abandoned. It was a bit further on, and all you'll find of the supposed Roman fortifications is a long, straight ditch and some earthworks.'

Kirk was breathing easily despite the uphill path; evidently he was in good shape.

'Do you get any hunters here?' Bruno asked, looking around to see if there might be any place for a sniper to get sight of the courtyard, but the trees, loaded with summer foliage, were too thick.

'No, we put *Chasse Interdite* signs up on the edges of our land and since we employ some locals and used only local craftsmen when we restored the place, people seem to accept that. We never hear guns nearby, which is a relief, since our young daughter likes to play in the woods with school friends.'

'How old is she?'

'Six. She normally stays around the house down the road where we live, but as soon as she hears there's a basset hound here, she'll come running.'

'Balzac is great with young children,' said Bruno, thinking

of Florence's twins. 'Is there another way back through the woods, to come out by your pool?'

'Yes. We'll go back the long way round but there's not much to see until we get through the trees. We'd better stay on the path because the cliff is pretty steep here, almost a straight drop down to the road.'

'Thanks for the tour,' Bruno said as they came out just above the swimming pool a short while later. 'I'll take a longer stroll around this afternoon when the special forces get here. They'll stay out of your way, and I hope the guests never have to see them.'

'I imagine the guests will be taking a few tourist trips, to the caves and a castle or two, maybe some vineyards.'

'They have plans to do so. I'll go with them and we'll have a car following, soldiers wearing plain clothes. I'm pretty sure we'll have a peaceful time and I'm sorry we have to impose on you.'

'That's fine, I understand. And it's a pleasure having your dog here. He seems to fit right in, as if he was always meant to hang around a chateau, looking very noble and decorative.'

'His pedigree is a lot grander than my own,' Bruno said, grinning. 'When Balzac mated for the first time the lady who was gracious enough to bestow her favours upon him was called Diane de Poitiers, after the royal mistress. It's very gracious of him to hang around with a commoner like me.'

'And was the mating a success?'

'Absolutely. We named one of their puppies Gabrielle d'Estrées.'

'Why does that name ring a bell?' Kirk asked, as though some fleeting memory was on the tip of his tongue.

'Have you been to the Louvre in Paris?' Bruno asked. 'One of the most popular paintings in the place shows two very white-skinned and topless beauties of the court sharing their bath, and one of them is gently pinching the nipple of the other. Apparently the gesture was meant to indicate that the one being pinched, Gabrielle, had succeeded in becoming pregnant by the king. They were two sisters, Gabrielle d'Estrées, yet another mistress of King Henri IV, being pinched by the Duchess of Villars. Or maybe it was the other way around.'

'He was enjoying the favours of both sisters?' Kirk asked. 'Must have been quite a guy.'

'He was known as *le vert gallant*, which is the delicate way they described a king who was a relentless man for the ladies,' said Bruno, smiling. 'He went for anything in skirts, from tavern maids to duchesses, and there was even some gossip about nuns. A true father of his people and probably the most popular monarch we ever had. We even named a dish after him, *poulet Henri Quatre*, chicken cooked in a pot, because he said he wanted every French family, even the poorest, to have such a meal every Sunday.'

Chapter 10

'I imagine you would rather I didn't tell Isabelle of your week with the beautiful Madame Cassandra,' said Marie-Do, teasingly, as they followed Balzac down the path to the house where Kirk and Cassandra lived with their daughter. Bruno was startled and not sure how or whether to reply when suddenly Balzac stopped, his tail up and one front paw poised. It was the pose he assumed when hunting and had sniffed or spotted something. With a rustling in the undergrowth, a small face emerged, broke into a wide smile, and then a little girl jumped out to throw herself on Balzac. The hound sidestepped and as soon as she fell on her hands and knees he began to lick her face with affection. They rolled over and over, hugging and slavering, and then she looked up.

'*Bonjour, monsieur-dame.* Are you the new guests?' she asked, in perfect kindergarten French. She was wearing shorts, trainers and a baggy blue T-shirt that bore the face of Snoopy. Balzac pushed her over again to resume the playful embrace.

'Balzac, *ici*,' Bruno said firmly, and his dog came to Bruno's side, giving Bruno an aggrieved look, as if enquiring why his master wanted to stop the fun.

'I just had lunch with your *maman*, and my name is Marie-Do. What's your name?'

'I'm supposed to be Patricia, but everyone calls me Patsy,' came the reply. The little girl was standing up politely, but her eyes kept drifting to the dog. 'Is his name Balzac?'

'That's right. He's my dog and my name is Bruno. I'll be staying here for a while, helping look after the other guests. Would you like to show me the garden and the house where you live? Balzac can come with us.'

'Oh, I really want a dog of my own,' she said, taking one of Balzac's long ears and using it to stroke her cheek. 'His ears are so soft. Can I play with him from time to time while you're here?'

Bruno got down on his haunches so he was close to Patsy's eye level, and said, 'You'll have trouble keeping him away.'

'May I feed him, please?'

'Yes, but not too much. I give him a small corner of my own croissant at breakfast but really he eats only once a day. There's one thing to remember and it's important: please don't give him chocolate or anything that's very sweet. I make my own dog biscuits for him and if you like I can let you have some to give him. Would you like that?'

'Oh, yes.'

'Okay, it's a deal,' he said, and put out his hand. 'Let's shake on it, and then Balzac can stay with you while Marie-Do and I finish our stroll.'

Patsy solemnly shook his hand, then looked down at Balzac and said firmly, 'No chocolate for you, Balzac, but lots of hugs.' Then she dropped to her knees and embraced him.

'It's obvious you like children,' said Marie-Do as they walked on. 'But you have none of your own, right?'

'I sometimes think I'm blessed to have a whole village-full in St Denis,' Bruno said, with a cheerfulness he deployed to mask his regret. 'I like coaching them in sports, tennis and rugby. It means a lot to me that all the kids know me by name and always say hello. I like being there to escort the little ones across the road to school and playing Father Christmas at the children's party that we organize every year at the retirement home.'

'So they grow up thinking the police are their friends?' she asked.

'I hope so. And they all love Balzac.'

'What do you make of this group of Kerquelin's friends?'

'Too soon to tell,' he replied. 'But given that they are probably the richest people I'll ever meet, they seem pretty human. Over the past couple of days I've come to know Nadia a bit, she's Kerquelin's younger daughter, and she seems refreshingly normal.'

'From what I've seen of him at work her father is a decent man, always amiable, unlike a lot of the higher-ups in the service,' Marie-Do said. 'He always has a friendly word for people, even the janitors. I'm told he also plays *le Père Noël* at our Christmas party in Domme but I haven't been there long enough to see it.'

'Do you miss Paris?' he asked.

'The city, yes, but the work at La Piscine, not so much. That was why I applied for this job, plus I've always wanted to live in the country. I'm Parisienne born and bred but I like seeing green fields and hills around me and this is a lovely part of France. But to get back to business, I thought we're supposed to have some soldiers to guard the place.'

'They'll text me when they arrive,' said Bruno, just as they reached the old house where Cassandra and Kirk and their daughter lived. Off to the side was a smaller house with a neat vegetable garden that someone had laboriously dug out of the slope. Chickens were clucking around the neat rows of lettuces and strawberry plants. As Bruno admired the scene a man rose from behind the tall and bushy rows of tomato plants and looked at them curiously.

'*Bonjour, monsieur,*' Bruno called out in a friendly voice. 'Are you Louis, Sylvie's husband?'

'*Monsieur-dame*, yes, I am. Are you the security people?'

'That's us. I'm Bruno and this is Marie-Do. That's a fine crop of tomatoes you have there. You must have put a lot of compost into that soil.'

'You'd be amazed how much compost you can get from the guests at this place, and then there are all the leaves and the grass cuttings and the ash from the wood fires. I've got three big crates filled and I'm going to have to build another.'

'Don't mind us, we're just taking a look around,' said Bruno. 'Is it an easy climb up this slope from the road?'

'I wouldn't try it, even when I was younger. When they were doing the restoration one of the carpenter's trucks got stuck on that hairpin bend and then the only way to get in and out even on foot was through the ruined village up on the hill. This was a castle in the old days, don't forget.'

'I see what you mean,' said Bruno, peering down the steep slope that fell away beyond the neat rows of lettuces. 'We'll carry on looking around. *Bonne continuation*, Louis.'

He and Marie-Do took the other direction, beyond the house,

and saw Patsy on the lawn tossing a ball to Balzac and then trying to wrest it from his jaws when he came back. It was a game the dog could play for hours.

'Are you happy staying here with Balzac?' Bruno asked the little girl. 'We're going to walk around a bit more. I wanted to see if there's a way to get to the pool without going through the courtyard.'

'Oh, I have a secret path,' Patsy replied. 'Just follow me and Balzac.'

Patsy scampered to the far side of the stretch of rough grass that lay beyond the lawn and then skipped between two trees, Balzac at her heels with the ball still firmly clutched in his mouth. She picked her way between bramble patches and slithered under a rough hedge and Bruno lost sight of her. Then he saw a flash of her blue T-shirt and Balzac sliding back down a steep slope. Bruno had to push his dog's rear end to help him up. Patsy stood waiting for him on the stretch of lawn beneath the long side of the house. Bruno needed to grab the sturdy trunk of another hedge to heave himself up, and then had to lie down and stretch down his arm to help Marie-Do up the slope.

'It's easier if you go around the next bush,' said Patsy. 'There's some stones that make a kind of staircase. Come on, this way to the pool.'

'Wait a second, Patsy, let me look at your staircase. Is that what your parents use to get up here?'

'Oh, no, they don't know about it. Only my secret friend who showed me the way does. I shouldn't tell you, really, but you helped Balzac get up. Just go back down, go past that bush you used and past the fallen tree and you'll see the steps.'

Bruno did as he was told, and after the fallen tree there were two stones that seemed deeply buried, but a chunk of each one protruded about a hand's width from the ground, one about half a metre higher than the other. As he looked, wondering how Patsy had clambered from one to the next, he saw there was a part of a tree root to one side that could have given her an extra step. And he noticed some crushed but still-green vegetation on the second stone, so he thought this route must have been recently used. Who was this secret friend Patsy mentioned?

Bruno looked carefully at the ground, and on the side of the fallen tree nearer the house there was a descending strip of more verdant green, as though it had been fed by some water draining down from the upper level. He peered more closely and saw the faint track of an unusual shoe, whose big toe seemed to be separate from the rest of the foot. It was far too big to be Patsy's. He held Balzac by the collar and pointed his nose at the footprint. Balzac sniffed, and then darted to the slope, which was too steep to climb, and then backtracked and cast around in the dense wood beyond the footprint to seek the scent. Bruno pulled out his phone, took a quick photo, and then tore a blank page from his notebook, covered the footprint and weighed it down with a stone. Then he followed Balzac downhill to the base of a tree with low-hanging branches, close to similar trees that would have allowed someone to swing from limb to limb without leaving a scent on the ground. Bruno climbed back to the steps, picked up Balzac and scrambled up to join Patsy and Marie-Do, and show them the photo of the footprint he had taken.

'Look what I found,' he said. 'That's an unusual footprint and

I never saw one like that before. Do you recognize it, Patsy, a shoe with the big toe separate from the other toes?'

'Yes, my friend has shoes like that. He said they are the right shoes for climbing and he's going to see if he can get a pair my size.'

'That's kind of him. He must know you like climbing. How long have you known this secret friend?' Bruno asked. Marie-Do was about to ask something but Bruno stilled her with a gesture.

'He came yesterday, dressed in a greeny-brown shirt and pants that were in wavy kinds of stripes. I heard him before I could see him, so I called out hello, and he put his finger over his mouth, like that.' She put an upright finger in front of her lips. 'But he was smiling and he looked nice.'

'Was he your age?'

'No, he was a young sort of grown-up, not as big as you and very thin and he had tiger stripes on his face, but he was very nice and showed me these steps and said it would be our secret path.'

'It sounds like you had an adventure, a bit like a fairy tale, with a secret path and a chateau and a new friend who turns up from nowhere,' said Bruno, squatting down to her level and smiling. 'Why do you call him a secret friend?'

'He wanted to keep the steps a secret so that only he and I would know, but I thought it might be a way for Balzac as well.'

'That was clever of you, and very thoughtful to help Balzac. Does your secret friend have a name, just in case I see him and then I can tell him that you're my friend too, and Balzac's.'

'No, I told him I was Patricia, but he could call me Patsy. He said I should just call him "secret friend". It was a bit hard to understand because he spoke funny, but not funny like some of the guests who come here who aren't French. I think my friend knows French but he had a special way of speaking.'

'Do you remember what his face looks like? Would you know him again if he wasn't wearing those funny green-browny clothes and had tiger stripes on his face?'

'Oh, yes,' she said. 'He looked a bit like Wang of the Sons of the Golden Dragon in Tin-Tin in *The Blue Lotus*. Do you know Tin-Tin?'

'I did when I was your age, very much, and when I was older, too. And I always liked Tin-Tin's dog, Milou, and Captain Haddock.'

'If you had a beard, Bruno, you might look a bit like Captain Haddock, but Balzac is nothing like Milou.'

'Have you seen your secret friend since yesterday?'

'No. But I have you and Balzac to play with now. Do you want to swim in the pool? There are extra bathing suits in the little cabin by the pool. Does Balzac swim?'

'He can if he has to, but he'd rather just paddle on the steps. Do you swim?'

'Yes, but only in the shallow end and I'm not allowed in the pool at all, not ever, if there are no grown-ups there to watch me. That's one of Maman's very strict rules, but I'm allowed to ride on Papa's shoulders when he swims. Can I ride on your shoulders, Bruno?'

'I have to be at work now but the very first moment that I can, I'll take you for a ride on my back. Is that okay?'

'Is it a promise?'

He took her little hand and drew a cross on her palm with his finger.

She skipped off along the chateau wall and Bruno and Marie-Do followed in her wake, Marie-Do demanding in a fierce whisper, 'So what's some damn guy in camouflage gear doing spying on this place?'

'Since he speaks French like a native my guess would be he's Vietnamese. There are more than 300,000 of them in France, and I knew some of them in the army, so he could be a scout for the special ops team that's joining us. I'll send the photo of the footprint to General Lannes.'

'Forward it to me, too. We have more Asian resources than he does,' she said.

Patsy was waiting impatiently with Balzac at the corner of the wall. 'Come on, you two slowpokes,' she called, and ran off out of sight around the corner. Balzac cast a reproachful glance at Bruno and then trotted after her.

Bruno and Marie-Do walked briskly along the chateau face, around the corner and across the veranda with its low stone wall and down the steps to the pool, where Patsy was encouraging Balzac to paddle on the top step where the water was only a finger's width high.

Some of the guests were lying on sunbeds and catching the afternoon sun. Bruno recognized the genial Indian, Krishnadev, and Hartmut, the German, who were lying side by side and talking together. A little beyond them was the American couple, Harrison and Lori, who seemed to be asleep. They had pushed their loungers together and were holding hands. Uncle Angus was in the pool, swimming lengths.

As Bruno approached, his phone vibrated to tell him he had an incoming text. It was from an army address, RPG2, which meant the second squadron of the Régiment des Dragons Parachutistes.

'The troops are here. I should go check with them and I should take Balzac,' he said to Marie-Do. 'What are your plans?'

'I'm not supposed to spend the whole day here, so I'd better get back,' she said. 'That Asian visitor could be a serious concern. Let me know if he turns out to be one of ours.'

Bruno looked at her levelly. 'Is there anything more about this meeting, this group, that you can tell me? Or do you have to hold some things close?'

She smiled at him, almost cheekily. 'I'm very particular about the things I choose to hold close, Bruno.' She put her hand on his arm. 'Why don't you escort Patsy to her parents and then you can take Balzac to meet the troops. Do you know yet which unit they are?'

'Parachute Dragoons, part of Special Operations Command. I've worked with them before.'

'Ah, yes,' she said, smiling archly. 'Your Croix de Guerre, but you don't wear the ribbon on your shirt.'

'I have to wear it on my uniform jacket, but I was never much good at sewing.' He shrugged.

'I'd have thought Isabelle would have been delighted to help you with that. I get the impression that you're the only guy she ever truly fell for.'

He looked at Marie-Do coolly. 'I fell for her, too. Should we arrange to check in formally with one another twice a day by phone, let's say 0900 and 1800?'

'Good idea,' she said. 'That reminds me.' She took from her shoulder bag a brand-new smartphone, still wrapped in plastic. 'Our secure phone system is not compatible with the one General Lannes gave you. This is one of ours. To open it, you'll need to log in with this ID I prepared.' She handed him a blank business card with some letters and digits written upon it.

'You'll need to create a personal password too, at least a dozen characters, usual mix of letters, digits and symbols, and then use the phone to take a photo of your own face. Next you'll be asked to give a fingerprint, right index finger. Then upload your photo to my email address, which you have. Wait until you get a text from me to confirm, and you'll be on our secure net. Only use that to contact me, okay?'

'Yes, thank you.' He put in the long access code she'd given him and then created a password.

'Now take a selfie,' she said. He did so and was asked for the fingerprint. He put his right index finger on the screen.

'Hit enter,' she said.

He did as Marie-Do said and 'Welcome' came up on the screen.

'That's it. Now call my office number.' She read it out.

He did so and was asked to give his fingerprint again. Afterwards, her phone rang and his own screen said 'call secured'.

'That's it. Like I said, only use that phone to call me, or anyone else on that DGSE network. If I'm not available you'll get a duty officer. Okay?'

'Got it,' he said.

'Perfect.' She leaned up and kissed his cheek. 'I'll get here at least once a day and we'll call each other anyway at 0900 and

1800, or at other times if our people here are on the move. I'll need to know all their plans.'

'Are your people finished with Kerquelin's house?' he asked. 'I think Nadia wants to move back in but I'd rather she didn't.'

'I think we're finished but you don't have to tell her that. I agree that it's better if she stayed here where there's security in place. I'd better get going. *Au'voir*.'

Bruno turned back to watch Patsy at the pool.

'Oh, come on, Balzac, you'll like it,' Patsy was saying appealingly, kneeling at the edge of the pool and splashing her fingers in the shallow water.

'Sorry, Patsy,' Bruno said. 'Balzac and I have to go to work and I think we should take you back to your house. I'll hope to see you later. That ride on my shoulders in the pool is a promise.' He squatted down again to her level. 'And if I should happen to come across your secret friend, I'll tell him that I know you and that you and I are friends, too. Is that okay?'

'Just don't tell him I showed you our secret path,' she said, nodding, and they shook hands on the deal. This time she made a little cross on his palm, before taking Balzac's paw and crossing the dark pads of his foot and then kissing the top of his head. He gave her an affectionate lick on the arm, removed his paw and trotted over to Bruno.

Chapter 11

Bruno set off uphill through the woods, using the sun to make sure he headed just a little east of due north. He was carefully checking all directions from the chateau. After some three hundred metres he saw to the east the brighter light of a clearing and headed that way. He emerged on a long, thin stretch of ground that ran north–south. It could almost have been the fairway of a golf course, some five or six hundred metres long and less than fifty metres wide. At the far end was a hedge, then some buildings that looked like private houses, which he had not seen during his earlier stroll with Kirk. He headed left and came to a dirt path that led to a narrow local road.

Now that the growth of home delivery had required all French houses to have a street address, he saw a street sign that told him he was on the Impasse du Camp Romain. It led through trees in each direction, to the north and to the east. He was about to head north when he heard a quiet voice call his name.

'That's me,' he said, stopping. He kept his arms out to each side, waited for a count of ten and two figures in military camouflage emerged, one from either side of the trees, each one carrying a SCAR, a special forces combat assault rifle, with some kind of screen, like that of a mobile phone, strapped to their helmets.

'Dragon-caporal Vernier,' said the shorter, stockier of the two, very quietly. He bent down and welcomed Balzac by name, delighting Bruno that his dog must have made quite a reputation as a tracker the last time he'd worked with troops from this elite unit. 'The lieutenant is expecting you.' He told the other soldier to stay at his post and set off through the trees. Bruno was almost at their camp before he made out the first of the low bivouac tents. A burly man of his own height rose to greet him, double black bars on his epaulettes.

'Lieutenant Berthier, Didier,' he said, holding out a hand to be shaken and then dropping to one knee to let Balzac give him a thorough sniff. 'Call me Didi. We're glad to see you, and Balzac.'

'Same here,' said Bruno. 'Tell me, do you have an Asian member of your squad who might have been around the chateau yesterday?'

'Our best scout is from a Vietnamese family, name of Tran, and he thinks you know his uncle. He came with us today. But no Asian that I know of was here yesterday.'

'Tran?' exclaimed Bruno. 'If it's the same guy his uncle was our best scout, too. Has a restaurant these days, in Bordeaux.'

'That's him,' said Didi. 'We're based at Martignas-sur-Jalle, just outside Bordeaux. We had a great feast at his restaurant when the squad got back from a tour in Mali. He told us all his old war stories from the Balkans.'

'If young Tran wasn't here yesterday, another Asian was around,' said Bruno. 'He was wearing camouflage and checking out the chateau. He had those special shoes with a separate big toe and speaks French well enough to convince a six-year-old that he's a native speaker.'

'We'll look out for him. Meanwhile, let me lay out my patrol plan. We're a half-squadron: twelve privates, two corporals, a sergeant and me.' Didi squatted down and pulled a large-scale map from his leg pocket. It went from Fénelon's castle at the bottom to just beyond Carlux at the top, and east for about three kilometres to where the river took a big bend south. The Château de Rouffillac was in the centre of the map, with enough detail to show its swimming pool.

'We'll be four hours on, four hours off, organized into four teams of three privates each, two with a corporal, one with the sergeant and one with me,' the lieutenant said. 'So at any given time we'll have eight men on watch, working in twos.'

'Make sure your men stay out of sight in daylight,' said Bruno. 'Where are you planning to post them?'

'I thought one pair at the hairpin bend in the path up to the chateau, another by the pool and watching the slope, another on the path from here, and the fourth close to the chateau. I'm not sure about those two separate houses very close to the west side of the chateau. Are they secure?'

'The larger one is where the owners live, a Monsieur Kirk and his wife, Cassandra, and their daughter, Patricia,' Bruno replied. 'She's six and made a secret friend of the mysterious man I mentioned. The smaller house is for the housekeeper, Sylvie, and her husband, Louis, who acts as gardener, driver and handyman. You should also keep an eye on that slope above the rocky outcrop that dominates the courtyard, since that's where the guests will probably eat most of the time.' He opened his phone to show the lieutenant his photo of the distinctive shoe.

'We'll check it out. Should I let the guys know you'll be patrolling around, Bruno? If so, we'll need a password and response.'

'Since you've just been to Mali, let's make "Bamako" the password, "Timbuktu" for the response.'

'Bamako–Timbuktu it is. You want to meet the squadron? They'll need to know your face.'

'Sure. And I think you have some equipment for me.'

Didi reached into his bivouac tent and handed over a small backpack, a separate belt pack and a helmet, saying, 'Have you used the FELIN helmet before?'

Bruno shook his head.

'It's a very smart version of the Spectra system blue helmet you used in the Balkans but it's electronic. It weighs just over three pounds, and although it isn't officially bulletproof it will stop anything but a straight-on hit and grenade fragments. Your two-way radio is in the helmet, and synched into our circuit. So is your night-vision. We'll have to test this tonight since there's a pull-down screen for silent orders which will also show you the positions of the rest of the squad. Recharge the batteries daily. Your flares, illumination grenades and spare magazines are in the backpack. And here's your weapon.'

He reached into the tent again {+ space]and brought out a SCAR like the one the sentries carried. 'Do you know this weapon?'

Bruno shook his head. 'A bit after my time.'

'It's the SCAR-L, the light version that takes the 5.56 milli-metre round. It has a double-action trigger – one pull gives you a single shot, pull and hold for a count of one and you'll get a

0

burst of three. It's a twenty-round mag. Keep pulling and it's empty in less than four seconds.'

'You still use a bayonet?' Bruno asked.

'In these woods, you bet. We used them in Mali on night assaults. You'll need to practise with the helmet. We can do that tonight, too. And then there's your camouflage vest, which gives good ballistic protection and holds the batteries.'

'I feel like one of Napoleon's soldiers suddenly thrust into a modern battle,' said Bruno.

'You'll pick it up in twenty minutes. Thirty maximum. It's designed to be intuitive. And the communications system and display screen make it very unlikely that you'll be shot by one of your own team because you'll know where they all are with a special colour. The bad guys stand out.'

'This really makes me feel like I'm stuck in the age of bows and arrows. I'm supposed to mingle with these guests, which will be a problem if I stroll around looking like a commando. I'll wear it for early morning and night patrols. Otherwise I have my sidearm. I thought I was getting this new undervest that's supposed to be discreet but still stops bullets.'

'It's in your backpack. Come on, meet the guys.'

Bruno recognized Tran at once, asked after his uncle, heard about the feast the squadron had enjoyed and then told him about the camouflage that Patsy had described, wavy stripes of green and brown. Did Tran or anyone else recognize it?

'Sounds like something you can buy here at any hunters' store in France,' said Tran. 'Military camouflage is dappled and hasn't used wavy stripes for years.'

'Right. I'll be at the chateau most of the time, unless I have to move with the guests or I get some free time. You have my contact details.'

He shook hands and exchanged a few words with each of the troops, before addressing them all. 'We don't know whether the threat is real but we're taking no chances. Nor do we know whether the threat is against Kerquelin and his daughters, or against this assembly of very important guests as a whole. Since Nadia Kerquelin, the young redhead, is committed each evening to take part in the re-enactment at Sarlat, either I will have to accompany her or two of you in civilian dress. I'll take that duty tonight. I'll arrange two tickets for you each night for the rest of the week. Good luck.'

'The sergeant and I have your number, in case we need to contact you and you're not wearing the helmet,' Didi said. 'We use silent texts wherever possible.'

'I'll stay in touch and make contact twice a day,' Bruno said. As he approached the chateau he stashed the assault rifle and camouflage gear in the trees before descending to the pool, where he saw the charming sight of Kerquelin's two daughters. Nadia was still a girl, just coming into her beauty, pale-skinned with that glorious red hair, lithe and slim in a black bikini. Claire, with her California tan, was wearing a backless red swimsuit. They were sitting at the edge of the pool, their feet dangling in the water, chatting with Hartmut, Angus and Krishnadev who were all standing chest-deep in the water. Harrison and Lori were at the deep end, tossing a water-polo ball back and forth with another couple, who had to be Gergen and his wife, Mavis, the lawyer.

'What time do you leave for Sarlat?' he asked Nadia. 'And are any others coming this evening?'

'We're all too jet-lagged,' said Hartmut, looking up from the pool. 'We'll go to the re-enactment later in the week.'

As he spoke, the plump and nut-brown Krishnadev scrambled out of the pool, dried his hands on a towel and came up to greet Bruno with a broad smile. The top of his head was bald but the rest of his hair was long and tangled, a little like Einstein, Bruno thought. And there was a jovial quality to the man that brought a warm smile to Bruno's own lips.

'I gather you are our bodyguard, so thank you for your attentions. Please, call me Krish,' he said.

'I'm just a local policeman, checking on security,' said Bruno. 'I don't think there's any serious danger but after the injury to Monsieur Kerquelin my superiors thought it best to take precautions. And please call me Bruno.'

'Uncle Krish is our good-luck charm and nothing bad can happen while he's here,' said Nadia, putting her arm around the Indian's shoulders. 'Claire and I need to get back to Papa's house first so I can pick up some clothes, since you and Uncle Vincent want us to stay here. Kirk and Cassandra arranged a room for us. We should leave here in about half an hour, let's say four thirty.'

'I'll come along,' Bruno said. 'I know you're driving your father's Range Rover so I'll see you at the car at four thirty.'

With the new backpack over one shoulder and the belt pack around his waist, Bruno went up to his room, plugged in the batteries and saw they were fully charged. He went downstairs again carrying his rainproof police jacket, slipped out of the front door and up into the trees, out of sight of the pool and courtyard. He found the camouflage gear and assault rifle where he had left them. Wrapping the weapon in his jacket, grateful that it was just over twenty-one inches in length with the stock folded, he returned to his room. He slipped on the new armoured vest, which did not show beneath his shirt, put on his police jacket whose length hid his sidearm, settled his képi on his head and checked his phone for messages. There was nothing urgent so he pulled out the phone Marie-Do had given him, opening it with his fingerprint. He then texted her that the troops were in place and that he would accompany Nadia to Sarlat that evening. Then he went to wait by the car, scanning through his emails until Claire and Nadia joined him.

'It must be a comfort, the two of you being together,' he said, half-turning to keep them both in view from the front passenger seat as Nadia carefully navigated the hairpin bend in the big car.

'Sure, but we're a pretty weird family. One father, two mothers, and I'm much closer to Claire than I am to my own brother by blood, and closer to Claire's mother than to my own.'

'Have you seen her yet?' Bruno asked.

'No, and I'm not answering her endless phone calls,' Nadia replied. 'I will be polite to her when I have to meet her but, as you know, she was never much of a mother to me. I was raised by nannies while she pursued her career and her social life in Paris, and from what little I saw of her there wasn't much difference between the two. When she was home, she lavished attention on my brother, "the heir", as she called him. I'm not sure he'll ever recover.' She tossed her head, accelerated onto the road that ran by the riverbank, then had to brake hard for the stop sign. Once she could drive on, she accelerated again, and gave Bruno a cheeky glance.

'I don't think I'll have any trouble with the gendarmes while you're in the front seat,' she said, grinning.

'Life is full of risks,' he replied equably. He turned to Claire. 'Will you be in the audience tonight?'

'Wouldn't miss it,' she replied. 'My little sister, playing the great warrior of France and standing in for Papa.'

'Not standing, sitting,' said Nadia. 'I'm not allowed to dismount under any circumstances. I just wave my sword and channel my inner Joan of Arc.'

'While making sure Joan of Arc doesn't turn into your inner Suzanne,' said Claire, gazing fondly at Nadia as she teased her sister in an affectionate, familiar way. These two Kerquelin daughters had turned out well, Bruno thought, whatever the trials of their upbringing.

'Did you see much of your papa when you were growing up?' he asked Claire.

'Lots,' she said. 'He came to the States often, even after he moved back to France, and always came to see me and my mother. In the winter he'd take me skiing to Vail or Heavenly, and every August I joined him and Nadia in Brittany.'

'He must have been on good terms with your mother,' Bruno said. 'Did she not marry again?'

'She was never married to him in the first place, didn't believe in it,' Claire replied. My mom was the last Latina hippy, lived in a commune, peace and love, rock 'n' roll and salsa. I must have been nine when I realized that every time he came to visit they slept together. It was during those Augusts in Brittany with Suzanne condescending to join us for the occasional weekend that my mom kept him sane while Suzanne was breaking his balls.'

'Suzanne can't have been that bad,' said Bruno. 'They stayed together fifteen, sixteen years.'

'You think?' said Nadia, her voice mocking. 'Over the last couple of years in Domme, it was just me and Papa when I came up for weekends. We'd play war games up in the attic. Papa would never criticize her, not even about the divorce. But you could see the pain on his face whenever he talked about her, which wasn't often, only when I pressed him. I even asked him outright whether he'd had to marry her when she got pregnant with my brother, which I think she did on purpose.'

'She wanted his money, and his status as the cyber-king,' said Claire. 'I think she was gripped by this fantasy of them as a star couple of Paris.'

'And she wanted to lord it over those smooth énarques who sneered at her as the token Arab when they couldn't lure her into bed,' said Nadia.

Bruno had not warmed to Suzanne in the hour or so they had spent together. She had been aloof, patronizing and demanding, all at once, a woman who saw herself as a chosen member of the elite. But now he had a sudden image of her as a vulnerable girl, fiercely intelligent, highly ambitious and determined to succeed. She must have fought to become one of the eighty or so young French superstars chosen for the Ecole Nationale d'Administration each year. And what a gruelling time she must have had there, probably the only one of Arab ancestry among a handful of women. She had probably been the most attractive, a target for the young elitists around her who believed that all France – and its women – lay at their feet.

And so it did. ENA had been founded by De Gaulle after the

war as a way to select and train the French administrative elite, the people who would design and implement the renewal of France. Several of its graduates, including Emmanuel Macron, became presidents of France. Others were ministers, corporate chieftains or the top civil servants in the prestigious ministries like finance and foreign affairs. With the coming of the European Union, most of the ENA staff and pupils had been moved to Strasbourg with a determined focus to become for Europe the architects and administrators that the earlier ENA had been for France. Bruno thought of himself as a convinced European but knew he was at the same time a fierce critic of much of the way it was run: a fishing policy that had devastated the fisheries, an agricultural policy created by those with little knowledge of life in the countryside, an industrial policy that spouted words of solidarity but undermined the skills and pride and jobs of the French workforce. Little wonder, he thought, that the Gilets Jaunes, who led that brief revolt of rural France against speed limits and higher fuel prices, had made the énarques the symbol of all that they thought was wrong with France. President Macron had responded by pledging to close ENA, but it had merely been reborn with a different name.

'It must have been tough for Suzanne,' he said. 'An attractive young énarque of Moroccan ancestry amid all those ruthlessly ambitious young men. I'm not surprised she fell for your father – he must have stood in striking contrast.'

'Don't tell me she's got her hooks into you already,' Nadia almost shouted, only half-joking.

'No. I thought she was half irritating, half terrifying,' Bruno replied. 'But I think I know how she got that way, how she became so determined to succeed at any cost after those nights at ENA when she probably cried herself to sleep.'

'I think I see what you mean,' said Claire, looking at the road ahead. 'I hadn't thought of it that way before.'

'From what I know of Papa, she was a lousy wife as well,' said Nadia, as they passed the imposing chateau of Montfort on its hilltop at the great bend of the river and she headed for the bridge at Vitrac. 'Papa stuck it out, did his best, mainly I think because of me and my brother. But it became steadily more impossible. He never said so in as many words but I got the impression that she was holding out for half of his money, but in the end he was able to hire better lawyers than she did.'

'I thought she did pretty well out of it,' said Claire. 'She got the apartment in Paris, a half-share in the place in Brittany and the chalet in the Alps. And Papa was always generous with her. He took care of my mother and me financially, gave me a good education and paid for law school, always remembered my birthday.' She pulled out a tissue to dab at her eyes and blow her nose, and then turned to Bruno. 'Do you really think he's going to recover? I mean a hundred per cent?'

'So I'm told,' Bruno said.

Nadia turned into the driveway of her father's house, only to find it blocked by the same big, black car in which Marie-Do had arrived at that same house when Bruno had first met her.

'Pull up behind that car so it can't get out,' said Bruno. 'That's the car used by the security team at Domme, who are only supposed to be here when accompanied by some of General Lannes's people. I wonder what they're doing here?'

Nadia parked, her front bumper almost touching the rear of the other vehicle, and they all climbed out, Nadia taking the lead up the steps and turning the door handle to find it was locked. She used her own key to enter.

'Allow me,' said Bruno, going in first. Once at the bottom of the stairs he shouted, 'This is the police, with the daughter of the owner. This is her home. Please show yourself right now.'

Marie-Do emerged from the kitchen looking surprised and saying, '*Bonjour*, Bruno. I'm here with Madame Kerquelin, who is moving in.'

'Over my dead body,' snapped Nadia. 'And there is no Madame Kerquelin. She's my father's ex-wife and has no standing here.'

Footsteps on the stairs signalled the arrival of Suzanne, wearing a bathrobe, her hair wrapped in a towel turban but wearing a pair of elegant black shoes. What sort of woman puts on high heels when she's just out of the shower wearing a bathrobe? Bruno asked himself.

'*Bonjour*, Nadia. I see you've brought your Mexican half-sister, and General Lannes's tame village policeman who seems to turn up everywhere. What can I do for you, my dear daughter?'

'You can pack up your stuff and get out. You're not staying here,' Nadia replied coldly. 'How did you get in? Papa was careful to change the locks during the divorce because he didn't want you back here either.'

'We used my key,' Marie-Do said, gazing uncertainly at Suzanne poised on the stairs. 'We have keys for all staff homes at the security office. I didn't realize there would be any difficulty.'

'Well, you know now,' said Nadia, so angry that her fists were clenched and her face red. Claire went up to stand beside her and put an arm around her sister's shoulders.

'I think it might be easier for us all if you were to leave, *madame*,' Bruno said. 'This is her legal residence and I'm sure we'd all like to settle this quietly without bringing any outside authority into this, which would certainly attract the media.'

'Ah, a subtle little threat,' Suzanne said coldly. 'I see that my dear daughter has wrapped you around her little finger, just as she did her father. It saddens me not to have some time with my daughter, but I'll start packing.'

She turned and climbed the stairs with as much dignity as bathrobe and high heels permitted.

Marie-Do rolled her eyes and let out a sigh of relief. Claire stifled what sounded like the beginning of a laugh and Nadia said politely, 'Thank you, Bruno.'

'You should unblock the driveway, Nadia,' said Bruno, and went outside. After a moment Marie-Do joined him at the bottom of the steps.

'Thanks a lot,' she said, her tone blending humour with bitterness. 'I suppose this means she'll move back in with me.'

'Is that where she's been staying?' he asked. 'I hope it's a big house. But can't DGSE afford a hotel for her?'

Marie-Do glanced up at the door and lowered her voice. 'I don't know if it's an official trip.'

Chapter 12

Nadia parked outside the building being used as dressing rooms for the cast, and soon learned that all tickets for that evening had been sold out. She swiftly arranged with Romain, the deputy Mayor, for Bruno and Claire to be invited to watch the show from the big upstairs windows of the Hôtel de Ville. Then she rushed off. Bruno and Claire had time to stroll around the crowded marketplace where the stallholders were in medieval dress, selling their food and drink until the show began. They looked, but didn't buy; Romain had assured them that wine, snacks and sandwiches would be served to the guests upstairs.

'This is an impressive show to be arranged by a small town like this,' said Claire as they wandered through the old town. 'I guess it lives on tourism.'

'In large part, Sarlat is the capital of the Périgord Noir.' He would have said more but suddenly his legs were embraced by two small people. He looked down to see the twins Dora and Daniel, and behind them their smiling mother, Florence.

He hugged her in greeting, picked up the children, one in each arm, and introduced them all to Claire, explaining that she was Nadia's sister and telling Claire that Florence was a

162

teacher at the St Denis *collège*, the reigning computer expert, star soloist of the church choir and a dear friend.

'Are you staying for the show?' he asked her.

'No, I have to get the children home to bed. They've been making friends with all the cows and goats but now they're drooping so it's time to go.' She turned to Claire saying, 'You must be the sister who lives in California. Nadia has told us so much about you. I do hope your father gets better soon.'

The two women chatted while Bruno asked Dora and Daniel if they had enjoyed their day and what they had liked most, but the twins wanted to ask him when he would take them swimming again. He'd taught them to swim and they never tired of it. Soon, he promised them, and the thought came into his head that maybe Patsy would like to meet them and they could all swim together when his work at the chateau was over. They all walked to Florence's car, and she set off for St Denis.

Having observed Bruno with the twins, Claire asked Bruno if he had children of his own as they walked back to the main square. He shook his head, still smiling at seeing the twins.

'Florence said her kids don't have a father but they do have Bruno,' Claire said. 'She kept her eyes on you the whole time we were chatting. She told me you'd changed her life by getting her a teacher's job in St Denis that came with an apartment. She added that she's never been so happy.'

'Florence is really somebody. She may even be our first female mayor one day,' he said.

'From the way she looked at you with the children, she obviously trusts you with them,' Claire said, with a cheeky smile.

'The children seem to have a real fondness for you. Maybe you played Santa Claus once too often.'

He wasn't sure what to make of the statement. He wondered if all Californians were so forward and direct.

'We're friends, several of us in a group, and we meet regularly, cook and go riding and spend a lot of time together,' he said, doing his best not to sound defensive. 'The kids are always part of that, almost as though they belong to all of us, a bit like the dogs. They reinforce something very special that I feel about St Denis, that we're all members of a village that's small enough for everyone to know each other. It's like a loose but affectionate and extended family. But I try to keep my private life separate from my town.'

'How very frustrating for the ladies of St Denis,' said Claire, taking his arm as they strolled back to the centre. Sarlat was not St Denis, where he knew everybody, but they frequently passed somebody who greeted Bruno by name, shook his hand or put up her cheeks to be kissed. And by way of courtesy, Bruno introduced Claire as the daughter of Kerquelin, the man whose fate had dominated talk in Sarlat in recent days. They all asked after her father's health and noted without comment the way Claire clung to Bruno's arm.

'This reminds me of high school, where everybody knew everybody else and who was dating whom and who had just been dumped,' she said. 'And I'm walking around with the school football star so people can't wait to gossip about that. How come you're so well known here?'

'Partly because of the reports in the local papers, but mainly it's the fact that I coach the rugby and tennis teams of the kids of St Denis. I always try to travel with them to matches with other communes in the area, attend the annual dinners of the different sports clubs, sit on various youth and sports committees in the region, that sort of thing.'

'Do you like that, being a public figure?' she asked.

'You're inflating my role,' he said. 'I'm simply in a job and involved in sports that keep me in the public eye. Given the way so many people in big cities seem to distrust the cops and the way they work, I prefer the way half of the kids around here grow up knowing me as Bruno, the sports guy who also happens to be a policeman. That's an important part of the job I do, a job I believe in. I can't think of anything more important than doing my job in a way that earns public trust.'

He broke off, feeling that he'd expressed himself clumsily. He tried to find the words that conveyed his real meaning.

'It only works because I learned my trade in the very small town of St Denis, and now since I'm police chief for the whole valley I'm trying to apply the same lessons I learned in my own village. I don't think it would work in a big city where most of the time cops have to deal with strangers, but around here I know a lot of people, probably know someone in their family. It makes a big difference.'

'Maybe we should get you to come give lectures at the police academies back in the States,' she said.

'I'd be very surprised if your cops in small towns don't find themselves working in much the same way,' he replied as they approached the steps up the Hôtel de Ville.

'So half of Sarlat and its surroundings will right now be gossiping about the way that you have been walking arm in arm through the town with some mysterious American woman,' she said as they circled the main square. 'By the way,' she went on, 'we have a mutual friend, or perhaps two. You remember Fernando Bondino of the California wine family? He says you got him off a murder charge. He said I should be sure to look you up when I came here.'

'I remember him well, a bit intimidating at first but a decent guy once you got to know him,' Bruno replied. 'He sent me a fantastic case of wine.'

'I know. He told me you were one of the few people who sent old-fashioned "thank you" letters. I had dinner with him and his French lawyer, D'Aubigny-something. They told me the story about that French-Canadian girl and her boyfriend who died in the wine vat, and how you found that she'd faked the evidence to blame Bondino.'

'Hector d'Aubigny-Dupuy,' said Bruno, remembering the case. 'Is he still connected to Bondino?'

'Very much so, and to us, our little investors' group. He's our French connection with friends at the Elysée. You know he was one of Macron's early backers?'

'No, I didn't know that but I'm not surprised. Are you planning to invest in France?' Bruno asked, trying to keep his tone casual.

'France and Europe,' she said, vaguely. 'D'Aubigny said you were an old-fashioned honest cop. High praise, I thought.' The door to the Hôtel de Ville was opened and they found themselves in an official receiving line. Seeing this, Claire drew herself up to her full height, tossed back her hair, smiled brilliantly, and just before she strode forward, hand outstretched to greet the Mayor, she murmured to Bruno, 'If Florence could only see us now.'

The remark took Bruno by surprise. He supposed it was meant to be a joke, a teasing and even flirtatious pleasantry, but it felt strange to receive an almost intimate comment from a woman he barely knew. Unbidden, the memory of Claire sitting by the pool in her swimsuit suddenly appeared in his head and he had to admit that it felt more than agreeable to think that such a fine-looking woman might be flirting with him. But then the Mayor took his outstretched hand, pulled Bruno forward and asked quietly for any news of Kerquelin.

'It's still early but I'm told the doctors are very hopeful he'll make a full recovery,' he murmured into the Mayor's ear.

'Is everyone satisfied that this was an accident, with nothing sinister involved?'

'That seems to be the way the higher-ups are thinking when last I heard, but we may have to wait a little longer. With a man of such prominence, and the Elysée taking an interest, the Police Nationale want to be completely sure. They still haven't been able to ask Kerquelin what he remembers.'

The Mayor nodded and steered Bruno to the stairs leading to the great chamber that overlooked the square. Claire had gone ahead as he spoke with the Mayor and now awaited him with a glass of wine in one hand and a ridiculously small open sandwich in the other. It looked like foie gras with a topping of onion confit.

'Wine is on the table behind me and there's a motherly figure who comes around with these miniature bites. The door to the kitchen is over there and we might want to secure a strategic position to pounce as she comes out with fresh supplies. We might starve otherwise.'

'You've been to this kind of reception before,' he said, smiling at her as she licked her fingers clean of crumbs. Bruno handed her his handkerchief, still neatly folded from the drawer from which he'd taken it that morning. She used it to dab at the corners of her mouth, handed it back and took his arm to steer him first to the wine and then out to a big window to see the audience beginning to take their seats on the benches.

'Should we wave?' she asked. 'Like the royal family on the balcony at Buckingham Palace.'

'In France, that's the Mayor's prerogative. Anyway, I thought you were planning to waylay the woman with the canapés,' Bruno said.

'I like the smoked salmon,' came a nearby voice, that of Yveline, in her uniform with her new rank as captain. Bruno introduced the two women, explaining that Claire was Kerquelin's daughter and Yveline was in charge of the gendarmes in St Denis.

'Four of us are here as a courtesy to help with crowd control,' Yveline said. She turned to Claire, saying, 'I hope your father makes a swift recovery.'

'How is it that Bruno always manages to secure the company of the most intriguing women in the room?' came a new voice as Romain joined them.

'You know what they say about men in uniform,' Claire said airily.

'I think it also holds true for women in uniform,' Romain said with a bow to Yveline.

Bruno introduced Claire to the deputy Mayor, who took her hand to raise it within an inch of his lips.

'This building looks more modern than most in the old town,' Claire said. 'How old is it?'

'It dates back to the thirteenth century, *mademoiselle*, when it was the House of Consuls, the local notables trying to assert their right to civic independence from the authority of the Abbey of Sarlat. It was then rebuilt in the early seventeenth century, and after the Revolution there was a bazaar on the ground floor. It has been the seat of the Mairie since the end of the nineteenth century.'

'Romain is the expert. He wrote the definitive history of the building in the bulletin of our local history society,' Bruno said.

'We take our history very seriously here,' Romain said, putting out an arm to steer the motherly woman with a loaded tray of smoked salmon canapés to their side. They all helped themselves, Claire deftly managing to take two. 'Did you know that when André Malraux was De Gaulle's Minister of Culture he made Sarlat the model of the cleaning and restoration of all our historic towns in France? Malraux had a special affection for Sarlat after being a leader of the Resistance in this area during the war.'

'History ancient and modern,' said Claire. 'When does the show start? I can't wait to see my sister all dressed up. And please call me Claire; *mademoiselle* may be a lovely word but it takes so much longer to say.'

'We start at eight.'

'Bruno is a historian, too, in his own way; a historian of food,' Romain said. 'He re-created a gourmet dinner for our history club of Neanderthal food using prehistoric cooking methods. He made a makeshift oven in a hole in the ground with a base of rocks and a fire on top, and when the fire died down he put on the ashes a shoulder of venison wrapped in moist deerskin, covered the hole and left it cooking slowly for hours.'

'How did it taste?' Claire asked.

'Excellent, with a blackcurrant sauce. He did some research with the archaeologists who have started analysing the tartar on teeth of old skeletons to learn about their diet and found that they ate a lot of duckweed, so he made a salad out of it with leaves of wild garlic. If you ever get a chance to try Bruno's cooking, don't pass it up.'

'I can second that,' said Yveline. 'Get him to make you his gazpacho, and that tomato *tarte tatin*.'

'Thanks for the tip. I'll bear that in mind, if I can tempt him to invite me. Maybe I can persuade him to cook for my friends at Château de Rouffillac one evening,' Claire said, with a glance at Bruno. She turned back to Romain and asked, 'Is your work as deputy Mayor full-time?'

'It could be, but I try to make time for my real job, teaching history and philosophy at the *lycée*.'

'I remember Nadia telling me she dreaded the four-hour philosophy paper she had to write for her *baccalauréat* exam,' Claire said. 'The questions seemed engraved on her brain: Does language betray thought? Is truth to be preferred over peace? It all sounded much tougher than anything we had to do in America.'

'Now you can understand why I left school when I did,' said Bruno. 'The army seemed like light relief by comparison.'

'We like to think of Bruno as the incarnation of honest, rural simplicity, the Périgord's version of Rousseau's noble savage,' said Romain, grinning. 'Until you see him on the rugby field.'

He was interrupted by the sound of a fork tapping on glass as the Mayor stepped forward to make a mercifully short speech of welcome to the guests, with a special thanks to Claire for her attendance and good wishes to her father. Yveline slipped out after brief farewells. The guests just had time to refill their glasses before being ushered to the open windows with their stone balustrades. There were chairs for the women but the men had to stand. Bruno couldn't help wondering whether to advise Claire to remain inside, but from her enthusiasm to see her sister perform he knew it would be hopeless. He just hoped the plain-clothes soldiers somewhere in the crowd below would provide sufficient protection if needed. The show was about to begin.

It unfolded as it had before: the trumpet; Sarlat crushed beneath the English yoke; the drunken English soldiers; Nadia's appearance and then the young squire's dramatic rescue, and Bruno saw Romain bend down to murmur in Claire's ear that the squire was his son. Then came the conspirators, the pledge to liberation, the tender scene when Nadia gives her scarf to the young squire who promises to wear it in battle.

'Now she has to dart off and change into armour,' Bruno explained. He was standing behind Claire and had bent down to speak quietly in her ear. She turned her head to listen and somehow her lips brushed his and lingered a moment. It wasn't a kiss, barely an encounter, but her eyes widened and she smiled at him, murmuring, 'A happy accident.' Then she turned back to the show, leaving him to wonder whether he had imagined it – until she reached back with her right hand to take his left and place it on her left shoulder, releasing it with a slow, lingering stroke of her fingers.

It was a movement that seemed French in its delicacy but American in its forwardness. He was in a situation where he didn't entirely understand the signals and rituals. A message had been sent but its precise meaning was elusive. If the message were an invitation, what did that mean, when Claire was only to be in the Périgord for a week? Was he being tempted into a vacation romance as if he were some convenient beach boy at a louche tropical resort? Had Claire been French, he would have understood the message to have been an invitation to explore at their leisure the possibility of a dalliance, even an affair. But she was, he suspected, far more American than French.

Moreover, he was on duty, charged with ensuring the safety of Kerquelin's daughters and their guests at the chateau. That was his priority, so this was no time to plunge with careless abandon into the beguiling attraction of some sexual adventure. Bruno didn't like to think of himself as a promiscuous man; the pleasures of the flesh were delightful but for him they were far too important to be treated casually.

Yet he caught the faint scent that rose from Claire's hair. You are building a vast and ornate chateau of dreams out of thin air, he told himself. Bruno withdrew his hand and dragged his attention back to the pageant unfolding on the square before them, the farm carts loaded with their secret cache of swords, the flagons of wine being offered by the market women to make the English soldiers drunk, the sounds of sheep and cattle, ducks and geese, the cries of the stallholders and the tempting smells of fresh pastries and roasting meat.

And then came the new sound of trumpets from the town's southern gate, the clash of swords and the shouts of fighting men. Below him the funeral party began pulling the hidden weapons from the coffin in the cart before them. The women in their low-cut dresses who seemingly had been bent only on seduction now pulled out hidden daggers to plunge them into the backs of the foolish foreign troops whose senses had been dulled by drink and sexual promise. There came the sound of hoofbeats, horses ridden fast, the cries of Montjoie, St Denis, and the Constable of France, Bertrand du Guesclin, helmet gleaming, sword held high and black surcoat flowing from the speed as he rode suddenly into the square.

'That's her,' cried Claire, rising to lean dangerously forward out of the window so that Bruno felt it necessary to put both his hands on her shoulders to keep her from toppling. 'That's Nadia.'

It was indeed a much smaller du Guesclin who reined back the great war charger into a slow walk and used a truncated sword to wave on the rank of mounted knights behind, before following them slowly to trot proudly before the benches packed with cheering crowds. She called out, *'Vive la France!'* but this time only the carefully planned number of French knights dismounted to attack the ragged line of English soldiers at the steps of the Hôtel de Ville below them.

'And see here the spirit of Jeanne d'Arc herself who comes to ride with the brave knights of our liberation,' came the solemn words of commentary. 'France, led by a woman, to the ultimate victory, Sarlat, the ancient town founded in Roman times, a town that grew under the shelter of the great abbey and the Holy Mother church, a town where the citizens themselves rise to fight and win their freedom, a France that is eternal and inspired by the bewitching grace of an indomitable daughter of her homeland. *La Patrie, Vive la France!*'

That was clever, thought Bruno, as the English soldiers, now prisoners, were led off and the knights and French infantry and the townsfolk gathered before the cheering benches to toast their victory in flagons of wine. There was a thunderous roll of drums, and from the gates of the old cathedral came a parade of churchmen, followed by a chorus of men dressed as priests and women as nuns. As they came to stand before the packed benches, the drum roll gave way to an organ playing the opening bars of a *Te Deum*. One of the monks came forward to deliver the solo before the chorus of nuns and the other monks broke in and then somehow the music turned into a stirring version of the 'Marseillaise' in which many in the audience joined, including Bruno and others.

'*Messieurs-dames*, and friends of Sarlat,' came the voice from the loudspeakers as the anthem ended. 'We toast our own Nadia Kerquelin, the young horsewoman who bravely stepped in to play the role of France's great hero, Bertrand du Guesclin. The role was first played by her father until his unfortunate recent accident. Our own lovely Nadia, whose home is in nearby Domme, symbolizes for us all gathered here in this ancient square the heroic and magnificent Jeanne d'Arc, who rallied the soul of our dear France to win back its freedom.

'And so from this heart of free France, we people of Sarlat thank you all for coming today to share in our homage to our brave forefathers who liberated this historic town in the year 1370, and lit a flame that has never been extinguished. Good night to you all. You will always be welcome back here in beautiful Sarlat. *Vive la France!*'

'She was great,' Bruno said as he and Claire and the others gathered in the great chamber for a last glass of wine, to congratulate the Mayor and to be told by Romain that the *Te Deum* had been composed by the celebrated young French composer Vincent Dumestre for a special event at the Château de Versailles.

Then the entire room began to cheer at the arrival of Nadia. Wearing a shortened version of her father's black surcoat with its white cross, she was bare-headed and had a sword in hand, her face flushed and her eyes ablaze with pride. Two paces behind her was the squire to whom she had given the scarf when she was still playing the role of the maiden. She was greeted by the Mayor who kissed her on both cheeks, and then by Romain, who did the same, and then embraced his son, the squire. They were handed a glass of wine as the Mayor called on all to drink a toast to Nadia's splendid reincarnation of Bertrand du Guesclin and of Jeanne d'Arc.

Only then could Nadia dart across the room to hug Claire and then Bruno, who showered her with compliments as Nadia asked if the show had been convincing. They assured her it had been a triumph.

'Don't hang around for me,' Nadia said. 'I have to change and then we have a cast meeting to work out a couple of glitches in the show. Romain will drive me back to the chateau, it's on his way.'

'If you don't mind, we'll wait here for you,' said Bruno. 'Don't forget I'm responsible for your safety, Nadia. Your godfather won't be happy if I let you out of my sight.'

'It's really not necessary,' Nadia said.

'Your godfather thinks it is,' said Bruno. 'And I'm under his orders.'

Chapter 13

Bruno did not sleep well. Claire and Nadia gave him chaste kisses goodnight at the door of the chateau when he said he had to make a last patrol of the grounds with Balzac. They would meet at breakfast with the others the next morning and plan the day. There was a tentative booking at Lascaux for the guests to visit the 18,000-year-old cave paintings in the morning and Josephine Baker's Château des Milandes in the afternoon. Harrison and Lori had read in a guidebook of the region's summertime night markets with food and wine, music and dancing in the squares of the old towns. Their enthusiasm had persuaded the others to join them, and they would attend the Monday one at Beaumont, Nadia's favourite of the old *bastide* towns.

As Bruno walked the grounds, all seemed quiet, the sentries by the pool and at the bend in the track watchful and remaining silent even when Balzac trotted up to greet them. A corporal gave him a silent thumb's up to signal all was well. He sent a text to Marie-Do on the phone she'd given him, reporting a successful event at Sarlat and a quiet night.

Harrison and Lori, Hartmut, Angus, Krishnadev and Gergen's wife, Mavis, were still up, drinking vintage Armagnac in the library after they had evidently dined well. They called on Bruno to join them when he returned to the chateau so he sat down, clearing space for his glass on a small side table, where he saw what looked like a scientific paper with the title, '2D Graphene: the next generation for semiconductors'. Hartmut quickly got up to remove it and placed an empty cognac glass on the table.

'You're going to love this,' said Harrison, handing Bruno a half-empty bottle. 'A Bas Armagnac, from Château de la Béroje, 1975, which is a lot older than my wife and almost as smooth.'

From the silence that fell Bruno realized that despite their invitation to join them, he had interrupted something. Angus had a notepad full of scrawled figures on the side table next to him. Hartmut was putting a copy of *Die Zeit* on top of the scientific paper. Krishnadev tried to smooth over the moment.

'How could a young man like you bear to exchange the company of two lovely young women like Claire and Nadia for this gathering of has-beens?' the Indian asked with a mischievous grin. 'Lori excepted,' he added, hastily, giving her an airy wave.

Bruno answered by holding up his glass, into which he had poured perhaps a finger's width of Armagnac. He toasted them and they all watched him as he took a sip of the drink.

'This is wonderful,' he said, truthfully. 'I've never tasted an Armagnac so old and so distinguished.'

They all looked pleased and he asked if they had spent a pleasant evening together. Indeed, they all chorused. Cassandra had arranged for a team of chefs to come from the Bergerac cooking school and they had prepared an excellent dinner. How had the re-enactment been at Sarlat?

'Nadia upheld the honour of her father very well,' he said.

'She was a great success and Claire was very happy with the evening. The deputy Mayor of Sarlat was very taken with her charm and beauty.'

Bruno thanked them, finished his drink and rose to go, wishing them a good night's sleep. He assured them that all was quiet and peaceful and he looked forward to seeing them at breakfast.

'Not too early, say eight thirty, even nine,' said Angus. 'We still have a little business to discuss here tonight.'

Bruno said that was fine and that their reservation at Lascaux was for ten thirty, so they should leave the chateau by nine forty.

He closed the double doors behind him and went to his room, where Balzac bedded down on his cushion. The window was open and the night was warm and peaceful. Bruno gazed out, seeing the moon's reflection on the swimming pool and aware of a light to his left. He realized the light must be coming from the library, and he could hear voices in English.

'This is no longer the age of geopolitics, not even geoeconomics, it is geotechnology, that is what will decide the future.' It was Hartmut's voice, loud and a little guttural.

'We all agree that we can't afford to fall behind China,' came a woman's voice that he thought might be Mavis's. 'That's the challenge this project will help us to meet.'

'Let's be sure the technology works, first,' came the distinctive, almost musical accent of Krishnadev. 'Just because China is pouring billions into it doesn't mean it's the best.'

Then two or three people spoke together, and Bruno picked up the words 'Taiwan' and 'graphene' but then somebody closed

179

the window. Bruno wondered what exactly they were discussing, because from what he could understand it sounded interesting. He washed his hands and face and looked at his toothbrush. He hated to lose that lingering taste of the Armagnac but he picked up his brush and toothpaste and cleaned his teeth. He turned out the light and went to sleep, thinking of Claire as she sat by the pool, and remembering that slight touch of her lips at Sarlat, and her hand stroking his.

Perhaps that was why he woke up at three, restless, the bedcovers awry, wondering why General Lannes insisted he stay here when Kerquelin's daughters were already being guarded by some of France's best soldiers. What was Lannes's motive for such a big operation with him and the special ops troops? He could hardly justify that on account of Nadia alone. And why should French taxpayers fork out to defend Kerquelin's old college pals? There had to be something of direct French national interest involved or the Elysée would never have approved it. He could understand the importance of Brice Kerquelin, but that would mean protecting his hospital ward rather than his friends. Unless, that is, the friends were involved with Kerquelin in an important project. Bruno tried to recall what he'd overheard from Hartmut and the title of that scientific paper he'd concealed. What was '2D graphene'? Given the European connection, he could see Hartmut being involved in some hi-tech project, but why the Americans? And what did China have to do with it?

He drifted back to sleep, waking before seven to take Balzac out for a run and to check on the soldiers, who gave him coffee and reported a quiet night before he went back to shower, shave, dress and check his emails before breakfast. Claire and Nadia arrived wearing shorts and blouses, carrying baskets filled with towels and suntan lotion, and looking lovely, even though they were bickering about whether they should both go to Lascaux and on to Milandes to keep their father's guests company.

'I see them all the time back in the States,' Claire said. 'I work with Angus, for heaven's sake. And I've been to Lascaux four or five times and to Milandes twice. They don't need baby-sitting, Nadia.'

'But I don't see them that often,' Nadia said. 'They are Papa's guests and they are our responsibility. So I think we should stay with them as much as we can, just out of respect for Dad. I think that's what he'd want.' She turned to Bruno. 'What do you think?'

'My orders were above all to watch out for the two of you but also to make sure that all the guests at Rouffillac were secure,' Bruno said. 'Whether that's because of your father's importance to national security or because his friends are somehow also important, I don't know. Given their hi-tech skills and the connections they maintain with your father, I suspect the latter but all that's way above my pay grade. You probably know more about that than I do.'

'Perhaps, but what should we do, Claire and I?' Nadia asked.

'I think one of you should always be with them, but you can divide up the responsibility. Nadia, you could spend the day with them before you leave for the performance in Sarlat, and Claire could spend the evening with them at the night market in Beaumont. There will be a discreet plain-clothes escort with you all the time, when I have to be somewhere else.'

'That makes sense,' said Nadia, and Claire agreed.

'When do you plan to take the guests to see Nadia play her starring role in Sarlat?' Bruno asked.

'Later in the week, maybe Wednesday or Thursday, there's no rush,' said Claire, and then added, 'Where are the soldiers staying?'

'In bivouac tents in the woods. They're used to it; so was I when I was in the army.'

Then Bruno's phone vibrated. It was a text from Lieutenant Berthier: 'Alert, intruder detained. Proceed to meet sentry by the pool. Didi'

Bruno texted back that he would be there right away. He excused himself and Balzac accompanied him down to the pool. He was greeted by Cassandra, swathed in an enormous towel after a morning swim, while Kirk and Patsy were still frolicking in the pool. He gave them a wave and climbed up the slope where a sentry rose from behind a bush to whisper that the lieutenant was waiting for him at the camp.

'*Bonjour*, Didi,' Bruno greeted him. 'What's this about an intruder?'

'We found our mystery man in camouflage with the fancy shoes,' Didi replied. 'He's a kid, works as a kitchen aide at the roadhouse downhill. It seems he makes a habit of sneaking up here every morning when that gorgeous blonde takes her morning dip. He's in the tent behind me.'

'You have the schedule for the guests' movements today, to Lascaux and then Milandes and tonight at Beaumont?' Bruno asked.

'Yes, the escort teams have been briefed.'

Bruno thanked him and ducked inside the tent to see a young

Asian in a camouflage T-shirt sitting cross-legged on the ground, his hands bound behind him and looking terrified at the gun being pointed at him by a watchful soldier. Bruno checked the feet to see those distinctive shoes with the separate big toe and asked the soldier to wait outside the tent.

'I'm a policeman and my name is Bruno. What's your name?' he began, his voice friendly.

'Nguyen, Jean-Marc Nguyen,' the prisoner said, a watchful eye on Bruno's dog. He was maybe seventeen or so, but he looked strangely vacant, and Bruno wondered whether he was giving him his full attention.

'I think we might both have the same friend, little Patsy, and she knows my dog,' said Bruno. 'Are you her secret friend?'

'Little girl of pretty lady?' Jean-Marc said, his face suddenly animated, almost cheerful. 'Patsy?' he added, a rising tone to his voice. In a European it might have been a question, but Bruno assumed it was the way he spoke.

'Yes, I know Patsy. She lives up at the house with the pool. Where do you live, Jean-Marc?' Bruno asked.

At the roadhouse, with his mother, who worked there as a cleaner, the youth replied. He said he came up to the pool every morning to watch the pretty blonde lady swim.

'Does the lady know you're there, watching?' Bruno asked, and the boy shook his head, saying he knew how to hide. He looked a little ashamed as well as frightened, as if he knew he was doing something wrong. Bruno got up, went outside to tell Didi to undo the handcuffs and that he'd be back with his Land Rover. He would take the youth down to the roadhouse to find his mother and check the story.

Fifteen minutes later he was at the roadhouse. He asked Jean-Marc to stay with Balzac and went in search of Madame Nguyen. She was a small, tired-looking Asian woman who looked to be in her forties, maybe a little older, and she was visibly nervous at the presence of a man in police uniform. He smiled, shook her hand, introduced himself and asked if Jean-Marc was her son. She nodded. He then explained why he had brought the boy back to her.

'He not well, ever since he was child, but he do no harm,' she said. 'He likes people, willing worker.'

Bruno gave her an encouraging smile as he wondered what small epic she had been through in her life. Obviously not a native French-speaker, perhaps arriving in France as a child, maybe with the boat people.

'Where is his father?' he asked.

She shrugged. 'He left when I have baby. I raise Jean-Marc and he work with me here.'

'Can you tell him not to go up to the pool to watch the pretty lady? It could mean trouble for him,' he said, leading her to his vehicle where Jean-Marc had now made friends with Balzac, who was lying contentedly on the youth's lap and enjoying being stroked. Bruno had a lot of faith in Balzac's judgement of people.

'Nice dog, *Maman*,' Jean-Marc said, and shook hands with Bruno before leaving with his mother who half-led, half-pushed him to the rear door of the roadhouse as she admonished him.

Bruno drove back to the chateau in time to get some fruit juice, coffee and a croissant from the breakfast table as the guests prepared to leave for Lascaux. He took his coffee and croissant outside and called Marie-Do to inform her that the mystery intruder had been identified and proved to be harmless. Then he used his other phone to call General Lannes. He spoke to a duty officer, explained again about the intruder, and asked if General Lannes could let him know if he was supposed to be on duty round the clock, and whether his priority should be the daughters or the guests. He added that Kerquelin's friends seemed to be talking of something called 2D graphene and asked whether that was significant.

'Where did you hear of this graphene?' Lannes asked, coming quickly to the call. Bruno explained the scientific paper he'd seen, which was hurriedly concealed, and repeated Hartmut's remark about geopolitics giving way to geotech and the alarm about China.

'Keep your ears and eyes open, Bruno. Are you satisfied with the special ops' security perimeter?'

'Yes, sir, they're very efficient. Nadia will be with the guests at Lascaux and Milandes today and then Claire will join them tonight when Nadia takes the stage again. I saw her perform last night and she was terrific. You'd have been proud of her. One more thing, is there any news about her father's condition?'

'Improving, and I'm told he may be released by the end of this week, but still no visitors. I assume you're staying at the chateau with the guests?'

'Yes, sir. I've been with them round the clock and on duty since making the security review with Commissaire Pantin on Saturday. Do you have any particular threat in mind, against the daughters or the other guests?'

'Nothing specific, and if you need to be elsewhere from

time to time I leave that to your discretion, but I'd prefer it if you were there overnight. As I said, keep your ears open and don't hesitate to search the guests' rooms if you think there's a reason to. Please give Claire and Nadia my warm regards and tell them that I hope to see them later in the week. Is that all?'

'Yes, sir,' said Bruno and Lannes ended the call.

Bruno went to the minivan where the guests were boarding. Nadia stood at the doorway, chatting with Claire. He assured them that there would be a plain-clothes escort shadowing their guests at all times.

'Aren't you coming?' Nadia asked, about to climb into the vehicle.

'I've got other duties,' he said, adding his goodbyes.

'I'm going to the pool,' Claire said. 'Will I see you there?'

'Sorry, I've got paperwork,' he said, and went upstairs to the library. There was no sign of the graphene paper he had seen the night before, nor of the notes Angus had been taking. He glanced quickly into each of the guest bedrooms, recognizing Angus's by the briefcase on the floor. The one with a woman's dressing gown on the bed had to be the room shared by Lori and her husband. The one with a copy of *Die Zeit* on the bedside table had to be Hartmut's and beneath it he saw the scientific paper on 2D graphene, with a second paper under it. He took a photo of the title pages with his phone, and another of some notes scrawled in the space beneath the title of the second paper.

He went to his room, sat down, looked up one of the photos and could barely understand the title – 'Synthesis, structure and applications of graphene-based 2D heterostructures', published by Chemical Society Reviews. The scrawled notes read simply: 'EU – 42B – Fr/De/Ned – GB??'

He tried to decipher it. 'EU' must be European Union, but what was '42B'? Then came 'Fr' for France, 'De' for Deutschland and 'Ned' for Netherlands and question marks over 'GB', which must stand for Great Britain. So it was a European project in which British participation was possible.

He opened his laptop and attached his secure phone to log onto the internet, where he copied the notes into his search box and then hit 'Enter'. At once a press release from the European Commission came up with the announcement of a 42-billion-euro project to double Europe's share of global chip manufacturing by 2030. That would explain the note about 42B.

Next he searched for material on 2D graphene and dozens of pages came up. As he expected, Bruno found that the term '2D' stood for something in two dimensions, which had length and breadth but no height. A sheet of 2D graphene was therefore only a single molecule thick, but extremely strong, and an almost perfect conductor of electricity. It was said to be the next generation of computing, replacing or augmenting silicon chips; to create more powerful and focused radio waves; and far more advanced solar cells, batteries and even desalination filters to make seawater drinkable.

He read that scientists at Manchester University had won the Nobel Prize in 2010 for developing 2D graphene, and had built both a new research centre and a technical institute to exploit their findings. The Chinese claimed to have filed the most patents for ways to use this new miracle of science. More research was under way in Russia, in the United States, in Japan, Germany and France. The promise sounded extraordinary; the products so far, however, seemed to be few. And who would be best placed to exploit it?

Like many French people, Bruno remembered the Minitel, the internet revolution that never quite happened – except in France. Launched in 1981 by the state's old post, telegraph and telephone giant, there were three million terminals in homes and offices across France by 1988, increasing by a hundred thousand more each month. From each one a user could buy rail or air tickets online, order and pay for goods from a mail order house, exchange messages, play computer games, consult databanks and join dating services. In 1986 French students even planned and coordinated a nationwide strike on Minitel. It seemed the internet age had been born in France, but the flowering of Minitel slowly wilted in the face of the World Wide Web, Microsoft and Apple, all strengthened by the huge financial lure of the American market and the global spread of the English language.

Perhaps 2D graphene was condemned to follow the same trajectory from its invention in the northern English city of Manchester, Bruno thought, only to see development and exploitation pass into richer hands in bigger markets. But if America and China were far bigger economies than France, Europe as a whole was of equivalent economic size. Was that the context in which Hartmut had spoken the previous evening? Krishnadev's concern about China was understandable. But why would he and Hartmut be discussing that with their American friends, unless he was thinking of the power of the American, Indian and European markets together to push back the Chinese challenge?

Bruno sat back, thinking that such ideas and developments were too grandiose for him, but there *was* something here that he could comprehend all too well. It was something strategic, about the shifting balance between power and technology that was as old as history; as old as the way the unbeatable English longbow had been defeated by French cannon, and as new as the humiliation of France in 1940 by the German panzer divisions. It was not that the Germans had more tanks; they simply used them better, with attached infantry and reconnaissance troops and dive bombers all knitted together by radio links into a coherent whole. And now it was about chips and the next generation of computing, about 2D graphene, and the massive amount of investment required to make each new technology work. He was too much a realist to think that this was possible for France, but perhaps for Europe

Bruno's thoughts wandered as he sat thinking about the loss to European science and technology because of Brexit, the sadness of his British friends at the result, and his own bafflement at the fact that barely 37 per cent of the eligible voters had carried the day. He also recalled that France in her own referendum in 2005 on the latest EU treaty had also voted No, but by 55 per cent. The EU had sensibly softened the terms and France had acceded.

Bruno sighed. He could no longer think of France alone. His country was now to be considered within a wider context of a Europe that was still in formation, without the sturdy bonds of language and history that held nations together. Perhaps the new Europe could be held together by a shared economic dream, a vision of technology that brought a tangible and shared prosperity. But technology, he knew, was seldom so generous in sharing its benefits. The wealth it created was too often garnered and secured by a visionary and perhaps a greedy few, rather than contributing to the enrichment of all. He thought of the untold billions now accumulating in the hands of the four or five leaders of the American visionaries who had led this revolution. Maybe that was the way it always worked; the profits went to the bold. And that was reasonable, he thought, if only they paid their taxes like everybody else, including him.

He was interrupted by a gentle knock at his door. He closed his laptop, opened the door, and saw Claire, modestly clad in a long silk dressing gown, her face flushed from the sun, her glorious ebony hair now damp and flattened from the pool.

'Are you going to stay here on your computer all day?' she asked. 'Maybe you can't swim. Is that the problem?'

He tried not to look at the swell of her breasts, the curve of her hips, the delicacy of her ankles beneath the fall of the gown.

'I love to swim,' he said, 'and I've been at the computer long enough, so maybe a swim is what I need. Give me a minute to change.'

He intended to close the door but she put her hand on his chest.

'There are just the two of us here,' she said softly.

And a squadron of special forces, he thought, doubtless reporting to Lannes, and perhaps Kirk and Cassandra and Sylvie and maybe even Patsy were around. He tried to summon a neutral smile, polite and friendly but less than welcoming.

'Please,' he said, 'excuse me while I change.'

She said nothing but remained standing in the open door, her hand playing at the cleft where her gown concealed her breasts, her glance raking him from head to toe. Her eyes were bold and her stance confident, as if she knew she was the dominant one here.

There were limits to the self-control a man could summon at such times, Bruno thought. His body was responding with increasing fervour to Claire's apparent invitation, even as some half-suppressed part of his brain shrieked that it would be a serious mistake.

But in the cruel daylight of reality, Bruno gently closed the door, saying in a voice so hoarse he hardly recognized it as his own, 'See you at the pool in five minutes.'

Chapter 14

He and Claire enjoyed a refreshing swim and then Patsy had appeared and demanded her ride in the pool on Bruno's back. Now Bruno was driving back to St Denis, reporting to Lannes and telling him the titles of the scientific papers on 2D graphene and what he had learned from his internet research. He also mentioned the role of the Paris-based lawyer and business consultant Hector d'Aubigny-Dupuy. Bruno was saving one final detail of his findings until he could learn a little more.

To do that, he was heading to the riding school, where his friend Jack Crimson now lived in a modest cottage close to his daughter Miranda and her children. Miranda had been helped to buy into the partnership with Pamela by her father's decision to sell a charming manor house that he said was far too large for him. Bruno had called Jack in advance to say he wanted a private talk. Although Jack was known locally as a retired diplomat and civil servant, Bruno knew that somewhere along his career between intelligence and diplomacy Jack had become a trusted friend of General Lannes and of several American and other NATO allies. In retirement, he stayed in touch with old colleagues, sat on a couple of corporate boards and was a trustee of think-tanks in Washington and Europe.

Jack greeted Bruno – and Balzac – and took him to the discreet terrace behind the cottage. A bottle of Lagavulin and two glasses awaited them with a bottle of Malvern water and a bowl for Balzac. 'Such a pleasure to see you both. I presume this is a business visit.'

Crimson began pouring generous glasses of Scotch and adding water as Bruno took out his phone, calling up a photo he had downloaded earlier from the internet and showing it to his host. Beneath a plaque saying 'GCHQ' stood the former British prime minister David Cameron beside Brice Kerquelin. Half-hidden among other dark-suited officials, male and female, almost as if he were edging out of the shot, was a slightly younger Jack Crimson.

'How well did you know Kerquelin?' Bruno asked.

'Not intimately, but we're friends as well as colleagues,' Jack replied. 'Am I right in thinking you are asking this on behalf of General Lannes?'

Bruno nodded and spoke again as Jack sipped his drink. 'The man standing beside Cameron is William Hague, the British foreign secretary of the day. So this is from sometime between 2001 and 2016. What can you tell me of the year Kerquelin spent at your GCHQ intelligence centre?'

Crimson looked at Bruno amiably, a half-smile on his face, but displayed no hint of surprise at the question, so different from their usual discussions of wine and dinner.

'You are probably aware that links between the British and French armed services and our security agencies have been much closer than most people assume,' Crimson began. 'It is logical enough. We are Europe's only two serious military and nuclear powers. We do not publicize the fact that French naval officers work alongside their Royal Navy counterparts in Britain, just as our officers work alongside yours here in France to coordinate the patrols of our nuclear ballistic submarines and to share intelligence. You know that Lannes and I are friends and have worked closely together. Under Tony Blair, we very wisely also began to share a great deal of electronic intelligence. France was never a full member of the Five Eyes, the US-British-Canadian-Australian-New Zealand intelligence gathering system, but once President Sarkozy made France a full member of NATO in 2009, France became to a great extent the sixth eye.'

'And that continues after Brexit?' Bruno asked. Crimson nodded.

'And the Americans agree to this?'

'They turn an amiable blind eye, excuse the pun. The cooperation is too useful to be interrupted.' Crimson took a large sip of Scotch and leaned forward. 'Bruno, you will recall that it used to be said that the sun never set on the British Empire. That is no longer the case, but it still never sets on the French. Consider the spread of your empire today. Just off the mouth of Canada's St Lawrence river you have St Pierre and Miquelon. In the Caribbean you have Martinique and Guadeloupe. In South America you have Guyana, Europe's space rocket launching station. In the Pacific you have Tahiti and New Caledonia. In the Indian Ocean you have the Ile de Réunion and in the Persian Gulf you have the new base in Abu Dhabi. Down near the Antarctic, you have a radar station and small military base at Kerguelen, south-east of southern Africa. That means French electronic intelligence stations cover the globe. In intelligence terms, these are your family jewels.'

Bruno nodded thoughtfully as he sipped his Scotch and water. He'd never thought of it that way.

'Brice Kerquelin understood that and made sure that we and the Americans and Germans also understood,' Crimson said, and then smiled. 'You know that he thinks he is directly descended from Bertrand du Guesclin, and also from the eighteenth-century Breton seafarer Kerguelen, who gave his name to those remote islands near the Antarctic. Brice was always a romantic.' Jack paused, added some more Scotch to his drink and offered the bottle to Bruno.

'No thanks, I'm looking forward to a ride on Hector before dinner.'

'Have you heard any more about Brice's condition?' Jack asked.

'Just that he's recovering,' Bruno said, and then tried to keep his tone light. 'By the way, did Brice ever talk to you about some kind of European internet or software consortium?'

Jack smiled at him amiably. 'Now I know you're up to something, Bruno, when you put on that casual voice. But yes, Brice was constantly grumbling at the way we let the Americans take over this whole new industry and make billions changing the world when we in Europe had the technology, the skills and the market size to do the same. But we never did. We lost our way. Brice used to talk about Minitel and the way Nokia used to dominate the mobile phone business, and SAP in Germany and Britain's ARM were more than competitive in software, and DeepMind was a world leader in artificial intelligence. He was beside himself with frustration when ARM sold out to Japan's SoftBank and DeepMind was bought by Google.'

'Did you agree with him?' Bruno asked.

'Very much, although I used to tease him about the money he must have made from those start-up shares he had from his time in Silicon Valley. He and I weren't the only ones who thought we Europeans should do better, particularly when the Chinese started to give the Americans a run for their money. Our Dutch and German colleagues felt the same.' Jack paused. 'I don't suppose this is simple curiosity, Bruno. Why are you raising this now?'

'Until he was injured, Brice was planning to spend this week at a reunion with his old Silicon Valley friends who now have their own investment club,' Bruno said. 'It's a venture capital group that includes a Brit, a German, an Indian and someone from Taiwan. And last night I overheard them talking about just such a European project, and also about 2D graphene.'

'I know a bit about 2D graphene, supposed to be the next generation after silicon chips,' Jack said. 'That's one area where Britain has invested a lot of money, in a research institute at Manchester University and a linked technical centre to develop commercial applications. The EU helped co-finance it but I don't know where that stands after Brexit. I can find out, if you like. I cannot think of a better idea than a European consortium with Britain involved and some American investors.'

'Maybe you should talk about this with General Lannes,' said Bruno, finishing his drink and rising. 'Thank you for the Scotch. I'll see you at dinner.'

Five minutes later he was in the stable giving Hector a carrot and telling his horse how much he'd missed him. From the way Balzac had run into Hector's stall and rubbed his face against the horse's leg until Hector had bent his great head to nuzzle him, the dog had missed him too. Bruno left them to their reunion while he checked the horse's legs and hooves, saddled Hector and had almost finished saddling Primrose when Pamela came into the stables wearing her riding boots.

'I thought it was your Land Rover I heard,' she said, hugging him. 'Are you staying for dinner?'

'If I'm welcome,' he replied. 'It's only been a couple of days but I missed you all – including you, Félix,' Bruno added, as the youngster came in, a smile spreading over his thin face when he saw Bruno and Balzac. He greeted Balzac first, which for Bruno meant Félix was getting his priorities right.

'Gilles left for the airport this morning so Fabiola will ride the Andalusian and Félix the warmblood,' Pamela said. 'She just called to say she's on her way so we can saddle those two. Miranda is out with the pony-trekkers so we'll take the other horses on a leading rein.'

Fabiola gave Bruno a cool nod when she arrived rather than the usual *bise* on both cheeks, which meant she was still cross with him about Kerquelin. Bruno was too happy to be back in the saddle to fret about it, enjoying how his sightline changed atop the big horse, the way his legs spread over Hector's wide ribcage and the feel of those powerful muscles beneath him. Hector seemed happy to be carrying his master again, and was eager to break into a canter even as they climbed the slope to the familiar ridge. Bruno used the reins to slow him but leaned forward to pat his neck and tell him they'd be galloping soon; Bruno himself could hardly wait.

As always, they paused on the ridge, the valley falling away gently below them to the river dotted with red and blue kayaks and flashes of yellow from the lifejackets. It reminded him of an Impressionist painting in which dainty flashes of red poppies stood out brilliantly in a field. The green of the grass and the honey-coloured stone of the houses against the clear blue sky and the darker green of the trees across the river reminded Bruno of another, similar painting. Was it a Manet? Or perhaps a Monet? He could never tell them apart and much admired those who could. Still, he told himself, he could usually tell a Van Gogh from a Renoir so he was making progress.

'Time for a run?' came Pamela's voice, breaking into his thoughts, and with a little, now automatic, pressure of one knee he turned his horse, flicked at the loose reins and felt Hector launch himself with a bound. Pamela and Fabiola were already ahead of him and Bruno knew that Hector would never stand for that. He bent down lower in the saddle, narrowing his eyes against the growing rush of wind and feeling the sudden smoothness of Hector settling into his stride.

And then the magic came, that sense across the species of intimate communion between horse and rider, of two creatures becoming one as Hector's stride devoured the ground between him and the two horses ahead, drew alongside and then with the grace of something much smoother than mere mechanics, Hector slid easily into some higher gear and surged ahead with only the remaining length of ridge between him and the edge of woodland that was becoming startlingly close. Unbidden, the sight of Claire at his door in the chateau popped into his mind, another kind of shared communion.

Even as he sat up in the saddle and felt Hector slowing at the approach of the treeline, Bruno felt a gust rise in his chest that was part laughter and part self-mockery at equating the entrancement of human flirtation with the joy of riding with Hector. But was it all that foolish, he wondered, to consider the rare but glorious moments when two distinct and separate beings could share a moment of mutual delight and understanding? At that moment, Hector tossed back his head in a way that Bruno saw at once as a request that he lean down to press his human face against his horse's neck and embrace his steed.

'What a glorious run,' came Pamela's joyful voice, still breathless after her own gallop. 'I almost laughed, Bruno, when I saw you up off the saddle, rump in the air like a jockey in the final stretch. And then I knew I was doing the same and that dear Primrose was damned if she was going to let Hector get any further ahead.'

'That was a ride to shake out all the cobwebs,' said Fabiola. 'All I could think of was moving as one with my horse, almost as though we shared a single consciousness. *Mon Dieu*, but I feel so much better for that.. Perhaps I ought to start prescribing it for my patients.' She put on a sonorous tone: '"Nothing wrong with you, Madame Duchamp, that can't be fixed by a headlong gallop on a really fine horse." It would be cheaper than tranquillizers and very much better for her.'

'Perhaps we might forge a useful partnership,' said Pamela. 'You can tell your patients that a ride before breakfast and another before dinner at the local riding school would make them feel much better.'

'That's not a bad idea,' said Fabiola. 'One of the interesting insights I get as a country doctor is to see how much healthier are the people who live on farms, or with animals, horses and dogs and even chickens. It seems as though we were meant to share this world with them and feel restive and troubled if we don't.'

'I usually try to take Balzac along whenever I visit the retirement home,' said Bruno, watching fondly as his basset hound pounded towards them, his long ears flapping as if he were trying to soar into the air and fly. 'He seems to cheer them all up.'

Pamela led the way down the bridle path through the woods that would bring them to the riding school, and Fabiola explained how animals seemed to comfort Alzheimer's patients. She described some promising Japanese experiments in using robots that looked like baby seals which could smile and blink and even purr when they were stroked.

They saw Jack and the Baron firing up the big barbecue as they walked their horses into the stable yard, unsaddled them and brushed them down before arranging their feed and replenishing their water. Bruno and Félix took off their shirts to wash themselves in the stable sink while the women headed for the bathrooms indoors. In the next stable, Miranda and her trekkers were taking care of the ponies. Florence's car was now pulling up, her twins jumping out as soon as it stopped to run to the stables to greet Balzac. Indeed, what a glorious run, Bruno thought, and now a Monday evening with his friends stretching ahead.

There were some unfamiliar bottles on the table on the terrace, the fruit of Jack's latest foray into the Bergerac vineyards. Bruno went to examine them but Florence came to him first and he greeted her with the usual *bise* on both cheeks. Her manner seemed a little cool, almost frosty.

'How was your evening with that sultry American?' she asked, forcing a grin. Her tone was pointed.

'Nadia's sister?' Bruno replied vaguely. 'They found room for us to watch from the Hôtel de Ville. Claire enjoyed the show. Nadia was terrific, as if born to the role. And unlike her dad, she didn't lose her horse, nor charge into the fray, so all went perfectly. A big success. Tell me, do you know this new wine Jack brought along?'

Thinking he'd changed the subject, he showed her the bottle with the label that said simply Ter'Raz and then looked at the second label on the back. 'It's an IGP, Indication Géographique du Périgord. So not an *appellation*, but it's from Chateau le Raz in the Montravel and seems to be made of the usual grape varieties. What do you think?' He poured out two glasses of the white.

Florence was not to be sidetracked. 'She seemed to be keeping a very tight hold on you after the two of you walked off.'

'It was just common courtesy to let her take my arm among those crowds,' he said, knowing that he was starting to blush. 'And with those shoes she was wearing . . .'

'Oh, yes, I'm sure you noticed those.' Her tone was strange; the only word that seemed to describe it was dry, very dry.

'What do you think of this wine?' he asked, trying again, handing her a glass and taking a sip from his own.

'I'm not in the mood,' she said, not taking the offered glass. 'And besides, I'll be driving the kids home after dinner.' She walked away, her back stiff, and began chatting to Pamela.

Feeling the two women's eyes on him, Bruno pretended nonchalance, poured a third glass, and with his own glass in one hand, the two filled glasses in the other and the bottle under his arm, he took refuge in the company of Jack and the Baron at the barbecue. There were three good-sized perch in the bucket at the Baron's feet, each fish as long as Bruno's forearm and weighing well over a kilo. The dark stripes were sharp against the greenish skin and the tips of the fins were still red.

'Looks like a great dinner,' said Bruno, giving his friends their wine and putting an arm around the Baron's shoulders. 'Where did you catch them?'

'In the lake at Queyssac,' said the Baron, turning from the barbecue to stare solemnly into Bruno's face. 'That's not important. What is important, Bruno, is that you can be an idiot about women. You never know when something is over and you seem incapable of recognizing your future when it stares you in the face.'

'He's right, Bruno,' broke in Jack. 'Everybody knows it. And we saw you trying to palm off Florence with a glass of wine. Are you blind?'

Startled, Bruno tried to make light of it, smiling broadly as he said, '*Putain*, what is this, an ambush?'

'Seriously, Bruno,' said the Baron. 'You rescue Florence and her kids from a wretched life in Sainte Alvère, you bring them to St Denis. You get her a job at the *collège*, you find her and her children a place to live and get me to help you decorate the place and make it habitable. You introduce her to all your friends, integrate her into St Denis and you become the nearest thing to a father those little children have ever known. You even taught them how to swim, for heaven's sake! And you still drop everything – including your trousers – whenever Isabelle, who puts her own career ahead of everything else in life, crooks her little finger. You must be crazy.'

'That's not all,' added Crimson. 'When that brute of a husband of hers got out of prison, you were the one who tried to fix things to protect Florence. When he turned up here at the infants' school and tried to grab his children, you stopped him and got him sent back to jail where he belongs. And then what do you do? You embrace the two little children and make them feel better and give Florence a big hug and tell her everything will be all right.'

'I don't know what the hell happened yesterday evening in Sarlat, or who you were with, but Florence has been moping ever since,' the Baron said. 'Your relationship with Florence is your own business, hers and yours, but you've certainly made yourself into a substitute father for her kids. Little wonder that Florence got her hopes up.'

The Baron paused and Bruno looked from him to Crimson and back again, trying to damp down his irritation at this intrusion by his friends into his private life. The Baron and the others were a kind of family, he told himself, and the Baron had long been telling Bruno it was time to forget his old yearning for Isabelle and move on. He knew they were right. And yet . . .

'We all know you're a fool when it comes to women,' said

Jack. 'Fair enough, most of us men are, much of the time. But we're two old men who have learned from our mistakes and we're your friends so please think long and hard about what we've just said to you this evening.'

'Here,' said the Baron, handing Bruno the bucket filled with perch. 'Go and gut these fish and season them while you're thinking about what we've just said before you bring them back.'

Without speaking, Bruno took the bucket of fish from the Baron, stared blankly at his two friends and then turned and went to the kitchen, trying to close his thoughts to anything but the way he would gut and season the fish.

To his surprise the kitchen was empty. Automatically he took a knife from the drawer, gutted and cleaned the fish, reached for the brush to spread on walnut oil, squeezed and sliced lemons, grated garlic, sprinkled salt and a little pepper. These were activities, he knew, that protected him from pondering what his friends had said.

Recognizing the truth of much that he'd been told, he stifled the little knot of resentment he felt at their frankness and intrusion. Bruno still wanted to think this through for himself, wondering if there might be something sensible he could say to his friends. He put the dressed fish onto a platter, took it out and handed it to the silent Baron.

'Do you think I haven't thought about this for a while?' Bruno said quietly. 'There are few women I've admired more than Florence, for her courage, her resilience, her kindness and good nature, and her sense of the public good. She's a wonderful friend and an admirable woman but I can see her *only* as a friend, one whom I love dearly but not in the way that she wants, that perhaps she deserves. I don't feel that spark that a man should feel for a woman, and I can't fake it. I've thought about this a lot, as I said, and I even told myself that Florence would make me a fine wife. But she deserves much better than that, a husband who desires her as much as he respects her.'

They heard him out and then the Baron shook his head sadly and Jack gave a long, deep sigh.

'Maybe I'd better go,' Bruno said. He went to his Land Rover and gave a low whistle, expecting Balzac to come. But his dog did not appear. *Merde*, he thought, even my dog is avoiding me. Then a shadow emerged beside his vehicle. It was Fabiola.

'I just wanted to tell you that an old friend from medical school made some enquiries for me about Kerquelin,' she said. 'You've been telling me for days that he's recovering at the Piqué military hospital under guard. That's not true. There's no guard there, and no Kerquelin. He's never been anywhere near the place. So what I want to know, Bruno, is whether you're lying or being lied to.'

'That comes as news to me,' he said, trying to absorb this new shock while he was still reeling from the first one.

'Something else,' she said. 'I had some of that blood on my clothes, and because my doubts were growing I took a sample to the lab in Bergerac and ran it through the Fourier spectroscope, checking on the proteins and nucleic acids. It wasn't human blood, Bruno. It came from a pig. He must have kept it in some kind of bag beneath his armour, and at the right moment let it all pour out. The whole thing was faked.'

He stared at her, stunned. 'I didn't know,' he said, his voice faint in his own ears.

Fabiola studied him, her face impassive as Balzac came up to stand beside Bruno and then lay down, resting his head on Bruno's foot. She glanced down at the dog and then she said, 'I believe you, Bruno,' and smiled. Bruno smiled back.

'Gilles will be furious that he's stuck in Kyiv while this story is breaking here in the Périgord,' she added. 'Can't you just see the headlines: "France's Spymaster Disappears", or "Did Superspy Fake Own Death in Sarlat's Mock Battle?"'

'You left out the part about his being a Silicon Valley billionaire,' Bruno said.

'Really? How interesting. Goodnight, Bruno. We all love you dearly and have your best interests at heart, even if you think we are all a bunch of interfering busybodies. And don't worry, I'll tell everybody you were called away on sudden police business.'

Chapter 15

Bruno was thinking about Fabiola's news rather than Florence when he let himself and Balzac into his office at the closed and silent Mairie. At his desk he called Alain, who had left St Denis with Rosalie that morning and Bruno knew he'd be on duty that night. After a brief greeting he asked Alain if he had access to the flight logs at his Mont-de-Marsan airbase.

'Yes, I do, right here at my desk. Since I teach radar operators and traffic controllers, we use those logs all the time.'

'Helicopters, too?'

'Yes, everything that touches the ground. We're the base for CEMA,' said Alain, referring to the air force's experimental centre, 'so we get all kinds of aircraft coming and going.'

'Remember last Friday when we were in Sarlat and that guy doing the re-enactment was injured?' Bruno asked. 'He was supposed to have been on a chopper that took him from Domme to the Piqué military hospital. Would that have landed at your base?'

'No, Piqué has its own landing pad for choppers. But let me double-check the log.'

There was a pause before Alain spoke again. 'Here we are. A Dassault plane, a prototype of the ultra long-distance Falcon 10X, landed at 2000 hours, filled its tank and took off at 2230, scheduled to fly to Cayenne in French Guyana. And we did have a chopper come in while the Falcon was on the ground. Let me see . . . it was an H135, that's an Airbus helicopter used for medical evacuations.'

'Where did that medevac chopper come from?' asked Bruno.

'Domme,' Alain replied.

'Let me get this right,' said Bruno. 'A medevac chopper comes in from Domme while that Falcon jet is on the ground having just flown in from where?'

'From Mérignac, that's a Dassault assembly site.'

'And Mérignac is what, just over a hundred kilometres from your airbase?' asked Bruno.

'About that. A very short hop. That's kind of unusual when the Falcon was flying off to South America.'

'Can you find out what the full flight plan was for the Falcon after Cayenne?'

'Yes, the log is in the computer.' There was another pause. 'The flight plan was filed for Papeete, Tahiti – we have an airbase there – and then to Nouméa, New Caledonia, another airbase, and then Sydney. There was a piece in one of the aviation magazines recently about Dassault doing a big sales pitch in Australia for its new business jet.'

'And coming back?' Bruno asked.

'No problem. Sydney to La Réunion in the Indian Ocean, that's just over nine thousand kilometres, and then another nine thousand kilometres back to Bordeaux. The Falcon could do that in twenty-four hours, including refuelling, no problem. They'd probably need spare pilots, but we've got French airbases all around the world. Makes you think.'

'It certainly does, Alain. If you hear of this Falcon coming back, could you let me know?'

'Will do. Normally you could do it yourself. Just go to FlightRadar24.com and you can track any commercial flight if you have the tail number. But this one probably won't show up on any public site, since it's a prototype. I'll keep an eye on it for you.'

'That's great, Alain, thanks. When should I expect you and Rosalie to come back here?'

'Weekend after next, if you can put us up.'

'No problem, you're always welcome.'

'What's all this stuff about – Domme and the Falcon?'

'I'm trying to work out what happened to the guy who was supposed to have been injured in Sarlat and taken to the Piqué hospital. You've given me an alternative explanation, so thanks.'

'Don't mention it. And by the way, give our best regards to our future new neighbours, Florence and her twins. She was telling us how much work you and the Baron put into decorating her place. Rosalie came away convinced that Florence and her kids think the world of you. I have to say you could do a lot worse.'

'Thanks, Alain,' Bruno said politely. 'I'll bear that in mind. Love to Rosalie.'

Bruno hung up and sat back, thinking about Kerquelin, flight times and possible explanations. There were obvious reasons why he might want to visit the space flight launch station at Cayenne, but why would he interrupt his reunion with his old Silicon Valley friends for such a trip? And why a jaunt to tropical Tahiti or New Caledonia? Had he really faked his own injury and his stay at the military hospital? Bruno now knew that Lannes had lied to him about the Piqué hospital. What kind of operation would lure the next head of French intelligence to abandon the Sarlat re-enactment of which he was the star and prime mover and travel halfway around the world?

Even as Bruno pondered Kerquelin's disappearance, the question of Florence kept nagging at him. He was obviously the target of a coordinated campaign by his friends. First the Baron and Jack, and Fabiola was in on it. And now Alain and Rosalie.

It was not only irritating, it felt somehow like a marriage being arranged by parents or the elders of a village, without the happiness or suitability of the two people as paramount. How dare they presume to make such plans on his behalf? Except for Alain, they weren't even family! Then Bruno paused, reflecting that his friends *were* in an important sense his family, and they were thinking not just of his future but also that of Florence and her children and of the community of St Denis.

From the Mayor down to the kids in her computer club, they had all been appalled at the prospect that Florence might emigrate to Canada if that was what it took to get away from her disastrous ex-husband. One way to lock Florence into St Denis was to tie her down with Bruno. And one way to ensure that Bruno would never drift off to Paris to join General Lannes's team and build a new life with Isabelle was to lock him in place with Florence and the twins. Yes, he could see the thinking behind that. But as far as Bruno was concerned, matrimony was his own concern. And even though the Mayor did it all the time, Bruno did not take kindly to being manipulated.

He had been lucky, Bruno reflected, that the one time he had broken his own rule about no affairs with local women it had been with Pamela, who was British and who had no intention of ever marrying or settling down with one man ever again. But aside from pushing marriage with Florence, his friends were clearly urging him to make a final break with Isabelle. Intellectually, he knew they were right. There was no future for him and Isabelle and never had been, only those snatched and brief reunions.

What cruel jokes the gods played on us mortals, he thought, that there were women a man knew in his bones that he should love, that he might even want to love, but that essential surge of primeval desire never even flickered. But that was not quite true in the case of Florence. A memory nagged at him, of the time at Pamela's pool where he had taught Daniel and Dora to swim and Florence had been looking entrancing in a green bikini. When the twins had each managed to swim up and back the length of the pool, Florence had jumped in to hug him and that delightful sensation of her bosom pressing against his chest had stayed with him.

With an effort, he hauled his thoughts back to the strange disappearance of Brice Kerquelin.The striking fact was not that Lannes had lied about Kerquelin being in the Piqué military hospital; he could understand the security concerns behind such a misdirection. It was that none of the local specialists on the kind of surgery that Fabiola assumed was essential had been summoned to operate in what was presumably an urgent case. So what of the possibility that the very public wounding of Kerquelin had been a deliberate misdirection and that he had taken that special Falcon flight and been engaged on some highly secret mission in the Pacific? This while his cherished group of old friends from Silicon Valley were gathered at Rouffillac talking about some European project to manufacture silicon chips and discussing the next generation of 2D graphene chips. And Bruno knew that another member of the group of friends had not yet arrived at Rouffillac – Sonny Lin, of the Taiwan Semiconductor Manufacturing Company, who would doubtless have more than a passing interest in graphene and in the European project.

Bruno began a computer search into the company and found that it was already building a $12-billion plant in Arizona, had agreed to build another in Japan and was said to be discussing a similar project in Europe. Some industry commentators had suggested this decision to build plants elsewhere was a 'silicon shield', a form of insurance against a Chinese invasion of Taiwan. Digging further, he came across articles in the English-language Chinese press suggesting that Taiwan might be secretly resuming its own nuclear weapons project, after their first attempt, the Hsin Chu programme, had been stifled by American pressure in the late 1970s.

Bruno widened his search for material on Taiwan's nuclear ambitions. The country had come within a year or two of developing a nuclear weapon, according to a US National Intelligence Estimate. An inspection report by the International Atomic Energy Agency in the 1970s found evidence of a secret weapon development project using a Canadian-supplied research reactor, heavy water from the United States, uranium from South Africa and technological advice from Israel. Taiwan then undertook to dismantle the weapons programme but work continued in secret until 1987, when Colonel Chang Hsien-yi, deputy director of the Institute of Nuclear Energy Research, who had been recruited by the CIA, defected to the United States with documentary evidence that a controlled nuclear reaction had been carried out and the Sky Horse ballistic missile was under development to deliver it.

Bruno whistled to himself in surprise and then sat back, wondering whether France might be prepared to offer its nuclear weapons expertise to Taiwan in return for a microconductor industry of its own. No, he told himself, that was taking speculation too far and he doubted that even if a French government were prepared to consider it, no such portentous news could be kept secret. But he remembered one of Gilles's articles in *Paris Match* after Russia's seizure of the Crimea in 2014, saying that the invasion might never have happened had not Ukraine in 1994 voluntarily surrendered its own nuclear arsenal of 1,700 warheads, a legacy from Soviet times.

He picked up his mobile phone and called Lannes's office, reached a duty officer and said Lannes should be told that the Piqué cover story was about to unravel after local doctors had verified with their colleagues that Kerquelin was not being treated there. Within minutes, Lannes returned Bruno's call.

'How did this get out?' Lannes demanded.

'On the doctors' grapevine, here and in Périgueux, Bergerac and Bordeaux,' Bruno replied. 'They mostly know one another and there have been pointed questions to the regional medical council. They are also questioning reports of Kerquelin's supposed injury since none of the relevant specialists were contacted.'

'How many doctors are we talking about?'

'I don't know, but they're a gossipy group. They went to medical school and did their internships together and they're always in touch with each other about getting specialists to operate or to find hospital places for their patients. Doubts began to arise when someone supposedly in Kerquelin's condition was sent to Domme and then by chopper to Piqué. It probably won't be long before your goddaughter hears about this and gets on the phone to you.'

'Have you talked to J-J about this?'

'No, but his forensics expert, Yves, is talking with doctors all the time, particularly those at the Bergerac lab, where apparently word is going around that Kerquelin's injury was faked, that the blood he was leaking had come from a pig. I'd be very surprised if Yves hasn't heard about this from them. It was surprising to me that Kerquelin's Silicon Valley friends at Rouffillac don't seem all that concerned about his condition, almost as though they know there's nothing to worry about.'

'I'd better make some calls and then we should talk again tomorrow. What's the plan for the guests tomorrow?' Lannes asked.

'St Denis market and the prehistory museum in Les Eyzies. One more thing, sir. At least some of the doctors have apparently established that no medical helicopter landed at Piqué on the night in question, and they're asking where it went after it left Domme. I think some of them have been looking at the flight plans that I'm told you can monitor on the internet.'

'I see. Thank you, Bruno. We'll talk tomorrow.'

'By the way, how is Monsieur Kerquelin?'

'Recovering, I believe. Goodnight, Bruno.'

'Oh, one last detail I forgot to report after visiting Kerquelin's home. There was on his bedside table a well-thumbed copy of a guidebook to Taiwan. I mentioned it to his ex-wife when I drove her from Bergerac to Domme but she had no explanation. I know from Nadia and Claire that he and his other Silicon Valley friends visited Taiwan last year as guests of their friend Sonny Lin of the Taiwan Semiconductor Manufacturing Company. I don't know if that is at all relevant.'

A sigh came from the phone. 'I have this funny feeling, Bruno, that you know or have surmised or made a wild guess about a great deal more than you are saying in this call. Why not tell me what you really think?'

It was quiet for a few moments and then Bruno spoke. 'You always asked me to be honest with you, so let me say that I think Kerquelin's injury was faked, and that he is somewhere in the Pacific with Sonny Lin of TSMC. I might even venture a guess that they are negotiating a deal to build a huge semi-conductor manufacturing plant here in France, which sounds to me like a very good idea, just so long as French nuclear technologies are not part of the bargain.'

There was silence on the line, and then '*Merde*, Bruno' came the voice of a very tired man. 'Why the hell are you not working with me here in Paris rather than down there in the Dordogne?'

'Because most of my friends are here and the food is better, sir, and the good wine is cheaper. And there's much more sunshine down here, glorious countryside and a lot less traffic, and I can keep a horse and a dog and go into my garden and dig up my own truffles.'

Bruno paused for a reaction but all he heard from the other end of the line was a deep sigh, then Lannes spoke: 'Goodnight, Bruno. We'll talk soon. I'm sure I don't have to ask you to keep your conjectures to yourself.'

Bruno sat thinking for a while, then Balzac rose from his cushion and adopted his usual watch position moments before Bruno heard the familiar sound of the lift reaching his floor. He went to open his door and saw the Mayor heading his way.

'I saw your office light on,' the Mayor said, 'so I tried to call you but you were busy and then I called the Baron, thinking you'd be there on a Monday evening. He told me you had left the dinner in something of a huff. Then he told me why.'

'I gather you and he, and most of my friends, think I've made a fool of myself over Isabelle long enough.'

'Not just her, Bruno. There was Oudinot's daughter, too, but Isabelle is the one who got her hooks into you and kept them there.'

'Isabelle is a remarkable woman,' said Bruno.

'She is indeed, and a woman who will go far, but she'll do so alone, at least until she finds the kind of well-connected Parisian who will make her a suitable husband to launch the next steps of her brilliant career.'

'I think I realized that a while back,' Bruno replied, and waited for the Mayor to drop the other shoe, Florence.

'What you didn't realize, perhaps because you were too close to it, is that *le bon Dieu* in His wisdom had sent you the perfect wife and future mother of your children,' the Mayor said. 'To be more exact, you found her, you saved her from a wretched existence, transformed her life and virtually adopted her delightful twins. You are her white knight on horseback, always there to rescue her from dragons.'

The Mayor paused, but Bruno said nothing. 'Come into my office and we'll have a glass of that excellent *gnôle* from Driant's still.'

Moments later, firewater in hand, Bruno sat in the familiar chair across the desk from the man he loved and respected as a father. But he still felt rebellious, uncomfortable with the way his friends sought to shape his future life.

'I don't intend to raise this matter again,' the Mayor said after an appreciative sip of his drink. 'You know my feelings on the matter and I have every confidence that you will eventually see sense, once you have exhausted every conceivable alternative. Who is it this time, one of Kerquelin's daughters? I hear the American one is, to quote one of my favourite authors, the kind of woman who could tempt a bishop to kick a hole in a stained-glass window.'

'That's from *Farewell, my Lovely*, by Raymond Chandler,' said Bruno. 'You introduced me to his books.'

'I was right to do so and I'm right again on your personal future, but enough of that. What do you think of our chances in next year's rugby tournament?'

Chapter 16

Bruno began to awake the next morning in his room at Château de Rouffillac with images of Claire in her dressing gown somehow merging with the memory of Florence's breasts pressing against his chest. He took a deep breath, sat up and saw Balzac standing by the bed looking at him, slightly concerned. Bruno got up, put on shorts, a T-shirt and running shoes, and trotted down the stairs with his dog for a morning run up the Roman earthworks. There he drank a cup of coffee with Lieutenant Didi.

'It's quiet now,' said Didi, 'but we had a sniff in the night.'

'A sniff?' asked Bruno. 'What do you mean?'

'Electronic interference that causes a flutter on our screens, which can mean that some unit is nearby with communication systems similar to ours. I reported it to headquarters and they say if it happens again they'll send a specialist unit to look into it.'

'What else might it be?'

'Sunspots, an electric storm, a car with a malfunctioning navigation system, trouble on transmission lines. It happens often enough.'

'I'd better report it,' said Bruno, and called the duty officer at Lannes's office to do so.

'What's the plan today, sir?' the lieutenant asked.

'Market day in St Denis, so we'll take them there, two of your men in plain clothes to follow, and then it's prehistory,' Bruno replied. 'I'm told that one of the guests, Hartmut, was at some point a student of a friend of mine, a German archaeologist who is married to one of the curators at the prehistory museum in Les Eyzies. So after a museum visit and lunch the pair of them are going to take all the visitors to a couple of the local sites and give a brief lecture.'

'I wouldn't mind hearing that,' said Didi. 'When we went to that restaurant of Tran's uncle he said you'd taken him to some of the caves and he was blown away.'

'Come back another time and I'll arrange something,' said Bruno. 'Have you seen Lascaux yet?'

Didi shook his head.

'I'll see if I can fix you an extra day here so you get the chance. I think everybody should see it. You'll never again think of our ancestors as primitive. They even invented rope so they could make scaffolding to let them paint the ceiling.'

Bruno's phone vibrated; Lannes was calling. 'Can you get me the tech who spotted that flutter,' Lannes said, less a question than an order. 'I have Colonel Tourbier on this call who is in charge of developing the FELIN information system.'

Bruno handed his phone to the tech sergeant and watched, fascinated, as he connected the phone into an outlet on his helmet, opened a laptop and sent the diagnostics he had run on the flutter to the distant colonel. Bruno could barely understand a word of the technical language the two men exchanged, but within minutes the lieutenant and two of his men were unpacking a drone from a small suitcase. The drone was shaped in the form of a cross, with each wingspan no longer than Bruno's forearm. They unplugged a camera system from the body of the drone, inserted a small box stuffed with mysterious electronics, and sent it soaring towards the rising sun. Within moments, data started flowing from the drone to the laptop and from there to Colonel Tourbier.

'It's carrying a scanner system to check possible interference or monitoring networks,' said the tech sergeant, looking up from his laptop. 'We'll soon find out who is out there, if anybody.'

'Unless it's a Micius,' said Lieutenant Didier, looking up briefly.

'What on earth is a Micius?' Bruno asked.

'Tell you later,' Didier replied, never taking his eyes off the drone control in his hands.

Twenty minutes later the drone returned, was packed away, Bruno's phone was handed back to him and arrangements were under way for a second squadron of soldiers to be deployed nearby that afternoon.

'So what's a Micius?' Bruno asked again when Didier seemed free to talk.

'It's a Chinese satellite communications system which allows quantum-encrypted communications, voice or video, over thousands of miles. State of the art. They even have a ground version, quantum-encryption data link between Shanghai and Beijing.'

'I'm not altogether sure what quantum-encryption means,' Bruno said. 'I thought this quantum stuff was way in the future.'

'Not any more,' said Didier. 'The good news is that it's not a Micius. The bad news is that we don't seem to know what it is. But somebody nearby is trying to tap into our FELIN helmet communications.'

'Do you know where they are?'

'The device they're using is across the river but it may be remotely controlled or on a drone, which means they could be anywhere. That's why we're getting a second squadron to help solve the mystery.'

'Campsites and *gîtes* tend to be full this time of year,' said Bruno. 'But there's no shortage of woodlands to the west, above Calviac, or across the river near the Fénelon chateau. And tell me, that flutter your tech sergeant noticed – was it just a probe to see who you were or was it supposed to interfere with your communications and your monitoring?'

'I don't know, but the techs are working on that.' He looked grimly at Bruno. 'This has just become a lot more serious. What inspired you to call it in?'

'Ignorance,' Bruno replied. 'I had no idea what it was about so I thought it worth checking. And now there are two other things I need to do, starting with asking why your sergeant's dinky piece of equipment could identify an electronic sniffer when we had no warning from that multibillion-euro electronic surveillance base at Domme. After all, it's really about their man Kerquelin that we're here.'

'What's the other thing you need to do?'

'Buy a little girl an ice cream.'

Thirty minutes later, showered and shaved and in civilian clothes, Bruno was knocking on the door of Kirk and Cassandra's house with Balzac, to ask if Patsy would like to join them for a walk down to the village. She was eager to do so, and Bruno handed her Balzac's leash as they set off down the lane, Patsy chattering happily to Balzac all the way. They skirted around the hairpin bend and along the river road to the small hotel-restaurant that dominated the little hamlet where young Nguyen worked and lived with his mother. Bruno bought a coffee for himself and an ice cream for Patsy and then walked around behind the kitchen where Nguyen's mother was attaching just-washed sheets and towels to long washing lines to take advantage of the sunshine.

'*Bonjour, madame,*' he said politely, adding that he was looking for Jean-Marc, but that there was no trouble; he just wanted to ask her son something. She looked a little suspicious but the sight of Patsy reassured her, so she pointed to a courtyard around the corner where Bruno found Jean-Marc also hanging washing on a line to dry. He brightened at once at the sight of Balzac. There was no sign of recognition between him and Patsy.

'*Bonjour*, Jean-Marc. I just wanted to ask you if you had seen anybody else, dressed a bit like you in your trips up the hill to the chateau?'

Bending down to stroke Balzac, Jean-Marc shook his head. 'Never.'

'Okay, that's all I wanted to ask, thank you,' Bruno said, and led Patsy and his dog back up the hill, Patsy chattering that Jean-Marc was shorter and much younger but he did look a little like her secret friend.

Bruno took Patsy first to his Land Rover to give her the bag of home-made dog biscuits he'd promised. He let her give one to Balzac, walked her home and then went to find Captain Didi. 'So we have had another intruder, also possibly Asian, who is not the boy who was watching the lady of the chateau take her swim,' Bruno told him. 'It was my fault, sorry. I jumped to conclusions. He said he knew the little girl because he must have seen her at the pool. But Patsy didn't know him so he's not the secret friend.'

'He'd have had trouble coming up here the last couple of days when we had patrols out and the detectors rigged.'

'Unless he was able to take advantage of that little flutter on your communications. How long did it last?'

'We can't tell. Colonel Tourbier has his experts working on that, and checking whether any nasty little bugs were inserted into our systems.'

'When does the new squadron arrive?'

'Sometime this afternoon. Can you help me to scout possible sites where they can set up?'

Bruno shook his head. 'Normally I'd be happy to help but I have to stay with the guests today. You'll have to spare a couple of plain-clothes guys to escort us. Still, I can point out some possible places on your map.'

Bruno walked back to the chateau in time to join the others at the tail-end of breakfast. There was fruit juice, strawberries and croissants left on the table, and a fresh pot of coffee. Bruno had arranged that they would lunch at Ivan's restaurant in St Denis after the morning's market tour. He then led them by the river route, past the towering old castles of Beynac and Castelnaud, and then turning off at St Cyprien to take the hill road to Campagne and St Denis, where the market was in full swing.

The stalls were almost overflowing with strawberries, peaches, apricots, squash, cucumbers and different kinds of lettuce. Stéphane's cheese stall could hardly be seen for the customers swarming around it, and the family from the Lac Noir farm were running back and forth to their refrigerated van to bring new supplies of duck breasts, legs, whole ducks and fresh foie gras. There were crowds around each of the stalls for wines – from the town vineyard, and the travelling peddlers from the Montravel and Saussignac, the Pécharment and Bordeaux. The children of the winemakers were kept busy rinsing out the glasses for free tastings, while the artisan brewers talked of their pride in their beers.

There were rivals for every trade: for the little round goat cheeses, fresh, demi-sec and aged; for the Basque sausage-makers from the Pyrenees; for the stalls with fresh oysters and mussels, shipped from the coast at dawn that morning. They competed for space with live chickens and a host of breads – rye, black, with bits of bacon baked inside, sourdoughs and with olive. There were home-made butters, yogurts and every version of fruit jam under the sun. There were queues at the Vietnamese stall with its hot *nems*, at the Mauritian stall with its curries, and an even longer line at the Guadeloupe stall with its empanadas and spices. A man with a huge vertical rotisserie was roasting chickens, quail and pigeons while great vats of *pommes de terre Sarladaises* bubbling below sent wafts of garlic to blend tantalizingly with the scents of roasting fowls. There were stalls of local honeys, of beeswax candles, of different kinds of mushroom, from the giant *cèpes* to the orange chanterelles, the pointed brown *morelles* and the black *trompettes des morts*.

And that was just the food. Beyond lay the stalls of kitchen wares, of boots and berets for farmers and wraparound aprons and bonnets for their wives. There were vendors of needles and pins and embroidery frames, of nutcrackers, playing cards, rolling pins and candlesticks. There was a knife-sharpener and a woman who fashioned the most alluring flies a trout had ever seen. She spent part of her time fending off the man with a cowboy hat and magnificent moustache who wove the best baskets in the region.

Bruno knew them all, knew their feuds and their friendships, their secret dalliances and their tussles with the taxman. Even those few he neither liked nor trusted he still respected for the stubborn valour that brought them out to set up their stalls before eight each morning, winter and summer, rain or storm or sunshine, always ready to do battle for a traditional spot. He warmed to their random acts of kindness, an extra hundred grams for a poor widow, a small baguette for a hungry kid, the unsold stock that was given to charities at the end of the working day. When Father Sentout came out to bless the market, one of the last priests in France to do so, they doffed their berets or bowed their heads in politeness rather than devotion.

Fat Jeanne, with her worn leather satchel, would collect the five euros the town charged for each metre-length of stall; Bruno was always nearby watching to be sure she was paid promptly and treated with respect. If there was a scuffle between two stallholders for a prize spot, Bruno would be there to re-enact the wisdom of Solomon, and find an equitable solution. He was welcome at all of the small tables that were erected behind and between the stalls for the *casse-croute*, the mid-morning snack when they ate bread and cheese and pâté and washed it down with glasses of red wine. The market of St Denis had been held each Tuesday morning for more than seven hundred years, and Bruno knew that he was only the latest in a long line of town officials who tried to bring a little order and fair dealing to this weekly example of raw village capitalism.

His guests, loaded with snacks and souvenir T-shirts, assembled at ten thirty at the Mairie, where he gave a brisk history of the town's founding in the ninth century as a *centaine*, a semi-military community behind wooden walls that would eventually be replaced by stone, to defend against the Arabs from the south and the Norsemen from the sea. He pointed to the stone cross, all that remained of the ancient nunnery, and recounted its brutal sacking in the wars of religion after the abbess embraced the Protestant faith. He spoke of the many blacksmiths' forges along the riverbank, who used the local iron ore that had given prehistoric artists their red colours, to make the swords and armour of the Middle Ages, and then the eighteenth-century naval cannon that were floated down on barges to the base of the French fleet at Bordeaux.

He took the visitors to the not very impressive small chateau of Vitrolle, which had been the secret Resistance headquarters in 1944; to the Chapel of St Martin, built by King Henry II of England as penance for the murder of his archbishop, Thomas Becket; and to the ancient river port of Limeuil, where the Vézère flowed into the Dordogne. They quickly understood the importance of such a port to local taxes that would pay for troops and castle walls. They evidently were more intrigued when he spoke of the bafflement of the archaeologists who had discovered, when a local bakery was being enlarged, a cache of several hundred flat stones, each engraved with an animal; horses, reindeer, bison, bear and one solitary fox. The best explanation the scholars could devise was that it might have been the first art school some twelve millennia ago. Then he took them to the town vineyard for a wine tasting before reaching Ivan's restaurant at one, as the market was closing and the stalls cleared away.

Bruno led the way to the restaurant and to his surprise he heard cries of welcome and delight from behind as he turned to see Mavis and Lori swooping as one upon someone Bruno could not see. It took him a moment, helped by the sudden stiffness of Nadia's posture and the anger in her eyes, to realize that it was her mother. Suzanne, evidently well known to the rest of the group, was exchanging embraces with Lori and Mavis and then being hugged by Krish and Hartmut, all insisting that she join them for lunch.

'Ambushed,' said Claire in a cold voice, 'and nothing we can do but make the best of it, Nadia.' She moved forward to exchange air kisses with Suzanne and Nadia then followed suit. Bruno greeted her politely.

'I see you're all in good hands,' Suzanne announced in English. 'But you might not know just how good. Your escorting policeman, Monsieur Bruno, is in fact a war hero, one of the very few of his generation who have been awarded the Croix de Guerre.'

Bruno felt himself start to blush as all eyes turned to him, and Suzanne went on to relate what, for Bruno, had been that endless moment of utter terror and confusion under the artillery bombardment at Sarajevo airport. He had no clear memory of the event, only that long burn scar on his arm.

Bruno brushed aside the compliment and explained that the food at Ivan's usually depended on the nationality of the women Ivan met on his vacation and brought back to St Denis. Diners had enjoyed the cooking of Ivan's Spanish, German and Japanese girlfriends as well as an Australian wine student who cooked Malay and Indonesian dishes. But today, Bruno said, Ivan had promised some classic French food from the Perigord.

'Has he yet brought back an Indian woman?' Krish asked, with a wide smile as he opened the door and held it for the others to pass through. 'Better still, he should bring three; one for the Punjabi style, another for the Bengali and a third for the Tamil. I had better warn him not to try bringing them all at the same time.'

Krish, with genial grace, seated Suzanne between him and Mavis, with Lori opposite, and Bruno found himself at the far end of the table, more than content to be squeezed between Nadia and Claire. Kerquelin's daughters seemed resigned to Suzanne's presence, even when they overheard plans being made for Suzanne to join them another evening, to see Nadia take her father's role in the re-enactment. Suzanne looked down the table as she said this, blowing a kiss and bestowing a brilliant smile upon her daughter, and calling out, 'So proud of you, darling.' Out of politeness, Nadia waved back.

Bruno and Ivan had chosen the menu with care: a chilled

soup of fresh green peas with crème fraîche, followed by trout caught early that morning and poached in white wine, served with new potatoes, salad and cheese, and then crème brûlée and coffee. With the meal everyone had drunk a crisp white wine from the town vineyard, a traditional blend of Sauvignon Blanc and Sémillon with a little of the local Muscadelle to add a sense of fruit with just a hint of sweetness. In the name of her father as host, Claire asked for the bill, but was beaten to it by Krishnadev, who said he had been so enchanted by the lunch that he was keen to find out what it had cost. Ivan handed it to him, and Krish pulled out his wallet and placed four 50-euro bills on the plate. Ivan thanked him and turned to leave, but then Krish pulled out a fifth bill and called across to Bruno, 'How do you say a tip in French?'

'A *pourboire*,' Bruno replied. 'But the service is already included.'

'*Pourboire* extra,' said Krish, beaming with pleasure and putting the banknote into Ivan's startled hand. 'Merci, *mon ami, très, très bon. Vive la France.*'

'In California, a meal like that for ten people with three bottles of an excellent wine like that would have cost at least a thousand bucks,' Krish announced as he rose from the table, taking Suzanne's arm as he escorted her to lead the way outside. 'Even in a Western-style restaurant in New Delhi it would cost five hundred. And apart from *Au revoir* and *Allons, enfants de la patrie,* I have now exhausted my French.'

He turned and patted Claire's hand. 'Thank you for indulging me. I know you only let me pay because I'm your favourite.'

Claire smiled fondly at him and said to Bruno, 'It's true.

When I was a little girl I would curl up and go to sleep in Krish's lap. It was the lovely smell he carried around with him, Indian spices. I never could stand aftershave on men.'

Krish glanced from Claire to Bruno and smiled. 'You see, Bruno, my secret weapon with the fair sex. But you don't smell of aftershave either.'

'No, I smell of dogs and horses, and so do many women in the countryside,' Bruno replied, with a grin at Claire. 'I thank you for that excellent lunch, and now I think we should head for Les Eyzies.'

At the museum, Bruno left them to Horst and Clothilde, went to a quiet spot by the river and called Marie-Do to ask if she had been informed of the electronic sniff that had alarmed Colonel Tourbier and triggered the dispatch of more soldiers. Yes, she replied.

'Bruno, you should know our work here is mainly about long-range and international communications. We're not really equipped for monitoring local stuff, plus we're short-handed, and then there are turf issues with Division R of the SI.'

Bruno groaned inwardly at the constant rivalry between the Piscine, for foreign intelligence, and the DGSI, Direction-Générale de la Sécurité Intérieure, for domestic security, which came under the Interior Ministry. Division R was the DGSI's bureau for surveillance, interception and monitoring communications.

'I understand,' said Bruno, 'but this time it looks as though somebody hostile may be targeting your Kerquelin and his Silicon Valley friends here at Rouffillac. You're the head of security at Domme, is there nothing your people can do to help?'

'With Kerquelin in the hospital and the chain of command

here all up in the air . . .' Marie-Do said, clearly flustered. 'Usually we'd get Suzanne to clear things at the Elysée but I don't
know where she is.'

'I do,' Bruno replied. 'She's at the Les Eyzies museum with
Kerquelin's friends. Leave it with me.'

Bruno called Lannes's office and asked to speak to the general. He described the lunacy of the Domme facility being
unable to use its own surveillance resources to protect itself
from local threats.

'I agree, Bruno, which is why the Elysée has just authorized
an emergency training exercise to bring together the army,
Domme and DGSI, all being coordinated by Colonel Morillon
of the cyberwarfare team at Rennes. And you may find this
hard to believe, but they've come across the same encrypted
phone system that you encountered in that Catalan operation.'

'That was Russian,' Bruno said. 'Are they behind this?'

'Not clear; Morillon's people are still working on it. The
special forces people are being joined later today by a team
of Morillon's cyber-nerds from Rennes, so we can monitor in
real-time what's going on. Where are you now?'

'At the Les Eyzies museum, with Kerquelin's friends and
daughters, and Suzanne has joined the group.'

'Damn that woman,' Lannes said. 'What are they doing next?'

'The curator is giving them a lecture then a prehistory tour.'

'Right. I want you back at Rouffillac to coordinate the new
teams. You know Morillon and Didi and his men and the people
at Domme, so you're the right man for the job. Get over there
right now and I'll be in touch later.'

'What about Kerquelin? I know he's alive, but where is he? When does he get back? Are these folk who are using Russian encryption systems trying to blow up the deal with Taiwan?'

'Maybe, but we don't really know yet. Morillon is the guy to find out. If that's all . . .'

'One final question, sir,' Bruno interjected. 'Jean-Jacques and Prunier. They have put a lot of effort and some extensive police time into the Kerquelin investigation. Will you tell them it was all a sham or would you prefer that I do it?'

'I'd appreciate it if you don't say anything about this, Bruno. This whole operation is now under the direct authority of the Elysée. We'll apologize later when the time comes. And remind me, what's the plan for the guests tomorrow?'

'They have a Montgolfier ride down the valley at daybreak, then take a helicopter to a tour of Roman Périgueux and the old town, then on to Brantôme for lunch, then they fly over the chateaus of Bourdeilles and Jumilhac and then have dinner at the Auberge des Truffes in Sorges, a special treat on which Kerquelin insisted, since they offer a special dinner with truffles in every course.'

'They won't need you for that, Bruno,' Lannes said briskly. 'I want you to stay at Rouffillac tomorrow, plan the locations and patrols for the reinforcements, check all the local *gîtes* and camp-sites, and then report back to me. I want those guys who have been messing with our electronics to be located and detained. Usual rules of engagement. You represent the civil authority with powers of arrest, and the special forces are under your command.'

Mon Dieu, thought Bruno. I don't even get paid extra for this.

Chapter 17

Bruno made his apologies to Horst and Clothilde for having to miss their tour, but before returning to Rouffillac he decided to consult the Mayor first. The complexities of the operation in which he was caught up were beginning to overwhelm him. He was being given huge responsibilities to command armed and elite troops, along with cyberwarriors and intelligence resources, and to protect important civilians in some crisis that could easily turn violent. The enemies and their capabilities were unknown. In the army, Bruno had never commanded more than twenty or so men as some part of a much larger military force in which officers devised plans and gave orders. It was up to sergeants like him simply to see that the orders were obeyed. This had become very different, an operation in which he was in charge and feeling more than a little out of his depth. Moreover, he told himself, right now the Mayor was his boss and needed to be briefed on the situation that Bruno faced.

'This assignment with General Lannes has taken on some strange aspects and it could turn very messy, so I thought I'd better bring you up to date,' he began, sitting in the familiar chair across the Mayor's large desk.

'It might be useful to have a record of this,' the Mayor said, pulling out an iPad and plugging in a microphone. 'The kids in Florence's computer club put this together for me so I can dictate into it and we'll soon have a written version.'

Bruno began at the beginning, how he had learned from Fabiola that Lannes had been lying to him: that Kerquelin had never been wounded, that the blood had come from a pig, and that Kerquelin had never been at the Piqué military hospital. Instead, he had been taken by a medical evacuation helicopter to the military airbase from which the latest Falcon executive jet then took off for Guyana in South America and then for Tahiti and Nouméa, presumably with Kerquelin aboard.

'What follows is my speculation, but Lannes didn't deny it,' Bruno went on. 'An important member of the group of Kerquelin's Silicon Valley friends was missing from this annual reunion, a Taiwanese named Sonny, a director of the Taiwan Semiconductor Manufacturing Company, the world's largest. Having agreed to build a new manufacturing site in the United States, the company is now negotiating to build one in Europe, using some of the forty-two billion euros the European Commission has decided to invest in creating a European challenger to the dominance of Silicon Valley, and it's about time, in my opinion.

'Why this is being done in secret by Kerquelin I don't know – perhaps out of fear of Chinese interference. I do know that Kerquelin's friends at Rouffillac have been talking about a possible successor material to silicon in semiconductors, a new material called two-dimensional graphene.

'In retrospect it was strange that all of Kerquelin's friends and his daughters seemed not very concerned about his health, almost as though they knew he would be fine. That leads me to suspect that they know all about his mission in the Pacific. But now we have two indications of possibly hostile action. The first is an Asian-looking intruder, spotted by the young daughter of the owners of Rouffillac. The second came this morning, some unknown but sophisticated electronic system trying to monitor or break into the military communications of the special forces who have been posted near Rouffillac to protect Kerquelin's guests and daughters. Whoever it is is using smartphones that use the same Russian encryption system we came across with the Catalan business. General Lannes was sufficiently alarmed by this to send in reinforcements today and to bring in our own military cyberwarfare specialists. Obviously, this is becoming serious, maybe even dangerous, and I'm supposed to be coordinating all this on the ground, even though I feel out of my depth. I thought you ought to know.'

'What do you think is going on?'

'Your guess is as good as mine, but I can imagine several scenarios. The Chinese might want to stop Taiwan becoming more and more of a crucial partner to the Europeans as well as the Americans. I can also see some possibility of industrial espionage by other tech giants. The Chinese are throwing massive resources into 2D graphene, trying to catch up with the Brits who developed the technology, and who may have their own man at Rouffillac, a Scotsman who is a trustee of Kerquelin's estate. Did I add that Kerquelin's early shares in Google make him one of the richest men in France?'

The Mayor's eyes widened and he sat back, steepling his fingers together as he gazed down at his desk in thought before speaking.

'Other than the Russian connection, there are two important facts here, it seems to me,' he began. 'The first is that Lannes has lied to you, even while you are the man he puts in charge of his operation, someone who knows the Périgord and who has in several operations never let him down. The second is that Lannes has now perhaps overreacted with this new flurry of reinforcements and cyberwarriors falling over one another.' The Mayor paused. 'Is he under some kind of extraordinary pressure?'

'Nadia is his goddaughter and he's very fond of her, and I recall that when I first told him about Kerquelin's supposed wounding in Sarlat, he seemed shocked and deeply affected, and I don't think he was faking. Maybe he didn't know then the full extent of Kerquelin's plan. At the same time, I gather that Kerquelin is likely to be the next head of La Piscine, and apparently his ex-wife saw his eclipse as her chance to make a bid to be the first woman to run French intelligence.'

'Amazing how in Paris it all comes down to individual personalities and their rivalries and connections,' said the Mayor.

'Kerquelin is still the missing man and he's the key to all this,' said Bruno. 'I get the impression that his daughters and friends are expecting him back among us by the end of the week. Lannes even said he might join him here.'

'Who else might have been on that private jet with Kerquelin?' the Mayor asked thoughtfully. 'I really don't think the Elysée would let Kerquelin play this hand solo. They'd want an insider, someone close to the technology and to the President. Let me think.' He turned off the recording system, looked up a number on his phone, and called it.

'Ah, *mon cher* Gervais, I hope you're well,' he began. 'I have a question for you. Who's the key high-tech person in the Elysée these days?'

The Mayor scribbled down a name on a notepad, and then asked, 'Would he be the son of our old colleague Lamartine?'

The Mayor nodded, and asked, 'This business with the European Commission for tech investment, more than forty billion, I hear. I was wondering to whom I should speak about getting some of that money for the Périgord?' A pause. 'So young Lamartine is also on the advisory board for the Commission, but based in Paris, is that right?'

Another pause. 'I see. But you don't know where he's gone. I'll give his father a call – he's retired in the Ardèche – and see if he can arrange for me to have a word with his son. I presume this is Edouard we are talking about, not the younger boy who went into the Cour de Comptes?'

Pause. '*Merci infiniment, mon cher*, and when can I tempt you down here for the finest food in France?' Pause. 'I'll look forward to it, Gervais. It's been too long.'

He ended the call and looked at Bruno, his gaze a mix of pride and innocence. 'Edouard Lamartine is the President's high-tech adviser at the Elysée, sits on the Europeanboard in Brussels that recommended the 42-billion-euro investment, and has been out of town on some special mission since last Friday. I think he'll be your man, taking care of the politics and the money while Kerquelin talks hardware and software and all the rest of it.'

'All that with just one phone call?' Bruno asked, grinning but impressed. 'This is the old Enarque network, I suppose.'

'France doesn't change, Bruno,' the Mayor said. 'In those years when the French state was being crafted, the crown created the Noblesse de la Robe, mostly lawyers like Montaigne and de la Boétie, men who knew how to make things work and remained loyal to the crown, unlike the aristocrats. Centuries later, de Gaulle understood that, which was why he founded the ENA after the war, a new class of *hauts fonctionnaires* to remake and modernize France. My old friend Gervais was a classmate of mine, and his son is also an énarque who now works in the Elysée.'

Bruno sighed. 'I haven't told you the worst part. I'm worried about J-J, and Prunier. They don't know about this. They've had teams of cops spending days going through videos from phones trying to find out what happened to Kerquelin, thinking it could be attempted murder. They'll never forgive me.'

'So, tell them,' said the Mayor. 'J-J is far more important to this town than General Lannes will ever be. And J-J has been your friend for far longer. Has Lannes explicitly ordered you not to tell the head of detectives? And what about Prunier, the chief of police for this whole *département?*'

'Lannes doesn't seem to give a damn that a whole team of cops is just wasting their time.'

'So tell them,' the Mayor said. 'I'm your primary employer and I think you should. Here.' The Mayor pushed his mobile phone across the desk. 'Lannes won't be tapping this one.'

Bruno picked it up and called the familiar number.

'J-J? It's Bruno. Listen, this will come as a surprise but I've learned that the attack on Kerquelin in Sarlat was a fake, all being run by Lannes. Fabiola has confirmed that they used pig's blood. Kerquelin was taken to Mont-de-Marsan on a chopper from Domme and then off to the Pacific for some super-secret purpose with a high-tech guy from the Elysée.'

'How long have you known this, Bruno,' J-J said after a silence that to Bruno seemed to be stretching beyond endurance.

'It began coming together for me last night and solidified today with some other stuff I've been learning, which led me to ask General Lannes for an explanation.'

'Did you get one?'

'Not really, but he didn't deny it.'

'And you could be in trouble for telling me this?'

'Maybe, but you've got a team of cops wasting their time on videos while people are getting burgled and assaulted and shops are being held up . . .'

'And I've been looking like an idiot day after day, giving nothing-to-say press conferences about our struggling through so many videos kindly sent to us by hundreds of honest citizens. *Merde.*'

'Don't say anything to the press, J-J. Keep up the pretence that you're checking the videos but get those cops back on the beat. And don't let Prunier blow his top and complain to the Prefect. I'll keep you posted as I learn more because this thing isn't over, and it's a lot more complex than it looks. I have to go. I'm sorry about this. If you want more background, come and see my Mayor.'

An hour later, when Bruno arrived at the intelligence base outside Domme where the reinforcements were to arrive, he explained to the receptionist who he was and why he was there and he was shown directly into a large office. There was not a computer in sight, only antique furniture, an even more antique tapestry on one wall, and the smell of excellent fresh coffee. He recognized his host as the man Suzanne had met for lunch, greeting him as Dominic. He was wearing an expensive suit and an Hermès tie and his white beard looked to have been trimmed that morning. He rose from behind a massive desk, went to a Louis Seize escritoire and poured out two demitasses of fresh coffee, handing one to Bruno.

'*Bonjour*, Monsieur Courrèges. I am Dominic Levalois and I'm nominally in charge here, although I seldom understand half of what my people are doing,' he said genially in the kind of stilted French that Bruno usually heard only in ancient films. 'I'm happy to extend you every courtesy and assistance in your assignment. I understand you are on the staff of General Lannes?'

'No, sir. I'm a *policier municipale* who happens to be on the spot with local knowledge that General Lannes sometimes finds useful. I understand that a squadron of special forces will be arriving here shortly and that Colonel Morillon from the cyber team in Rennes is also involved.'

Dominic gave a graceful nod and sipped his coffee before speaking. 'A communications suite is at your disposal and we shall give what help we can, but I should warn you that our capabilities here are more international than local. You will find Mademoiselle Pantin and Madame Kerquelin in the communications suite but I am, of course, at your disposal should you require my services.'

Bruno tried to hide his surprise that Suzanne would have abandoned her daughter and her husband's friends to return to Domme. But the fact that she was here told him something; that she thought this was the crucial spot to be. And he guessed that her instincts for power were much sharper than his own.

A young woman dressed austerely in black with her hair in a bun entered the room without knocking, shook hands with Bruno and then pinned onto his lapel a visitor's badge. There was a small, grey, metallic square in one corner which Bruno assumed was to track his movements and prevent him going anywhere unauthorized. Silently, she escorted him to a large lift and pressed a button marked '-3' and they emerged into a subterranean room the size of a basketball court, filled with rows of desks holding computers and wall screens but relatively few people, most of them very young. She led him through a frosted glass door to a smaller room where Marie-Do and Suzanne were sitting at a round table with a middle-aged man who gave Bruno a curt nod as Marie-Do rose to shake Bruno's hand. Then, to Bruno's surprise, Suzanne advanced with a broad smile to proffer her face to receive a *bise* on each cheek. Politeness required that he comply.

'Bruno, I have to thank you for being so helpful with Nadia. My poor daughter is understandably distraught by what happened to her father and you seem to have the gift of calming her down.'

'I think you and I both know, Suzanne, that there's nothing wrong with her father,' Bruno said calmly. 'His injury was faked, and right now he is somewhere in the Pacific negotiating a deal to build an advanced semiconductor plant in Europe.'

'*Zut alors*,' she said coolly, with a lingering half-smile, as Marie-Do gasped in surprise. 'It seems that General Lannes has been unusually indiscreet or that you are far more in his confidence than one might assume.'

'General Lannes said nothing to me about this. Traditional police work sufficed. We can be in touch from here with Colonel Morillon, can't we?'

Marie-Do was already tapping at a keyboard and the screen on the wall flared into life, at first blank but then with the familiar image of the man running France's cyberwarfare centre.

'*Ça va*, Bruno? That home-made foie gras you sent me after that last operation was terrific. Any news of our musical friends, the Troubadours? After that incident I downloaded some of their music. Great stuff. I'll have to come down and listen to them live.'

'You'll be a welcome guest in St Denis, *mon colonel*. I'll cook you a real Périgord meal. I assume you already know Madame Kerquelin and Mademoiselle Pantin. Do you have any news for us?'

'We're still working on that sniffer but we have tracked some interesting phones in your proximity that are using the same encryption that we managed to break in that last operation against the Fancy Bears of Moscow – the same Russian-made phones, same software – and we're sending you some intriguing but kind of confusing tapes in languages we can't handle. At least three people on the phones speak street-slang Arabic and two speak something else. Our linguistic expert says that just like the Americans used Navajo Indians for real-time communications against the Japanese in the Pacific war, the Russians are using some of their ethnic minorities to frustrate eavesdroppers like us. He thinks it might be Tartar, so we've called in a linguistics professor from the Sorbonne to help translate it.'

'Can you send me the Arabic tapes?' Suzanne interrupted.

'They've already gone to Mademoiselle Pantin's secure inbox,' Morillon replied. 'The sniffer that alerted the special forces is something else. It's Israeli, state-of-the art, probably obtained by the Russians during the war in Syria. The Israelis must have thought they were better off with the Assad regime remaining in power than any Islamist group that might replace them so they provided the Russians with some very high-tech equipment.'

Marie-Do handed a headset to Suzanne, who at once sat down to listen to the Arabic tapes, opened a notepad and uncapped a Mont Blanc fountain pen. Not a woman to wield anything less, Bruno thought.

'We're monitoring the phones in real-time and will automatically forward everything we get to Pantin,' Morillon went on. 'And if anyone in Domme can translate Tartar, we'd like to know what it says.'

'Hold on,' Suzanne said, still scribbling on the notepad. 'It's Syrian Arabic, Aleppo accent, but strange, modernized. One speaker said in half-English they had "pimped the software", whatever that means.'

'It's from rap music, American slang,' said Marie-Do. 'Pimped means upgraded, made fancy.'

'This next one is timed at dawn yesterday, another voice, still Aleppo dialect, saying someone he calls the Asian is on a recce,' said Suzanne. She paused, focusing on the voice on her headphones. 'The next transmission, timed at forty minutes later, has the same voice saying: "The Asian is coming back in."'

Bruno tried to imagine it. A dawn reconnaissance from someone, possibly Chinese or perhaps Tartar. Could that be little Patsy's secret friend, the one who showed her the stepping stone? Was he making a recce of Rouffillac or somewhere else? And he was away forty minutes, so his base was less than twenty minutes away by foot. That made things a little easier.

'Have you a location for these phones?' he asked Morillon.

'They're piggy-backing, using a remote terminal to forward the call, rather than doing so directly. That means a locked transmission system to a drone or a mobile repeater in a car, so I can give you that location but not the one for the original caller. According to the map it's near Château Fénelon. The repeater is circling, but the map shows no roads that would allow that so I assume they're using a drone.'

'Wait,' Morillon added, glancing sideways at the laptop on his desk. 'We've been working with the Brits on new voice-recognition software so I plugged these voices through and we have another result. We've come across the Arabic-speakers before. One voice is distinctive, very guttural, as though he had some kind of throat injury. He's the one that was speaking to somebody else in a language that we think might be Tartar. There are all sorts of different variants, Crimean Tartar, Kazan Tartar and so on. And the person he was talking to must have been some distance away, I mean thousands of kilometres, because of the time lag.'

'Where did you hear him before?' Bruno asked.

'Syria, Ukraine, Central African Republic, and that time

he was on a Wagner network. Wagner is a private company of Russian paramilitaries, officially known as PMCs – private military consultants. Many of them are ex-Spetsnaz, Russian special forces. The Kremlin likes Wagner because they can use them and retain deniability. There have been all sorts of nasty reports to and from the UN about their behaviour in Sudan and Central Africa.'

'How many different voices are you getting from that rough location around the Fénelon castle?' Bruno asked.

'Four so far. Could be more. But just one guy on the other end. We're still trying to run down his location but I suspect we'll get another remote terminal. He could be sitting in Moscow or Aleppo or even Beijing for all we know at this stage.'

'We've had an unknown intruder at the Rouffillac chateau, seen by a child who suggested he was Asian,' said Bruno. 'Could that be this Tartar? And we have no idea what he was up to. Could he have been planting stuff to tap the place?'

'Have you checked the windows and the phone lines?' Morillon asked, turning away briefly to answer a phone on his desk.

'I can get one of our people from Domme to do that,' said Marie-Do, picking up a phone from the desk. She pulled out a notebook from her bag to check an extension number, dialled and then began talking urgently into it.

Morillon turned his face back to the screen. 'I've just been told that the language we can't translate is not Tartar but something else, maybe Tungusic and some other derivative of Manchu. Our Sorbonne scholar is going to call a colleague in Germany.'

'Wait,' said Suzanne, raising her head from the pad on which she'd been scribbling notes. 'I know someone in London who teaches at the School of Oriental and African Studies. She might know. Send me a sample and I'll get it to her.'

Marie-Do turned up the audio on her laptop as the bursts of sound came in. Bruno could make nothing of it. It didn't sound like a Chinese or Arabic dialect, but something entirely different. Suzanne called, spoke briefly in English, and then put the phone close to Marie-Do's speaker. Suzanne, Bruno and Marie-Do watched the phone intently and Morillon was staring from his screen until an English female voice interrupted.

'It's a variant of Tungusic called Evenk,' came the voice. 'There are fewer than a hundred thousand of them, reindeer herders in Siberia, north of Lake Baikal and the Amur River. One of the speakers seems to be called Alalet, and the other one Dular, and they're being very rude about someone called Naryshkin.'

Suzanne's eyes widened and, on the screen, Morillon almost jumped out of his seat. Marie-Do looked at Bruno and murmured, 'Sergei Naryshkin is head of Russian foreign intelligence.'

'How do you mean, the Evenks are being rude about him?' Suzanne asked.

'They say Naryshkin is always telling the boss what he thinks the boss wants to hear, and he's always getting in the way – that's Alalet speaking,' came the English voice again. 'And Dular replies that it's just because this Naryshkin studied French that he thinks he owns the place and any operation having to do with France. Then Alalet says that Naryshkin's guys always screw things up.'

'Thanks, Dorothy,' Suzanne replied. 'Please send me a full translation as soon as you can.'

'*Putain*, this is gold dust,' said Morillon.

'I'd better call the Elysée,' said Suzanne, 'and Bruno, you'd better call General Lannes. Morillon, please see if we have any known Evenks in the database for GRU or FSB.'

Bruno knew that FSB was the Russian security service and GRU was the Russian military intelligence arm. He tried to call Lannes but his phone seemed dead.

'You'll have to go upstairs and outside to get a connection,' Marie-Do said. 'Only approved phones work here in the underground.'

'Will I be allowed back in?' Bruno asked.

'I'll get Dominic's assistant to go with you.'

Marie-Do took him out to the lift, whose doors opened. The assistant was inside, waiting for him. They went up, and then outside into the open air, large domes and banked antennae blocking much of his view. Bruno reported to Lannes what he'd heard.

'I don't know who these two Evenks might be but it sounds to me as though we might have two competing Russian operations under way here at the same time,' Bruno concluded.

'Thank you, Bruno, I'd worked that out,' Lannes replied. 'Make sure Suzanne gives you the full translation once she gets it and send it straight to me. Have the reinforcements arrived yet?'

'Not that I've heard, but they're expected. I'll brief them on patrol routes and so on. I'm worried about them being too visible in uniform.'

'We learned something from the last operation, Bruno. They're coming to Domme in buses, dressed as hunters, and since it's the school holidays we'll base them in the schools at Souillac and Sarlat. Capitaine Duvalier is in command, you know him.'

'I thought he and his squadron were going to Mali?'

'They're back, and they should be with you within the hour. Duvalier will text you when he gets to Castelnaud.'

'If I go back underground my phone won't work.'

'In that case come up for air every fifteen minutes.' Lannes ended the call.

The assistant led him back to the lift, about to take him once more into the subterranean depths when his phone vibrated, the screen reading 'caller unknown'. But he recognized the voice.

'Duvalier. Glad you're back safely from Mali.'

'Good to hear your voice, Bruno. We're just approaching Domme airport. Can you meet us there?'

Thirty minutes later, he was shaking hands with the squat, solidly built young captain and then being introduced to the two lieutenants and the six sergeants of the squadron. They were all new to him.

'You're doing the briefing, I'm told,' said Duvalier.

Bruno pulled out his local, large-scale map and pointed to Domme airport. 'You are here, and west is Château de Rouffillac, where the people we have to protect are staying, and where another half-squadron of special forces is posted. But their helmet communications have been compromised by an electronic intruder using a drone that was circling Château

Fénelon here, across the river to the south. We think they are a team of at least four, probably Russian special forces with Syrian mercenaries, based somewhere in the vicinity. As you can see, east and west of Fénelon it's mostly woodland. That's your patrol area. I suggest you base one half-squadron here at Veyrignac and the other to the east, here at Masclat, just across the border in the *département* of the Lot.'

'Rules of engagement?' Duvalier asked.

'Shoot if your lives or the lives of civilians are in danger,' said Bruno. 'Your job is to find this group, or its drone operator, locate their base and then report back for further instructions. Do your best not to engage them since it's possible there is a second team operating and this first team might be good guys. There seems to be some rivalry.'

'We aren't wearing our helmets and anyway you say they've been compromised,' Duvalier said. 'How do we communicate and how do I stay in touch with my men?'

'WhatsApp,' Bruno said with a shrug. At least it's encrypted. It's not great but the best we can do. This is all being put together in a hurry.'

'Who are these people we're protecting?'

'Civilian cyber-experts from various countries, men and women, whose security has been deemed vital to French interests by the Elysée.'

'And these Russian troops, Syrian, whatever, are they armed?'

'We presume so, armed and with considerable and recent combat experience. Sorry, Captain, it's not a clear mission and it's not a pleasant job. And since it's not hunting season, if any militant Greens see your men wandering around armed, they'll probably start complaining to the media, to the politicians and everyone else. If you get a contact at any time, night or day, call or text me.'

'Okay. Where should I set up my command post?'

'On high ground, probably up on the ridge above Sainte Mondaine, where you'll have a good view of the Fénelon fortress.'

'Do we shoot the drone down if we spot it?'

'No,' said Bruno. 'It makes more sense to use it to guide you back to their base, or at least to their drone operator.'

Bruno's phone vibrated on his belt and he saw it was Cassandra calling from Rouffillac. He answered and heard the panic in her voice as she explained that Sylvie had slipped while cleaning the bathrooms and broken her wrist and the guests would be arriving soon and expecting dinner. Louis had taken her to the hospital at Sarlat. Could Bruno help?

'What was she planning to cook?' Bruno asked, thinking that Louis's *potager* was full of salads and tomatoes, and he'd seen some plump artichokes near the laden peach tree. Nobody was going to starve.

'There are chicken breasts in the fridge and she made apple pie, and there's a cheese board and a big pot of crème fraîche.'

'Don't worry,' said Bruno, thinking of the well-stocked pantry. 'Have you got rice and fresh bread?' She said yes.

'Then we'll be fine. Do you know what time the guests get back?'

'In about an hour.'

'If you could set the table, get the tray of drinks ready, open the red wine from Les Verdots and put the white wine from Château Bélingard in the fridge, then leave it to me.'

Chapter 18

Bruno parked in front of the chateau and went straight to the *potager*, hoping his memory had not misled him. He was almost sure he'd seen some tarragon, the real French version with its strong anise flavour, not tasteless Russian tarragon. He was right, there were some plump bunches of Frenchtarragon and the peaches on the tree looked perfect. He pulled off one that was almost glowing red in the sunlight, bit into it and felt the juice overflow and run down his chin. Bliss.

In the courtyard, Bruno found Kirk setting out the drinks and Cassandra fluttering nervously around the table settings in the dining room while Patsy sat in the big chair at the head of the table, playing at being hostess. Two bottles of red wine had been uncorked and stood on the sideboard and Bruno saw there was a bottle of very good cognac beside them. He grabbed it and went into the kitchen and checked that there was Dijon mustard, chicken stock and sherry vinegar in the pantry. He took a basket, went back to the *potager* for artichokes, peaches and tarragon, took them into the kitchen, removed his jacket and washed his hands.

First, he stripped the leaves from half the tarragon and put them to one side. In the fridge there were a dozen chicken breasts in the large pack from Leclerc supermarket. He shrugged. It could have been worse. He found a decent knife, cut the breasts into three and then peeled and finely chopped three fat shallots. Cassandra and Patsy came into the kitchen, asking what they could do to help.

'How is Sylvie's wrist?' Bruno asked, avoiding the question. 'Have you heard from the hospital?'

'Louis called to say it wasn't a bad break but they had to wait for the plaster to set before they could come home,' said Cassandra. 'Sylvie wanted to know if they should bring back pizza or something but I said you were taking care of dinner.'

Bruno put a kettle on to boil and found the biggest pot in the kitchen for the artichokes. 'Once I start cooking we'll only need about half an hour so we'll wait for them to be settled with their cocktails. Where do you keep the rice?'

'I know,' said Patsy and darted into the pantry to emerge with a kilo pack of basmati rice. 'Sylvie lets me help sometimes when she's cooking. What are you going to make?'

'Chicken tarragon, served with rice,' said Bruno. 'Then I'll make a vinaigrette for the artichokes that we can have for a first course and then a salad.' He looked at his watch. 'You said you expect them all back in about forty minutes from now, and then say another forty or fifty minutes for them to freshen up and have their drinks. So I'll time the artichokes to be ready in ninety minutes and the chicken and rice for thirty minutes after that.'

Bruno rummaged in the cupboards for a large roasting pan and then for a large stainless steel bowl. He melted a hundred grams of butter in a pan, stirred it into an equal amount of olive oil and poured the blend of fat over the chicken chunks that he'd placed in the large bowl. He washed his hands again and then manually massaged the oil and butter mixture thoroughly into all the chicken pieces. He put the well-greased chicken into the roasting pan, with the remaining tarragon twigs tucked in between and around them. He wiped his hands clean of the fat.

Putting the chopped shallots into a large frying pan, he added olive oil and sautéed them gently on low heat, stirring steadily until they were transparent. Then he added half a litre of chicken stock, a wine glass full of cognac and half a glass of sherry vinegar. He added salt and pepper, used a wooden spoon to blend it all together and then turned up the heat until the mixture began to boil. He lowered the heat, let the ingredients simmer gently for about two minutes, and then put the pan to one side. Thirty minutes before serving the dish, he would add two-thirds of the litre pot of crème fraîche and the remaining leaves of tarragon to this sauce, pour it over the chicken, cover the pan and bake it for thirty minutes at 180 degrees centigrade.

'You make it look very easy,' said Cassandra. 'And you aren't even looking at a recipe.'

'Practice,' said Bruno with a smile. 'It's an easy dish to make. I'll write it down if you like, so you and Patsy can make it together. Can I leave you to make the salad so I can jump into the pool and cool off?'

'Can I come, too, and ride on your back?' Patsy asked, jumping down from the stool on which she'd perched to watch Bruno prepare the food.

'It will be very quick, just in and out,' said Bruno. 'I'll go and change and see you at the pool.'

Less than five minutes later Patsy was sitting on his shoulders while Bruno swam a stately breaststroke up and down the pool, ignoring Patsy's pleas to go faster, but then delighting her by swimming a few strokes underwater so that only her head remained above the surface. He clambered out of the pool, Patsy still clinging to him and asking him for a piggyback ride home. He plucked her off, set her down at his feet and began to towel himself dry.

'I saw my secret friend again today and told him about you and he said he'd like to meet you,' Patsy remarked casually.

Bruno looked up from drying between his toes. 'But I don't know him,' he said.

'He knows you. He said he does,' she said airily. 'He said that he liked what you did about Africa.' She dipped a toe back in the pool. 'I said I didn't know you'd been to Africa, and he said he wasn't talking about the place but about a person.'

Bruno swallowed hard. There was only one person called Africa with whom he had been in contact, and he'd been there when she had died; he had helped to make it look as if she had fired first. 'What did your friend say exactly, Patsy? Can you remember?'

'Just that he liked what you had done and wants to have breakfast with you at the café down at the bottom of the hill in the morning when they open,' she said, her little face knitted with concentration as she tried to remember. 'And if I came too, he'd buy me an ice cream, so you have to say yes.'

'I'm really not sure I know him, whatever he says about knowing me and this Africa person,' Bruno said. 'Africa is a place.'

But Africa had also been a person, Bruno knew, the third generation of women of that name, each one of them an intelligence agent, the first two for the Soviet Union, the last one for Russia. All three embodied a long line of devotion to Moscow that had begun in the Spanish Civil War, played a role in the assassination of Leon Trotsky, and an even greater role in defending Fidel Castro's Cuba. The last woman of the line had almost succeeded in using a drone-launched mine to massacre musicians and the audience at a free concert in St Denis. It was being given by friends of Bruno's, a band called Les Troubadours who had produced a hit record in support of Catalan independence that became notorious after being banned by the Madrid government.

The woman known as Africa had incited Spanish nationalist extremists to target the band and the concert, in order to divide Europe by setting Spain and France at odds. When she realized the mine had failed, thanks to Bruno, she shot her Spanish partner, who had operated the drone, and seemed ready to give herself up to Bruno and Yveline, who was armed with a sub-machine gun. But slipping and sneezing on a hillside path Africa had drenched in red pepper to defeat Bruno's tracker dog, she had seemed to be aiming her own gun at Yveline, who had fired and killed her in self-defence. That was Bruno's version and it had been officially accepted. So why was Africa coming back to haunt him in the form of Patsy's mysterious secret friend?

'You won't be awake when they open at seven,' Bruno told Patsy. 'And that's certainly not a good time to eat ice cream.'

'Why?'

'The cold is a shock to the stomach that early in the morning, when your tummy has been resting quietly all night,' he said, thinking it wasn't a bad explanation, dreamed up on the spur of the moment.

'So why does Mommy have orange juice from the fridge first thing in the morning?' Patsy asked. 'And why does she let me have a sip with her?'

'Ah, mummies have special powers,' said Bruno vaguely, but was saved by the sight of the minivan coming up the drive. 'Look, here come the guests. I have to get changed and do the rest of the cooking.'

He managed to get upstairs, change into civilian clothes, and get down to the kitchen again without being noticed, until Claire came into the kitchen and said, 'I hear from Cassandra that you're whipping up some kind of gourmet dinner for us after Sylvie had to go to the hospital.'

'I had to throw everything together at the last minute but let's hope people enjoy it,' Bruno said, putting on the big electric kettle to boil water for the artichokes. 'It's tarragon chicken and rice, with some lovely, fat artichokes to begin.'

'Sounds good,' she said. 'Are you staying for the talk afterwards? It's Krish tonight. He's always great.'

'You have a talk every evening after dinner?' Bruno asked.

'Usually. Angus will talk about the group's investment portfolio tomorrow. I'm sorry I missed Hartmut's presentation on that first evening when we went to see Nadia in Sarlat. He got people really interested in graphene, and then Harrison and Lori gave a fascinating talk on that Soviet science city in Siberia, Akademgorodok, with the special foods and luxuries and the idea that all those bright scientists would intermarry and breed a new generation of super-smart little Soviets. It didn't quite work but it's still in business, more like a venture capital centre these days.'

'It sounds very interesting,' said Bruno. 'Would anybody object if I sat in on this evening's talk?'

'After you've cooked us dinner? I would think not,' she said cheerfully. 'By the way, Dad sent us a text saying he's hoping to be with us the day after tomorrow. He's determined to see Nadia perform his role at Sarlat.'

Bruno threw her a quick glance, trying to hide his skepticism. 'Amazing that he's recovered so soon,' he said.

Bruno began to melt a quarter kilo of butter to go with the artichokes and at the same time he made a vinaigrette with olive oil, chives and sherry vinegar for those who preferred it.

'You might want to tell the others that dinner will be served in five minutes,' he said, pouring the crème fraîche and tarragon mixture over the chicken breasts and putting them in the oven. He filled a kettle to boil water for the rice.

Cassandra and Kirk came into the kitchen asking if they could do anything to help, so Bruno asked them to take the artichokes to the table and Claire took out the bowl of melted butter and the vinaigrette while he stayed a little longer to stir the rice before going out to the dining room to join them. He was greeted with a glass of Bélingard white wine and a chorus of thanks for the artichokes.

'The man who makes this wine, Laurent de Bosredon, maintains that he is the proud owner of the oldest vineyard in the region and one of the oldest in France,' Bruno said. 'He has an old stone seat on his land that archaeologists say was where the druids made sacrifices. The name of the chateau, Bélingard, comes from the old Gaul words for garden of the sun god. And there are ancient vines nearby.'

'We'd better add that to the list of vineyards Brice planned that we should visit on our wine tour,' said Angus.

Bruno excused himself to bring in the next course. In the kitchen, he fluffed up the rice before putting it into two large bowls which Kirk took to the table. Then Bruno added the last of the tarragon leaves to the chicken, stirred them into the creamy sauce and brought it to the table in the roasting dish in which it had been cooked.

'It smells divine,' said Lori, bending over the dish before backing away to let Cassandra serve the portions of chicken breast and leaving the tarragon twigs. For the next few minutes there was silence, broken only by the sound of cutlery and sighs and murmurs of appreciation as the food swiftly disappeared. Kirk opened two bottles of Les Verdots red to go with the cheese.

Finally, after the cheese and salad and Sylvie's apple pie they adjourned to the library. Cassandra brought coffee and Kirk offered cognac, Armagnac and a Talisker malt Scotch as a *digestif*. Angus reminded his friends to be ready to leave for their balloon ride at six thirty the following morning. Then Krish rose to speak.

'I am humbled to be speaking in this room where Thomas Jefferson sat to write letters and his journal nearly two and a half centuries ago. Recalling that great man and the American and French revolutions through which he lived may help us to put our current concerns into some perspective,' Krish began, before launching into a strikingly well-informed analysis of the current global situation and what he saw as the looming crisis in China.

He started with the country's demographics, and the distortion of the population imposed by thirty-five years of a one-child policy. He cited a report in the Proceedings of the National Academy of Sciences which calculated that some 12 million female foetuses had been aborted since families tended to prefer that if they could have but one child it should be male. The usual ratio of births among humans was 105 male infants for every 100 females. In China, it was 118 males for every hundred females in the year 2005. The one-child policy also meant that China was now one of the fastest-ageing populations in the world, and that the number of Chinese of working age had been declining since 2014. The relative shortage of women meant that many millions of Chinese males were likely to have trouble finding mates and having children; the Chinese had developed a term for such men, calling them 'bare branches'.

'China is also likely to be hard hit by the environmental crisis,' Krish went on. 'A quarter of the population lives in coastal regions, which means that some 300 million people are highly vulnerable to rising sea levels. Above all, China faces a crisis in its supply of fresh water. China's crucial main rivers, the Yangtze, the Yellow river and the Mekong, all come from the Tibetan plateau, where the glaciers are melting at an alarming speed.'

Krish opened a notebook, looked up and said, 'Let me quote Qin Dahe, the former head of the China Meteorological

Administration, who issued the following assessment in 2009: "Temperatures on the plateau are rising four times faster than elsewhere in China, and the Tibetan glaciers are retreating at a higher speed than in any other part of the world. In the short term, this will cause lakes to expand and bring floods and mudflows. In the long run, the glaciers are vital lifelines for Asian rivers."

'Let me cite another source,' Krish went on, and quoted a study led by the University of Leeds in Britain, which concluded that over recent decades the Himalayan glaciers had lost around 40 per cent of their area – shrinking from a peak of 28,000 square kilometres to around 19,600 today.

'Bear in mind that the Tibetan plateau is sometimes known as the Third Pole, being the greatest concentration of fresh water other than the poles,' Krish added.

He closed the notebook and went on to explain in his own words that China was not the only country dependent on the water from the Tibetan plateau and the mountain ranges that surrounded it. India, Bangladesh and Pakistan depended on the Indus, the Ganges and the Brahmaputra rivers. South-east Asia depended on the Mekong.

'Moreover, the plateau is also a vital factor in India's other supply of water, the monsoon,' Krish went on. 'The air over the plateau is warmed in summer and rises, creating a low pressure zone that draws in air from the Indian Ocean, which brings moisture with it. That moisture falls on India and all of southern Asia as the vital rain of the monsoon.'

He paused, looking almost grimly around the room from face to face, letting the tension build.

'We are facing a situation in which three billion people in China and the Indian sub-continent, nearly half the human race, appear to be faced in the next few decades with an existential crisis over their water supply,' he said. 'I need hardly remind you that the three of them, India, Pakistan and China, possess nuclear weapons.'

Krish paused again, casting his eyes slowly over each member of his audience. 'This is a situation which has filled me with despair for the future. But earlier this week, I heard something that gave me hope. It came from our friend Hartmut, in his talk on the potential of 2D graphene for the future of microchip technology. But he also said, almost in passing, that 2D graphene also had the potential to transform the efficiency and economics of desalination of sea water. I know we use the term "game-changer" very loosely these days, but affordable and massive desalination could really transform the prospects for human survival in southern and eastern Asia. I urge us all to consider whether this technology should not go right to the top of our own investment planning. We certainly are unlikely to lose money by doing so, and we might just save humanity.'

Chapter 19

Bruno was still glowing from his morning run when he saw the guests off to their balloon ride down the Dordogne valley. He returned to his room to shower and change into civilian clothes, and then he and Balzac walked down to the roadhouse restaurant in the hope that he might meet Patsy's secret friend. As a precaution, he had used a burner phone he kept in his Land Rover to send a brief text message to Isabelle to say where he was going and why, adding the telltale reference to the woman known as Africa. If he failed to check in with her within the hour, he suggested she should report to Lannes.

The place was not busy but there were some guests in the dining room. A breakfast buffet table offered fruit juices, croissants and various jams, slices of ham and cheese, bowls of fruit salad. On a black slate, the management had chalked that *œufs à la coque ou brouillés*, boiled or scrambled eggs, were available on request. A noisy machine delivered espresso or café au lait, tea or hot chocolate, all for a cent less than eight euros. Bruno helped himself to orange juice, a double espresso and a croissant and took a solitary table by a window. No sooner had he sat down than the door to the men's toilets opened and a stocky

262

man in sunglasses came out wearing jeans, a baseball cap and a grey polo shirt. He filled himself a breakfast tray and took a place at Bruno's table. His hands were large for his frame, the fingers long and elegant, and the first dark spots of age had emerged just below the knuckles.

'*Bonjour*, Monsieur Bruno,' the man said in serviceable French with an unusual accent, and then removed the sunglasses. If he had to guess, Bruno would have said he was some kind of Inuit.

'Thank you for coming, and I am so glad you brought your dog. I believe his name is Balzac,' he went on, offering his hand to be shaken. He had a firm grip and an amiable smile showing good teeth and the flash of gold from a filling.

'Are you Dular or Alalet?' Bruno asked, shaking hands. 'Or do I just call you Patsy's secret friend?'

'Call me Dular,' came the reply, as he bent down to fondle Balzac and give him a corner of croissant. 'From the precautions you have taken, it seems that you know there is a great threat to Brice Kerquelin and his friends at the chateau.'

'Yes, but a threat from whom?' Bruno asked. 'And who exactly are you?'

'I'm usually known as Nomokonov. My great-great uncle was a famous sniper in the Great Patriotic War who claimed 367 kills. He died when I was a little boy, but his fame secured me an education, a place at officers' school and a career with the GRU. I hold the rank of *polkovnik*, or colonel. The threat comes from some of my wilder colleagues in Russian intelligence.'

'Why did you want to see me?' Bruno asked.

'Because we looked into the crazy stunt that Africa and her

people tried to pull off with those Spanish fascists,' Dular said. 'One of her reports mentioned you, so through *Sud Ouest* I ran a search for your name and found a great deal of interesting material about you, your work as a local policeman and even your dog. I think we share a common goal in preventing any foolish attack on Monsieur Kerquelin and his friends.'

Bruno tried to conceal his surprise by taking a bite from his croissant and then keeping his eyes on Dular as he chewed, finally washing it down with a sip of coffee before speaking. 'The only sign of any hostile activity we've seen so far was a probe from nearby on our communications system, and we think it came from a drone,' he said.

'If it was circling over Château Fénelon it was probably my team,' said Dular. 'The real threat comes from some of Africa's old friends at Moscow, the ones from Khimki, better known as Unit 74455, and the real crazies of Unit 29155.'

'But they are GRU, like you, military intelligence,' said Bruno.

'It's a big organization, almost as big now as it was before they slashed us back after they fired Kobelnikov in 2009 . . .' Dular broke off. 'You don't know what I'm talking about, do you?'

'Not in the least,' Bruno admitted.

'No matter. They were looking for a scapegoat after the less than impressive military action against Georgia in 2008,' he said. He went on to explain that Kobelnikov had been blamed and dismissed from his post as head of GRU. New men came in with grandiose talk about modernization, bringing the GRU into the twenty-first century, cyber-warfare, social media and fake news. The Spetsnaz was placed under the direct orders of the general staff, losing its precious autonomy. The GRU's name was changed to the GU. The Wagner Group was launched, as a supposedly private group of paramilitary consultants, and therefore deniable.

'Then they started playing God, using fancy software to get into political campaigns in the West and playing favourites,' Dular said. 'So there is the Sandworm team, Unit 74455, that got into the Clinton campaign's computers in 2016 and tried to sink Macron in 2017. They hacked into the Ukraine power grid in 2015 and tried to sabotage the Winter Olympics in 2020. There is Unit 26165, the Fancy Bears, who hacked into the German Chancellor's office in 2018 and tried to sabotage the Dutch investigation into the shooting down of that Malaysian airliner. And there is Unit 29155, the psychos, who used nerve agents in Britain to kill Sergei Skripal, tried to launch a coup in Montenegro and blew up that Czech weapons warehouse in 2014. They were behind that Catalan operation that you know about.'

'None of those operations could be called an unqualified success,' said Bruno. 'Even when they succeeded, they left Russia's dirty hands all over it. And mostly they failed, or were found out.'

'Exactly, and that's why some of us want to stop this particular operation against Kerquelin.'

'Why?' asked Bruno.

'Killing American, European and Indian civilians is a very bad precedent,' Dular said, tapping the table to reinforce his words. 'And we don't think it's healthy for most of the new cyber-technologies to be American or Chinese. We think Kerquelin is right to partner with Taiwan to build a European semiconductor industry, and we wonder who is really behind this plot to kill him and his friends, or at least, who is paying for it.'

'Is that because you in Russian intelligence would find it easier to steal that technology from Europe?' Bruno asked. 'Or are you worried about the Chinese?'

Dular grinned. 'Russians have worried about the Chinese since they were conquered by the Mongols eight centuries ago.'

'Putin has a funny way of showing it,' said Bruno.

Dular threw up his hands. 'Putin will do anything to bring back that Greater Russian space he talks about.'

Bruno finished his coffee and sat back. 'You do realize that I'm just a village policeman who sometimes gets caught up in things that are way beyond my usual work?'

'Maybe, maybe not,' said Dular, slicing a sliver of ham and feeding it discreetly to Balzac. 'But you have the ear of General Lannes and I want you to tell him about this conversation and meet me again here tomorrow. As soon as we know when and where these thugs are assembled nearby, I'll let you know. In the meantime, tell Lannes that they have been using the area east of Grenoble as a base for years. It's a summer and winter resort area, lots of rentals, Airbnbs. It's near the Swiss and Italian frontiers and their people fly to Nice or Paris, rent cars, take trains.'

He pulled out a wallet from his hip pocket and handed Bruno two passport-sized photos.

'These guys are the ones known to the British police as Alexandr Petrov and Ruslan Boshirov, the ones accused of trying to poison Serge Skripal in Salisbury with the nerve agent. Their real names are Alexandr Mishkin and Anatoly Chepiga. Mishkin is a doctor, studied at the Kirov military medical academy. He was awarded Hero of Russia status in 2014 and also goes by the name Nikolai Popa. I've written these details on the back of the photos. If Lannes runs them through surveillance cameras around Grenoble, he'll get some hits.'

'Very kind of you,' said Bruno, drily. 'Why should we believe a single word you say?'

'I don't care what you believe. I just want you to make Lannes aware of my credentials, that I want to cooperate and that I come bearing gifts. Your work, Bruno, is then done.'

Dular pulled a twenty-euro note from his wallet and put it on the table, saying, 'This time you are my guest, but perhaps some day I will have the pleasure of eating at your table. Our file on you says that your cooking is highly regarded.'

'How will I contact you after I speak to Lannes?'

'I'll see you here tomorrow. Or you could call him now, while I get us two more coffees.'

Bruno took photos of the two headshots with his phone, turned them over and photographed the details on the backs, and texted them all directly to Lannes. Then he called Lannes's office number, spoke to the familiar voice of the duty officer, explained the photos he had sent, gave the name of Colonel Dular Nomokonov, and related what he'd been told about Unit 29155 having a regular base camp west of Grenoble. Almost immediately Lannes came onto the line as if he'd been listening to Bruno's explanation.

'Is he still there?' Lannes asked.

'Yes, he's just coming back to the breakfast table.'

Bruno handed over the phone to Dular, saying simply,

'Lannes on the line'. Then Bruno rose, picked up the double espresso Dular had brought and strolled away out of earshot with Balzac. He thought it wise to give Dular some privacy but not before he'd heard Dular speaking Russian and Lannes apparently replying in the same language.

Had he known Lannes spoke Russian? Bruno recalled that Lannes and Jack Crimson had worked together on an Anglo-French project to rescue Mikhail Gorbachev from his house arrest in Crimea during the abortive coup of 1991. The coup had collapsed in the face of Boris Yeltsin's defiance in Moscow, and Gorbachev had been freed while the Anglo-French plan was still on the drawing board.

Bruno stood on the covered terrace, looking across the river to the Fénelon chateau, thinking that Fénelon had been no stranger to the intrigues and power games of his own day. The reactionary clerics at court who supported the absolute monarchy of King Louis XIV had targeted Fénelon as a dangerous liberal, at the same time that Tsar Peter the Great was establishing himself as another absolute monarch. And Tsar Peter had succeeded so well that Russian power had loomed over Europe ever since, a tradition Putin sought to continue.

There was a line of Fénelon's that had always appealed to Bruno and it had stuck in his memory: 'Each individual owes incomparably more to the human race, which is the great fatherland, than to the particular country in which he was born.' Even today, he thought, not all French citizens would agree with that, nor many British or Americans, let alone Russians. The patriotic instinct was strong, and reinforced by schools and history textbooks and politicians.

Much as he admired Fénelon's sentiment, Bruno wasn't sure if he entirely agreed. France, and the ideals of its revolution, had a profound grip upon him, just as Pamela was devoted to Scotland and Jack Crimson loved his Britain, even though they had both been dismayed by the vote for Brexit. Like Bruno, they shared a hope, often sorely tested, that the European Union could yet match their dreams of a wider homeland rooted less in national pride than in the shared heritage of Greece and Rome, Renaissance and Enlightenment, *Liberté, Egalité, Fraternité*. Bruno gave a half-shrug, half-grimace, as Balzac stirred and Dular appeared at his side, handing Bruno back his phone.

'There is news,' Dular said. 'Lannes has decided to come down here this evening, as soon as he's arranged the security sweep in the Alpine base of Unit 29155. And he asked me to give you this and ask you to take it to your technical experts at Domme.' He took from an inside pocket an unfamiliar phone and handed it to Bruno, saying, '180615 – remember the code'.

'Why are you doing this?' Bruno asked, scribbling down the number and noting that it happened to be the date of the battle of Waterloo, while trying to conceal his confusion. He found it hard to think of this man as a traitor to his own side. But handing over an operational phone would almost certainly be seen as treachery by Dular's colleagues in GRU.

'Would you be convinced if I said it's because I don't want to see Europe at war again?' Dular said. 'I saw enough of it in Chechnya and Syria. And if I said that I think there are stupid people in the Kremlin who puff themselves up with foolish dreams of new glories for Greater Russia? Would that be enough to convince you? How about if I said that I like Kyiv and Odessa and don't like seeing them bombarded by heavy guns and multiple rocket launchers?

'We've forgotten the main lesson of the Cold War, the need to contain conflict,' Dular went on. 'The Korean and Vietnam wars stayed within their region even when other great powers intervened with troops, weapons and supplies. Great power boundaries were respected. NATO didn't intervene when Soviet troops crushed revolts in Hungary and Prague. Since 2014 the US has given Ukraine more than two billion dollars in military aid, the Poles, Germans and Brits another billion and the British are training their troops.'

'Ukraine is an independent country,' said Bruno. 'Moscow formally recognized that independence when the Soviet Union broke up, and again when Ukraine gave up its nuclear weapons.'

'True,' said Dular, 'but such details are irrelevant to those who dream of Russia's historic mission to reunite the Slavic people. They prefer to remember American assurances that NATO would not expand one inch beyond East Germany. So they claim poor, innocent Russia was betrayed by the cynical falsehoods of the West.'

'I presume such people do not include you,' said Bruno. Dular grinned and nodded. Then Bruno, curious as always, asked a question that had been nagging at him.

'Where do you usually work? Don't you stand out too much in Europe or America?'

Dular laughed, eyes crinkling in amusement rather than mockery. 'You don't know much of the world, if that's how you think. I can pass as a Canadian all across Canada, as an Alaskan in America, as a Hokkaidan in Japan, and I pass unnoticed in

China and Korea. Even in Brazil and Peru there are people who look like me. Sometimes I even get away with saying I'm from Greenland, which is more than you could do.'

He stuck out his hand. 'We'll meet here again at six this evening, with General Lannes. And you have to get my phone to the techs in Domme, in the hope that they can then monitor the movements of Unit 29155. If we cannot, General Lannes agreed with me that we should evacuate everyone from the Rouffillac chateau, including our little friend, Patsy.'

'And I suppose I would be the one to arrange alternative accommodation?' asked Bruno, and Dular nodded cheerfully.

'You are the local man so that would be your job. Logistics and good staff work are the keys to any successful operation,' he said.

Chapter 20

When Bruno went to deliver Dular's Russian-made phone to Marie-Do at Domme he was taken down to the same subterranean room where Colonel Morillon's face beamed again from the same giant screen. A female technician who looked like a teenager asked him for the access code. He told her the digits, 180615. She tapped the keypad, the screen lit up and the phone opened. She plugged it into a mysterious black cube, then connected one wire from the cube to a laptop and tapped the code into a keypad. Then she asked Morillon, 'Are you getting this?'

Morillon glanced away from the screen and said, 'It's scrolling and it looks very like the architecture we got from that Africa woman, Bruno. Not exactly the same but close enough. Thanks again.' Then Morillon spoke to the teenager, asking, 'Can you bring up a map and see if we can spot the linked phone locations?'

Bruno saw the familiar map of Domme and its airport on the screen and then a flashing red point that he assumed was the phone he'd brought from Dular. If Morillon could locate similar Russian phones on the map that could be very useful, Bruno thought as Marie-Do escorted him out. He heard something from Morillon about the phone being cloned as the glass door closed behind him and he was escorted to the lift and up to the main floor again.

'Is Suzanne still staying with you?' he asked Marie-Do as she led him out to the parking lot where he'd left his Land Rover, with Balzac perched on the passenger seat so he could watch the passers-by and the occasional take-off from the nearby airstrip.

'Yes, unfortunately,' she said, a little crisply. 'She's a pretty demanding guest, as you might expect. A strange family, the Kerquelins.'

'The two daughters seemed very normal to me, and very likeable, and even Suzanne is an impressive woman in her way,' Bruno said, surprised that Marie-Do had not noticed Balzac. 'And Kerquelin must be a remarkable man.'

'Remarkable to have put up with her as long as he did?' she asked.

'No, in his brain and skills, and his hobbies, the military re-enactments he enjoys,' Bruno said.

'A dangerous hobby,' she said as Bruno climbed into his vehicle, where Balzac gave him a lavish welcome with a cheerful little bark of greeting to Marie-Do.

As he drove back towards Rouffillac, Bruno wondered where to relocate Kerquelin's guests at the height of the tourist season. Suddenly inspired, he called Clothilde, the curator at the prehistory museum in Les Eyzies, to ask if there was any room at the residential centre for archaeologists at the Château de Campagne, where up to twenty people could be housed for conferences.

'Yes, at this time of year most of them are out living in tents at their excavations with their students,' she said. 'Why?'

Bruno explained that a sudden security concern had arisen, adding that the people at risk were the extremely rich friends of Kerquelin she had met the previous day. In return for emergency accommodation, they could doubtless be persuaded to make a generous donation to the prehistory museum. Intrigued by the prospect, Clothilde at once promised to arrange it and Bruno then called Claire, asking her to warn all the others at the Rouffillac chateau of the move. 'A precaution,' he told her. 'We've had a new security alert.'

Next he called Lannes's duty officer, to point out that since Rouffillac was being evacuated and alternative accommodation arranged for the guests, the bulk of the soldiers at the chateau should be assigned to provide a loose escort for Kerquelin's friends at Brantôme, Bourdeilles and the restaurant at Sorges, just in case their plans were too well known.

'That's at your discretion,' Bruno was told. He closed his phone and instantly it signalled a new incoming call, the screen saying it was Gilles.

'Welcome back. How was Ukraine?' Bruno said cheerfully.

'It was terrifying,' Gilles replied. 'Look, Bruno, I'm at Charles de Gaulle airport and I need to speak to General Lannes. It's really urgent and it's not about journalism, just something he very much needs to know. Trust me on this.'

'I know he's travelling today but I may be in contact with him tonight,' Bruno replied cautiously. 'Is there anything I can tell him that he won't get from whatever you publish in *Paris*

Match? Otherwise text me something and I'll make sure he gets it. Are you coming straight down here?'

'No. I have to go to the *Paris Match* offices and then talk to some people. Should I email or text you?'

'Phone may be more secure,' Bruno said, wondering what had got Gilles, usually a level-headed guy, so worked up. It would have to be something very special for Bruno to risk Lannes's anger at being put in touch with a journalist. 'And Lannes will probably pay more attention to Jack Crimson than to me so you could go through him, unless it's not something for foreign ears.'

'That's a good idea, but I'll text you anyway,' Gilles said, ending the call. Curious about his news, Bruno kept glancing at his phone after he put it into the cradle on his dashboard. Finally it gave the buzz of an incoming text.

Long interview with highly credible Russian defector. Paratroop colonel father-Russian, mother-Ukrainian. Says Moscow planning full-scale invasion, including naval blockade and airborne assault on airfield near Kyiv. Our diplomats sceptical. Am calling Jack.

Bruno gaped at the screen in something close to shock. There had been rumours of a wider war ever since the Ukraine crisis had erupted in 2014 with Russia occupying the Crimea and some Russian-speaking border regions. The skirmishing and cyber-attacks had never really stopped. But naval blockades and airborne assaults aimed at the Ukraine capital were something else. Certainly it would be the biggest military operation in Europe since NATO deployed 30,000 troops in Kosovo in 1999, maybe even the biggest since 1945.

Since France was a full member of NATO, it would be one of the first potential allies the Ukraine government would inform along with the Americans, British and the Germans. There had been no sign of any special alert at the Domme base, Bruno reminded himself. That meant nobody in Paris was concerned that any kind of military action was imminent. It was now August. If action was not imminent that meant September, which would be uncomfortably close to the autumn rains and mud of October. And that would quickly give way to winter on the steppes. Unless the Kremlin was extremely confident that the Ukraine government would collapse quickly, it would take an extremely bold military man to launch a major ground operation before the spring.

Bruno pulled into the side of the road, went to the back of the Land Rover and took his burner phone from his sports bag. He checked that it had enough juice, plugged it into the place that used to hold a cigarette lighter and called Isabelle's burner phone. It cut out after three rings, which meant she would call him back as soon as she could. He drove on towards Rouffillac and was about to turn off up the steep road when his burner rang. That would be Isabelle. He pulled off to the side again and answered.

'Have you heard of some kind of alert about a Russian attack on Ukraine, a big one, airborne assault and naval blockade?' he asked.

'Another one?' came that familiar voice that always sent little currents of excitement running up his spine. 'Must be the third or fourth this year. It's like that story of the boy who cried "Wolf". It's not that we don't believe it but that we don't yet see the build-up for anything that ambitious, even if the Kremlin thought it might make sense. I'm at the Gare du Nord, about to catch a train for Brussels to discuss it in the coordination committee. What have you heard?'

'My friend Gilles from *Paris Match* has good contacts who invited him to Kyiv to interview a Russian defector. He's just back and taking it very seriously.'

'That's why they invited Gilles, to take the bait,' Isabelle replied. 'I think he must have talked to the same defector who gave an alarmist briefing in Kyiv this week to NATO military attachés. It all sounded plausible but the satellite intel is showing no immediate preparations and some of the ships they'd need for a blockade are still in dry dock. We're more worried about next February, when Russia is holding joint military exercises with Belarus, which would put their troops within striking distance of Kyiv. I have to go, hugs to you and Balzac.'

She ended the call while he was still thanking her and as soon as he put the burner phone back in his bag, the phone in the pouch on his belt vibrated. The screen told him it was Jack Crimson.

'*Bonjour*, Jack,' he said. 'I assume you've spoken to Gilles.'

'Yes, and I tried to calm him down,' came the reply. 'If the Russians were going to start anything serious before the winter we'd have seen the build-up by now.'

'I thought the Russians were supposed to be good at operating in winter.'

'Yes, but logistics are their weak point, or one of them,' said Crimson. 'They would need to have a lot more equipment in place than they have now, both in the Donbas and in Crimea.

And I think they would want to make sure they have secured their links with the Chinese. We hear Putin is planning a trip to Beijing for the winter Olympics in February so I don't see him moving before then. I'm not saying it won't happen, just that I don't think they could mount much of an attack for the next two or three months. NATO expects something in February when Russia has scheduled military exercises in Belarus. Gilles told me that this defector was vague about timing. He's already talked to NATO military people in Kyiv and there's some concern about a sudden decapitation attack against the leadership. But I think Kyiv is well aware of that and international consequences would be very serious. How is that other business you were asking about, the graphene and semiconductors?'

'I'm not entirely sure but I should know more this weekend.'

'It's your turn to host the Monday dinner, I believe,' Jack said, a little tentatively. 'If we're still on good terms after that slightly edgy conversation with the Baron about Florence.'

'Of course, that's what friends are for,' Bruno replied, almost automatically, but realizing with some surprise as he spoke that it was true.

He ended the call feeling all the clearer in his own mind about his confused feelings for Florence after being pressed by his friends to confront them. Fond of her and full of admiration as he was, Bruno was not in love with her. Moreover, if this past week had taught him anything, it was that he couldn't fully devote himself to a wife and family when he was at constant risk of being conscripted into one of General Lannes's schemes, or onto some criminal investigation with J-J and Prunier. And there was no other job he wanted to do.

Pensively, he drove up the hill to the Rouffillac chateau, wondering how best to report that the guests would not be returning. He would also have to persuade Kirk and his family to decamp for a few days. The place would be guarded and all precautions taken, but the dangers were real and unpredictable. Clearly, he could not reveal what he'd learned from Dular. He began drafting a few phrases in his head once he'd parked and gone looking for Kirk, who was down at the pool with Cassandra and Patsy. Kirk walked up to greet Bruno, telling Patsy to stay with her mother.

'Your guests won't be coming back tomorrow and perhaps not at all, I'm afraid,' Bruno said. 'The security alert has been stepped up, our military team reinforced and I've been ordered to tell you that the French authorities strongly urge you to stay elsewhere until this is over. Do you have somewhere else you can go?'

'Yes, we have an apartment in Sarlat where we lived when the chateau was being fixed up. We usually rent it out by the week but it's empty right now, and if there's any danger I'd rather have Cassandra and Patsy there.'

'Thanks,' said Bruno. 'The sooner the better.' He handed Kirk his card with his mobile number and made a note of Kirk's. 'I'll tell you what I can when this alert is over. We may have to bring some of the soldiers inside the buildings but we'll try to keep the place tidy.'

Kirk gave a rather twisted grin. 'I hope that promise about the insurance your security people gave me will cover bullet holes.'

'What about Louis, and Sylvie?'

'The place in Sarlat will be big enough. We'll be fine.' He

stuck out a hand. 'Good luck, Bruno.' Then he took Cassandra and Patsy back to the chateau to pack some valuables.

Bruno called the lieutenant and heard his phone ring. The officer was approaching him, wearing his helmet and grinning at him.

'We got the new alert thirty minutes ago, and there's something interesting happening with the captain's team,' he said. 'Put your own helmet on and you can follow it.'

'I will,' Bruno said. 'Listen, since this place is now empty and will stay that way, could your squad provide a loose escort for the guests today and tonight? Leave two men visibly on guard here, but just in case our plans are known, I'd like to be sure our guests are protected. They'll be spending the night at the archaeological centre attached to the Château de Campagne.'

'No problem. Now put this helmet on, you'll want to hear this.'

Bruno pulled the FELIN helmet and the power pack and combat vest from his vehicle and put them on, instantly hearing the terse exchanges of troops in a potential hot zone: 'Garage clear' ... 'Pool house clear' ... 'Vehicle empty, engine cold.' Then a voice of command, 'Gas masks on. Stand by, gas grenades.'

Then came an amplified voice: 'Come out one at a time with your hands up.' Another voice, also amplified, said something in Arabic, presumably the same command.

There was a faint flurry of Arabic, as if coming from inside a house.

'Come out one at a time.'

'Lie down flat on the ground, face down, hands on top of your heads.'

And in a different tone of voice, 'Cuff them, secure weapons, check the house.'

Then a new voice: 'House clear, weapons secured.'

'Sergeant, check for documents, IDs, passports.'

Bruno waved a hand in front of the lieutenant to get his attention and asked, 'Is there an override for me to speak? Or ask him how many prisoners he has.'

The lieutenant nodded, pressed a button on his throat mike, and then spoke. 'Dragon Three to Dragon One. Permission to speak.'

'Go ahead Dragon Three.'

'We are monitoring your transmissions, Dragon One. Chief of Police Bruno wants to know how many prisoners. Over.'

'Hi, Bruno. We have two, no longer armed. Come on down.'

'Query, are both prisoners Arabs?' Bruno asked, speaking into the lieutenant's mic. He could never get the hang of these things.

'Affirmative, and we have their drone and box of tricks.'

'On my way, but one Asian and a third Arab are still on the loose,' said Bruno, and then asked the lieutenant, 'Do you know where they are?'

'It's on your screen,' he replied. 'Turn this switch to enlarge the location and you'll see the blob, that means several of our guys together. That's where they are, somewhere in a little *lieu-dit* called Lajougi, south of the castle.'

'Tell him I'm on my way,' said Bruno, calling Lannes's number as he left to find out which idiot had given the order to make the arrests when Dular and a third Syrian were still on the loose.

'SOP,' he was assured by the duty officer. Standard operating procedure. Whenever armed terrorists were located, in the absence of orders otherwise they were to be detained and disarmed. And Lannes, Bruno thought, who would be authorized to give such alternative orders, was otherwise engaged.

As Bruno crossed the bridge, his phone vibrated and it was Fabiola. Earplugs in, he answered.

'Have you heard from Gilles?' she asked, in a voice that carried alarm signals.

'Yes, from Paris. He was heading into the *Paris Match* offices after getting back from Kyiv,' he replied. 'He sounded very harassed.'

'He'll be more than harassed when I see him,' she snapped. 'He had time to call you and I hear from Miranda that he spoke with Jack but not a word for me, not even a text to say he was back and okay. And I've barely slept since he left; you know what troubles he got into there last time. Dammit, Bruno, I thought he was different, not driven by this macho career thing like you. I thought he was a writer, a man of the pen, not some gun-happy cowboy who leaves the little woman fretting her heart out at home. *Merde*, Bruno, you men are all alike!'

Chapter 21

Captain Duvalier was looking pleased with himself as he sat in the shade of an awning watching his two prone prisoners while his men were bringing out material from inside the house. There were three Kalashnikovs, two cheap shotguns, a mixed box of stun and fragmentation grenades, body armour, a laptop, two iPads and three of the Russian mobile phones that Bruno now recognized. There was also the military-grade Martlet drone, its sensor pack and its control box.

'What do you plan to do with them?' Bruno asked, thumbing through two Syrian passports. They had recent Bulgarian entry stamps, which made their presence legal throughout the European Union, at least for the remaining nine weeks from the entry date. There were also quasi-military pay books for the Wagner Group, which showed that they had been employed since the summer of 2017.

'Hand them over to the civil authorities,' the captain replied. 'That's you.'

'Not in this case,' said Bruno. 'This is no longer the Vézère valley so I'm out of my jurisdiction. You have to call in the Sarlat commissioner, or the Police Nationale. On what charges are they to be detained?'

'No idea,' Duvalier replied cheerfully. 'Unauthorized firearms, illegal entry, suspicious behaviour. We'll think of something.'

'I'm all in favour of initiative but next time please call me before you make an arrest,' said Bruno. 'There's a third Syrian around somewhere, and a fourth guy, and I hope they haven't seen the others arrested and pushed the panic button.'

He called Marie-Do at Domme, reported that they had the drone with its box of tricks, plus two Syrian mercenaries and their illegal weapons. Did she have a facility where the prisoners could be locked up? No, she replied, but she would like to have the drone and its sensors. He suggested it might be useful to have an Arabic-speaker interrogate the prisoners, and he gave her the address where they were. She said she was on her way. Then he called the chief of police at Sarlat who said that since Bruno was on the far side of the river, it was not within his jurisdiction. Bruno should try Villefranche. Instead, he called Yveline at the St Denis gendarmerie to explain why he might need a spare cell or two.

'You see the trouble you've caused by not calling me first?' he said as Duvalier grinned at him. Bruno shook his head and went inside, looking for hiding places. The house was a low-rent *gîte*, a new two-bedroom house built from a kit, with a small garden, terrace and pool, a gravel driveway and garage. It would probably rent for four hundred a month, and nine hundred or a thousand a week in the high season.

In his search, Bruno found a sealed plastic bag with six thousand euros in hundred-euro notes inside the toilet cistern. Tucked into a pile of maps and local guidebooks he found a notebook with Arabic writing and phone numbers. Inside the pool house he found a ratty old garden umbrella that looked unusually bulky. He opened it to find a gun case and a Dragunov sniper rifle inside along with two packs of 7.62 millimetre ammunition. A sniper scope was in its separate long case. He took it out to show Duvalier.

'Just in case you want to shoot something at a thousand metres,' Bruno said, and tossed the gun case onto the captain's lap. Then he waved the plastic bag with the cash. 'This was in the cistern. I think you need to work on your troops' search skills. There was also a notebook.'

'Sorry, but we knew the experts would follow up,' Duvalier said.

'Maybe you should apply for a course on how to spot booby traps,' Bruno said amiably. 'And just in case the third Syrian shows up, maybe we should get out of sight.'

'Sorry again, it's strange to act like we're in hostile territory here in the heart of France.' This time Duvalier stood up, looked around and saw that his sergeant already had the troops out of sight. He dragged one of the Syrians carelessly into the garage. Bruno brought the other prisoner, more gently, and the Syrian said, 'Shukran.'

'Afwan,' Bruno replied, which was very nearly the limit of his Arabic. He stayed in the garage until Marie-Do arrived with Suzanne and a young male technician, who almost leaped onto the box that carried the various attachments for the drone. He looked inside and rewarded Bruno with a wide beam of delight. He pulled a laptop from his own shoulder bag and various cables and was about to begin downloading when Bruno asked him to take his stuff inside the house and out of sight.

'I'll take them one at a time,' said Suzanne, eying the two trussed Syrians. Bruno handed her the passports, pay books and the notebook and told her about the sniper's rifle. Then he led the Arab who had thanked him to a chair in the sitting room and watched Suzanne leaf through the notebook and other documents before taking another chair and smiling at the young man who could have been little older than Nadia. She established that his name was Ha'adin and began what sounded like an amiable conversation.

They spoke for a while, the Arab's answers becoming longer, and then Suzanne asked Bruno politely if he could make tea. The boy had said there was some in the kitchen cupboard. Bruno called in Duvalier to take his place, found the kettle, tea bags and cups and made tea for five, taking the last two cups to Marie-Do and the second young Arab in the garage.

'She seems to have got Ha'adin to talk,' he said, and saw a flickering in the Syrian's eyes, suggesting he'd understood.

Bruno left him under the eye of the sergeant and led Marie-Do to the kitchen, closed the door and explained how they came to have two prisoners and the drone.

'So the whole group of them are staying elsewhere tonight?' she asked. 'That's a relief, I suppose. But what about Kerquelin?'

'I think he's been on a long trip with a computer expert from the Elysée, secretly negotiating some big deal with Taiwan about building a massive semiconductor plant in Europe, probably in France,' he said. 'That's why they faked his injury. What I can't figure out is why the Russians seem to be trying to block it, or at least to attack Kerquelin's reunion. I thought they had their hands pretty full with Ukraine.'

'This is all well above my pay grade, and also above yours.'

'Not in your case, Marie-Do. You're head of security at Domme, and you're not supposed to know that your top man is not in the hospital but on the far side of the world? It's crazy. We need to trust our own people more than that.'

'And how did you get through all the security layers around this, Bruno?'

'Routine police work, checking the hospitals, checking Kerquelin's background, wondering why his kids weren't nearly as worried about his health as they should have been. The core of it was the way other doctors could not believe the appalling treatment he was getting if his wound had been genuine.'

'Isabelle told me you were a born detective! It did seem bizarre, taking him to Sarlat hospital, then Bergerac, then Piqué, but we always assume the medics know best.'

'Yes, but that's just half the puzzle. Kerquelin and his health and whereabouts are one thing, but this Russian operation, spying on the reunion of Kerquelin's friends, is something entirely different. At least, I think it is. I don't see a connection.'

'If the Russians have a target it may be someone else in that group of his friends – the Indian or the German or the Microsoft guy.'

'That's a thought. It sounds to me as though you've been doing some research of your own,' said Bruno.

Marie-Do shook her head. 'No, just chatting with Suzanne, looking for things to talk about. But this sniper rifle, could they have planned an assassination?'

'No other reason to have one,' Bruno replied firmly. 'But they couldn't do it from here. The range is too far, and to be high enough and close enough any sniper would have had to find a spot within the patrol area we set up with the special forces.'

'So they are safe enough for now?'

'I hope so,' Bruno said, shrugging.

'But there's still another Syrian out there,' Marie-Do said. 'He sounds like the key figure.'

'Can't Morillon track him and the other Russians on that network through their phones?' Bruno asked. 'I thought that was happening when I was with you this morning.'

'I don't think I should answer that,' she said.

Bruno shook his head. 'You don't have to trust me but you should ask yourself two questions: how I knew Morillon from our previous work together; and who brought in the Russian phone this morning with the access key?'

'You did, and I have already asked myself those questions.'

'And the answer is that Lannes told me to bring that phone in and he was the one who briefed Morillon that I'd obtained it, and that he should make video contact with you pending my arrival. And I'm confident Morillon explained that. Now there's another question. What if we were set up to bring reinforcements here, chasing the lure of the Syrians, while leaving Kerquelin's friends less protected?'

'That would only make sense if the Russians knew where they would be today and tonight, and could strike while most of our troops are down here.'

'Exactly,' said Bruno. 'That's what worried me. And too many people know today's programme. That's why I arranged for some soldiers to escort the group in plain clothes and to stay with them overnight. You still want to worry that I'm not fit to be trusted?'

'No, I'm sorry, I didn't mean it like that,' she said. 'This is not security as I was trained to organize it, with checks and routines and controls over files and communications. This feels more like mobile warfare, with snipers and drones and grenades. I'm still trying to adjust.'

'You've never organized a drill for dealing with a terrorist attack on Domme?' he asked. 'Maybe you should, and start by finding out how long you will have to hold out on your own before military reinforcements arrive.'

She stared at him until the door opened and Suzanne entered.

'The boy is going to the toilet, under escort, and perhaps you could make more tea,' she said. 'We've established that the other one here is the *saya'ad*, the sniper. The third Syrian is their sergeant and the fourth man is a senior intelligence officer and some sort of Mongol who was with them in Syria and in Mali, an operation nominally run by a private military group called Wagner. Ha'adin was paid thirty dollars a day, most of which was sent to his family; he called them once a week to be sure the money came through. He's never been to France before. His job is to operate the drone, to ensure it isn't spotted and that the spare batteries are fully charged. Other than that he has no idea of the mission. I'll try the other one next. I imagine he'll be less forthcoming.'

At that point came a shout from outside, immediately followed by a burst of gunfire, three or four rounds, Bruno thought, coming from somewhere behind the house.

'Get down on the floor,' he shouted to the two women,

MARTIN WALKER

and ducking, he scuttled to the kitchen window and risked a swift glance. Nothing to be seen. There would be little protection in the thin walls of breeze-block and plaster. Drawing the Sig-Sauer automatic from his holster he crawled to the kitchen door, and reached up to open it.

'*Dégage*,' came a shout. Bruno thought he recognized the sergeant's voice when he shouted again, '*Tout va bien.*' Bruno went out through the front door and saw Captain Duvalier getting to his feet at the corner of the house, his assault rifle at the ready. Bruno joined him and together they walked to the rear where the sergeant and a young soldier were standing over a prone man wearing camouflage at the edge of the pool. Blood was already seeping across the flagstones and had almost reached the Kalashnikov, whose strap was still wrapped around an outflung wrist.

'He just came out of the bushes, saw me when I shouted to him to stop and then he pulled the gun off his shoulder so I shot him, sir,' said the young soldier, looking nervous and glancing back at the motionless figure by the pool.

'It's all right, Flantin,' said the captain. 'He was aiming at you and your life was in danger and you shot. You did the right thing. Better him than you.'

'You, Monteil, get a cloth from the kitchen and stop that blood dripping into the pool,' the sergeant shouted to one of the group of soldiers now coming to see what had happened. 'The rest of you get back on watch. There may be another one.'

Bruno knelt down and put a finger against the side of the stranger's neck. There was no pulse. 'He's dead,' he announced, and tried to avoid getting blood on his hands as he checked the pockets of the camouflage jacket for any papers. There was a Wagner Group pay book in one pocket, a notebook in another and black cloth chevrons on the epaulettes of the camouflage jacket.

'May I see that?' asked Suzanne, now beside him, her hand outstretched for the notebook. He gave it to her along with the pay book. She skimmed through the latter and tossed it back on the body.

'How come he got so close before being challenged?' Bruno asked, not looking at anyone in particular. He saw the sergeant gave a quick glance at Captain Duvalier. Then a soldier came around the corner carrying a bunch of rags, which he placed at the poolside to stop blood from leaking into the water.

'I suggest we put the dead man into the garage, wrapped in something, and out of the sun. And get that blood cleaned up,' Bruno said. 'I'll have to report this to Lannes's office, but I think the rules of engagement have not been broken. We can let him do the paperwork with the magistrate. I'll draft a statement and so should Flantin. Let me look it over before it gets filed.'

Along with Suzanne he went to the room where the first young Syrian was waiting under guard and murmured in her ear, 'Ask him about the one he calls "the Asian".'

'First things first,' she said, and told the soldier on guard to bring the handcuffed prisoner Bruno thought of as 'the Sniper' to the pool and show him the dead man. Bruno followed, not sure what she had in mind but suspecting he would not like it. As the young Syrian stared down at the body, Suzanne stood beside him almost crooning some words of Arabic into his ear. Then she slapped him gently, almost playfully on the cheek and had him hauled back indoors. As she turned to follow, Bruno asked her to wait a moment.

'You're not supposed to lay a hand on any prisoner, Suzanne. And I strongly advise you to use your phone to record your interrogation, so there can be no legal difficulties when he comes to trial. Now I have to draft a formal report on the death, in which my verbal recommendations to you will be recorded. This is to protect you, me and the special forces.'

'Do what the hell you like,' she snapped in reply, and stalked off. Bruno sighed, staring after her, and went to his vehicle for a notepad, wrote down the date and began drafting his report.

Acting under the joint authority of the Ministry of the Interior and the Ministry of Defence, a security exercise involving the 13th Regiment of Parachute Special Forces, Captain Duvalier commanding, was held at the government communications centre of Domme, in the *département* of the Dordogne. Representing the Interior Minister, Chief of Police Bruno COURREGES was the designated liaison officer.

On the above date shortly before noon COURREGES was informed that a patrol had spotted two unknown men in camouflage dress and carrying assault rifles. They were seen behaving suspiciously at a *gîte* near the *lieudit* of Lajougi, near the Château de Fénelon. The two men were detained and found to speak little French. COURREGES joined them shortly afterwards, found that they spoke Arabic and summoned an Arabic interpreter from Domme. Mme. Suzanne KERQUELIN volunteered to assist and arrived at the *gîte*, accompanied by Marie-Dominique PANTIN, head of security at Domme.

COURREGES was able to establish that the two men held Syrian passports and carried quasi-military pay books from the Wagner Group, a Russian-based private security company known to have conducted paramilitary operations in Syria and Africa. One of the Syrians was identified by his colleague as a specialist sniper and a Russian-made sniper's rifle with specialist sights was found hidden in the poolside building.

While the two Syrians were being questioned, a third Syrian in camouflage uniform with sergeant stripes and carrying an AK-47 assault rifle, approached the building and was challenged by a sentry, private first-class FLANTIN, Jean-Michel. Instead of halting, the third Syrian unhooked his AK-47 from his shoulder and prepared to open fire. Recognizing that his life and the lives of others were in danger, FLANTIN opened fire in accordance with the Rules of Engagement in force, felling the intruder, who was then pronounced dead by Chief of Police COURREGES. The intruder also carried a Syrian passport, in the name of Hamid al-Arayun and a Wagner Group pay book under the same name. COURREGES warned all personnel of the rules of arrest and interrogation in force, and in the absence of other facilities arranged for the two Syrian prisoners to be detained at the St Denis gendarmerie, where they were charged with firearms offences.

Bruno called Marie-Do and Captain Duvalier to join him, read aloud his report and asked if they had any questions or comments. They each said no, and Bruno added a note of that. He dated and signed the report, which covered two pages of his notebook, and Marie-Do and Duvalier added their signatures. He then photographed the pages with his phone and texted them to General Lannes's address, with a copy to himself at the Mairie, another to Marie-Do and, once he had Duvalier's email address, a fourth to the captain.

Ten minutes later came a reply from Lannes: '*Lu et approuvé.*' Read and approved. It went on: 'Meet me at Domme, 17h.'

Chapter 22

Bruno, Marie-Do and Suzanne returned to Domme together, leaving Captain Duvalier with his men, his prisoners and the dead man. The ride was almost silent, the two women sobered by the sudden shock of gunfire and violent death. France's external security service must live a relatively sheltered life, Bruno thought, and as he opened doors for them, observed, 'At least we now know the security alert was no false alarm. There are real enemies out there.'

'I've never thought of being in a sniper's sights before,' said Marie-Do, her voice not quite level. 'I'd assumed somebody was being overcautious. I think we'll need to tighten security here in the future.'

As Marie-Do escorted them past the desk where a young woman nodded as she checked them through the electronic gate, a guard stopped Bruno, saying, 'General Lannes wants to see you.' He led the way to a lift, went down one level and escorted Bruno to a small office where Lannes sat alone, his laptop open before him. Bruno went in and the guard withdrew.

'*Bonjour*, Bruno. Thanks for your report, and please sit down. I need to ask you, on the record, a serious question,' Lannes began, his face unreadable as he turned on a small tape recorder.

'How did you learn that Brice Kerquelin was not at the Piqué military hospital?'

'From doctors' gossip,' Bruno replied.

'And how did you learn about his flight in the Dassault Falcon prototype?'

'Air traffic logs on the internet,' Bruno replied.

'Anything else, Bruno?'

'I also learned from politicians' gossip that he was accompanied by Monsieur Lamartine, France's representative on the European Union's committee on the development of cyber industries. I was interested because I had heard from Kerquelin's friends over an after-dinner drink at Château de Rouffillac, where I was assigned at your orders, that he and they were interested in 2D graphene for the next generation of semiconductors. And that there was talk of a related EU investment project for some forty-two billion euros. All of this was clearly relevant to my mission, to oversee security of Kerquelin's family and friends at the chateau. And I conveyed my impressions to you, sir.'

'Quite right, so you did.' Lannes turned off the tape recorder. 'There are people in Paris who fear we have a leak and are looking for someone to blame. You are evidently not the source, since you kept nothing from me. What are your plans tonight?'

'I was going to Campagne, where Kerquelin's guests were to spend the night after their dinner at Sorges. But if you assume after arresting the Arabs from the Wagner Group that it would now be safe for them to return to Rouffillac . . .'

'No, I don't. This is not over, as we now know from your

friend Dular, whom we are going to meet shortly at the place where you and he met before. We need to eat somewhere discreet where none of us will be recognized and he needs a new place to sleep before tomorrow's probable dramas.'

'Rouffillac is empty tonight, and there's food in the kitchen there that I could cook,' said Bruno. 'And Dular can stay in a spare room.'

'Okay. Thanks to the phone Dular gave you and which you passed on to Colonel Morillon, we're tracking the phones of the GRU group that is currently near Grenoble. We believe they will be heading this way tomorrow to ensure that Kerquelin's plans do not bear fruit. He's due to land tomorrow at Mont-de-Marsan with Lamartine and Kerquelin's friend from Taiwan. They were then planning to join their friends at Rouffillac tomorrow night. The Russians have other ideas.'

'If you can track their phones, why haven't they been picked up?' Bruno asked.

'Because we need to catch them in the act, armed and equipped,' Lannes said flatly, but there was an excited glint in his eye. 'Right now, they are just tourists. If Dular is right, they plan to hit Rouffillac tomorrow. Dular has assured them that everything is in place for their mission.'

'Do you plan to stop them with the special forces?'

'If we must. I was hoping you might have a less dramatic idea, this being the tourist season.'

'The obvious way would be roadworks, or to stage a traffic accident, or perhaps a wildlife collision, deer or wild boar. But we'll need some notice of their route.'

'Okay. But we've got to go and meet Dular now,' Lannes

said, rising from his chair and putting the tape recorder into his briefcase.

Dular was already at the far table on the long porch of the roadhouse, nursing a cup of coffee. He was dressed in cycling clothes, shorts and riding shirt. A helmet was on the table and a small bag was at his feet, just the size to fit on the stand behind the seat of his mountain bike. Balzac bounded ahead to greet him. Dular grinned and gave him the complimentary cookie that had come with his coffee before rising to shake hands.

'The special forces stumbled across your base and were too enthusiastic,' Bruno said. 'I'm sorry, but one of the men is dead. The two Syrians are being questioned.'

Dular shrugged. 'No friends of mine, just hired help, cannon fodder using Wagner Group cover. My colleagues can be ruthless.'

Bruno nodded and Lannes said, 'Will your bike fit in the back of Bruno's car? We'd better get going. We're going to the Rouffillac chateau to show you how our capitalists live.'

'Almost as well as our oligarchs, I expect,' said Dular. He put his bike into the Land Rover. Once the door was closed he looked at the venerable vehicle, rolled his eyes and winked at Bruno.

They headed for the familiar gravel road up to Rouffillac, Lannes beside him and Dular in the back, renewing his friendship with Balzac. Bruno parked and led them along the long wall of the chateau, left to the promenade with the glorious view along the river, and left again into the courtyard, where he went to the hiding place Kirk had shown him for the key. Once in the kitchen, Bruno examined the contents of the fridge, the bread bin and the larder. He nodded with approval at the jars of Sylvie's pâtés that were lined up on the larder shelves: wild boar, venison, rabbit and veal. A well-smoked ham hung from a beam, with braids of onions and garlic hanging alongside. Fresh bread had been delivered that morning and there was plenty of cheese and butter in the fridge. He brought a jar of the venison, bread and butter to the table, along with plates, knives and forks.

'We won't starve,' he said, tearing a baguette into three and opening the venison pâté as Lannes and Dular each took a seat. Lannes took a bottle of Lagavulin from his briefcase, saying 'I recall your saying this was your favourite of the malts, Bruno.'

'You're right, and thank you for bringing it,' Bruno replied. He then brought to the table three suitable glasses and a bottle of flat mineral water. 'I'm going to show you how to drink it the Scottish way.'

'No ice?' asked Dular.

'Not the Scottish way,' said Bruno. He poured a healthy measure into each glass, and said, 'Raise it to your nose and take a deep sniff.'

They did so, eyes widening. 'Now lower your glass, open your lips and take another breath through your mouth so the aroma goes straight to the throat.'

They did so again, each bringing forth an appreciative murmur of surprise and satisfaction.

'Now take a tiny sip but don't swallow,' he said. 'Roll it around and let it evaporate and then take a deep breath through your mouth, deep into your lungs.'

This brought forth more widening of the eyes, grunts of surprise and appreciation as the warmth went deep into their chests. Bruno then added a splash of water to each glass and said, 'Now you can drink, but only a small sip, not like vodka,' and raised his glass to them.

'*Slava Bogu*,' exclaimed Dular when he put down his glass, still half full. 'Glory to God, that is truly something very special. Lagavulin. I'll remember that.'

'Now we have you warmed up in Bruno's special way, what do you think is planned for tomorrow?' Lannes asked.

'Unit 29155 will try to kill Kerquelin and his friends, once they have him located. That's my job.'

'Will you do that?'

'No. I will be in the hospital after being hit by a car while riding back to the *gîte* you found earlier after supposedly locating Kerquelin's friends. You will have to ensure that I will have suitable injuries by the time I report back to Moscow. They will need to see X-rays and other convincing evidence of my injuries. That is the only way to explain where I was when the *gîte* was attacked and why I could not warn my comrades of danger.'

'You could stay in France or elsewhere in the West, well hidden, with a new identity,' Lannes said.

'They would find me, like they found Skripal, Litvinenko, Berezovsky, Golubov, Perepilnichny, Patakashvili . . . and you know what happened to them.' Dular took a drink of Scotch.

'No, we have to do it this way,' he insisted. 'You have to leak a news item about this Canadian tourist who was injured in a hit-and-run, with a photo of the crushed bike, my smashed helmet and of me in the hospital,' he went on. 'You will also launch a serious search for the missing driver and feed some useful fool of a journalist with the story that the hit-and-run was a French security job. Moscow will arrange for a relative from Canada to come and visit me and fly me back to Toronto. Then they will somehow get me to Russia, X-ray my injuries and interrogate me, and it's up to me to convince them that the whole plan must have been blown. The Syrians you have in custody must be put on trial, and you must give big publicity to the man who was killed by French security forces. That will help my cover.'

'I think we can do a better job of hiding our defectors than the English did, or rather, failed to do,' said Lannes.

Dular shook his head. 'No, this is the only way. And as far as I know, but this may have changed, they will be coming in a van or in a van and a car. Their cover is that they are Polish water-skiers training for the European championship at your club at Tremolat. There will be four guys and two women, and they will drive here tomorrow. They will have water skis and photo albums of themselves on the water. They will expect to see me and get a briefing on the latest info. If I don't show, that won't deter them. This is a contract job for the Chinese so it must not be allowed to fail.'

'A contract job?' said Bruno, startled. 'Is that why the Syrians were carrying Wagner Group pay books?'

'Wagner Group, Liszt Group, Stravinsky Group, they just pluck names from a hat. They are all offshoots of GRU.'

'Why the Chinese?' Bruno asked.

'Because Russia wants Chinese support over Ukraine. And China sees Taiwan as part of the Motherland and wants to keep the semiconductor industry to itself,' Dular said. 'That's why

Beijing wants to make a public example of Sonny Lin and of Kerquelin for trying to take away what China wants to make its monopoly. If the others get caught in the crossfire, and if Russians take the blame, so much the better for Beijing.'

'Why would Putin want to help China get a monopoly?' Bruno asked.

'Who says Putin is behind this operation?' Dular almost snorted. 'Why not some ambitious underling who wants to present Putin with another great success for the Motherland, like Syria was saved by Putin, or what he's doing in Madagascar. It's insane. Russia has never had anything much to do with Africa but it makes Putin feel more powerful, thumbing his nose at the Americans and their feeble NATO allies. He refuses to see that the Chinese are just using him.'

'We should eat,' said Bruno. 'You can make a start on the pâté while I get some things from the garden.'

He took a wicker basket from a shelf beside the kitchen door and strolled around the chateau walls to the *potager*, taking a fat frisée lettuce, two young courgettes, half a dozen tomatoes and three fat peaches. Back in the kitchen, he washed the lettuce, vegetables and peaches, sliced the tomatoes and courgettes and then went into the larder to carve three thin slices from the ham, and take two fat onions and a head of garlic.

He'd missed some of the conversation because he was surprised to hear Lannes say to Dular, 'I assumed you were to be the sniper, because of the Olympics.'

'What do you mean?' Bruno asked, curious.

'Winter Olympics at Sarajevo, 1984, almost won bronze

medal in the biathlon, cross-country skiing combined with shooting,' Lannes replied.

'Luckily, I'm too old for sniping these days,' said Dular. 'One of the Syrians was very good, but this was never about sniping. They wanted to send a message, not just to Taiwan, but to France and Europe and to those hi-tech investors like Kerquelin's friends. Do not try to take Taiwan's crown jewels away from their rightful owners, the Chinese people, or you will suffer personally.'

'And all without leaving a single trace of Chinese involvement,' said Bruno.

'Yes, and courtesy of the Kremlin, because Russia wants to play in the big leagues,' said Dular. 'None of it made much sense to me, nor to many of my old colleagues in GRU, until we factored in the Ukraine. Otherwise for Putin, it runs entirely against the grain. He doesn't want to be a Chinese satellite. He's a Scythian, one of the chosen, with a divine mission.'

'What do you mean, a Scythian?' Bruno asked, pushing aside the chopped vegetables and starting to chop the smoked ham.

'There's a poem, "The Scythians", by Alexander Blok,' Dular said. 'It's about Russia's divine mission to be the people of the heartland, facing east against the Mongol hordes, while also facing west against the Europeans.'

Dular raised his eyes to the ceiling and recited some lines in Russian: '*Millioni vas. Nas, tmi, i tmi, i tmi. Poprobyitye, srazitess snamy. Da, Skiyfi - mi. Da, Aziati - mi.*'

Then he gave a translation: 'You are millions, but we are numberless hordes. We are Scythians, just try to take us on. Yes, Scythians and Asians.'

Dular paused and looked solemnly at Lannes, before adding, 'It goes on later, "We gaze and gaze at you, with hatred and with love. You have long since forgotten such love, a love so fierce that it can crush and burn."'

'I've heard Putin with my own ears,' Dular went on, his voice emphatic. 'He never stops complaining that Europe ignored the sacrifice Russians made, to save you from the Mongols, to save you from Napoleon, from the Nazis. He's a pan-Slav believer, that's why he'll never rest until he can bring back Ukraine into the pan-Slav host.'

'So why is he doing China's bidding in this Taiwan operation?' Bruno asked, tossing the chopped ham into the largest frying pan he could find. He added olive oil and a little butter and turned on the gas.

'He might not know about it,' Dular replied, 'just as I doubt whether he knew about that foolish Spanish business that you were involved in, Bruno, when Africa was killed. Little operations are not ordered by him. Maybe he knows that there are measures being taken to gain Chinese support but won't know the details until some minion can come along and report success.'

Bruno tossed the chopped ham, garlic and onions together in the pan and began to stir, adding salt and pepper. He put on a kettle to boil and then ripped up the washed lettuce before making the dressing.

'You make him sound like some mad medieval king who dreams of glory while his peasants starve outside the palace walls,' Bruno said.

'A new Ivan Grozny? A new Ivan the Terrible?' Dular asked,

chuckling at the thought. 'From time to time, I've thought that myself. But look at the alternatives. Tell me honestly, who would you like to see in the Kremlin instead? Your choice is Putinism without Putin or some ghastly gang of oligarchs with a Yeltsin-like figurehead in charge.' He pushed his glass across to Lannes for more of the malt Scotch.

'The reality is that Russia dreads the future,' Dular went on. 'What do we live on? We don't have a real modern economy, we just export oil and gas. So do we continue to sell it and watch the Siberian permafrost melt and hundreds of millions of sun-broiled Asians trek north into Russia to find safety? Or does Russia nobly stop living on oil and gas, which means we then just as nobly starve? Do you have any other realistic options open for us?'

Bruno turned the ham, onions and garlic and added the chopped tomatoes and courgettes. He poured the boiling water from the kettle into a saucepan, added salt, took down a jar containing spaghetti and inserted a generous handful, gently pressing at the point where the spaghetti began to bend so that the still-dry pasta gently folded into the boiling water. He took a bottle of Bergerac red wine, a Château Bélingard, from the rack beneath the draining board, opened it and poured a small amount into the sauce and stirred it in. Then he poured himself a glass. One malt Scotch was enough for him.

'Dinner is ready,' he said.

Chapter 23

Bruno was in the back of the control truck from the DGSE base at Domme, watching the progress of the two red indicators on the map. The larger one was the four phone signals from a car with four of the attackers in it; the smaller one was the truck, loaded with waterskiing equipment, with two phones for the driver and one other. The attackers had set out early that morning from near Grenoble, and taken autoroutes through Lyons, Clermont-Ferrand and Brive and were now driving south to Souillac. It was the logical route and Bruno felt relieved. Had they turned off at Brive to descend through Montignac and Sarlat he would have been forced to shift his troops and resources very quickly.

Bruno had asked Guyon, the fight choreographer, for his help. Guyon had driven to Rouffillac from Sarlat as soon as his part ended in that night's show. He and Bruno had huddled over maps, gone down to the road and paced out distances under the moonlight. Guyon had stayed at the chateau overnight and in the morning he and Bruno went back to the road beside the river, checking, checking and re-checking their plan.

Bruno's first plan had been to block the two vehicles at one of the payment stops on the A89 autoroute. It was possible from the kiosk to lock a barrier in place even if the toll was paid, and he had planned to block their exit with large trucks, each containing armed gendarmes. Lannes vetoed that, saying the drama would almost certainly be filmed on mobile phones from other cars and he didn't want the arrests all over the internet. So Bruno and Guyon had now planned a roadblock that could be swiftly mounted from cover, with thick woodland on the other side of the road where the soldiers could be posted.

The place they had chosen was less than a mile from Rouffillac, so the approach road from the west at the junction by the bridge could be closed off, and a temporary stop could be put on the canoes coming down the Dordogne river. A heavy tow truck from the gendarme's garage would be manoeuvring to tow a broken-down old tractor, and Bruno himself would be waving down any traffic. Folding metal signs warning 'Slow – Accident Ahead' were in place, but face down. Once the target vehicles reached Souillac, they would be erected to alert oncoming traffic.

Bruno had wanted the tyres of the two target vehicles shot out but Lannes vetoed that too, because the noise would attract attention. Instead, he had two sturdy logs, narrow enough to be pushed under the vehicles, but too big for the front or rear wheels to go over them. That would have to do. Guyon had assigned himself to drive the big garbage truck that was waiting among trees on a small side road. As soon as the two target vehicles passed, Guyon was to pull out and block the road behind them. At this spot trees flanked the road on each side, so there could be no going around him.

Bruno and Guyon were quietly proud of the plan and Bruno

stressed to the special forces that they must emerge quickly enough from their roadside cover to have automatic weapons pointing at the target vehicles from both sides the precise moment that they had come to a halt. The occupants would be hauled out, handcuffed and pushed into the back of Guyon's truck. They would then be taken to the gendarmerie at St Denis, the only one nearby able to hold so many prisoners. General Lannes and the diplomats would then take over. That was the plan. Bruno, however, had seen too many plans crumble in the face of unexpected reality to assume it would all work as he had hoped.

'Time for me to get into that truck,' Guyon said, clapping Bruno on the shoulder as their hands clasped. 'And as we say before going onstage, *merde*.'

'*Merde*,' Bruno replied; it was also what soldiers told one another before going into action. Then he climbed into the back of the gendarme control truck with its screens, technicians and radio links.

Bruno and Guyon had timed the journey from Souillac to Rouffillac at fifteen minutes, and the targets had yet to reach the Souillac turn-off. He forced himself to sit still, even though he wanted to walk off his nervousness. He knew that the best thing he could do for his colleagues was to appear cool, calm and confident.

'They've come through Souillac,' said the radio technician. 'You said to remind you to put up the accident warning signs.'

'Thanks,' said Bruno. He climbed out of the van and walked up the two hundred yards to put the warning signs in place, half-blocking the road, forcing oncoming vehicles to slow.

Back in the truck, he glanced again at the screen. The two red indicators had just followed the bend to the right, away from the bathing spot known as the Dordogne Plage, and were driving straight towards him while the river curved in a great bend to the south. There were about seven to eight minutes still to go. He plugged a tiny bud into his ear and checked that he could hear the technician sitting beside him.

'Tell me when they are back on the straight stretch,' he said. 'I'd better go to the stop point as soon as the tractor's in place.'

He flipped the microphone switch so he could speak to all the others of the network, and said, 'This is Bruno to all stations. Bridge checkpoint, close the road as planned and confirm. Bruno to tractor, proceed onto the road for your breakdown. Bruno to tow-truck, get ready to follow the tractor and erect the accident warning signs. Bruno to all forces, stand by.'

He stepped out of the control truck, saw that the turn-off from the bridge road behind him had been closed, and set off up the road, watching for the tractor to lumber out onto the road, put one wheel in the ditch and stall. It came out, sure enough, but when the rear wheel went into the ditch, it stayed there, digging into the dry earth, and one front wheel rose into the air. The driver jumped out as the two front wheels rose. Like a praying mantis, it stood there, not blocking the road. At last the driver scampered off into cover and the tow-truck lumbered forward, blocking the road. The driver's assistant jumped out, swung the bow hook on the tow chain around and dropped it onto the metal bar at the front of the tractor, the extra weight bringing the wheels down to the road again, blocking it.

Bruno had been holding his breath and now exhaled to see the two vehicles with the attackers coming towards him. He took his position in the centre of the road, his hand up and a hint of a smile on his face because he could see two hundred yards beyond him Guyon's big garbage truck lumber onto the road to block any retreat. The two Russian vehicles were now trapped between Guyon behind them and the tractor with its attendant tow-truck ahead.

Bruno slowly walked forward, his hand now waving, rather than palm up in the universal signal to stop. The driver's window opened and Bruno lazily assumed there would be a polite enquiry. Instead, there was a gun and Bruno dived to the ground just as the soldiers surged out of the treelines to each side, yelling and menacing and trying to shove the logs between the wheels of the lead car. One of the soldiers fired bursts into the open car window in the belief that he was saving Bruno's life.

There was more gunfire. Howling soldiers slammed the car windows with the butts of their guns, only to dive for cover as the inmates opened fire. Guyon's truck coming up from behind veered to the side of the road and slammed into a rear corner of the van whose side was painted with the cheerful, sunlit image of a water-skiing girl in a bikini. The van then toppled over and spun into the path of the first car, which was trying desperately to race backwards out of the trap. Instead, it stalled as it hit the van, and stopped, steam pouring from the engine.

Silence fell, save for the sound of steam rushing from a punctured radiator. Gingerly, Bruno rose to one knee. Then from somewhere, a last gun fired and Bruno spun around and fell, numbed with shock and the realization that the final bullet of this disaster for which he was responsible had hit him. And he'd forgotten to wear his protective vest. Maybe it was fitting.

Still woozy from the painkillers, but aware that he was in a hospital bed, Bruno slowly recognized the familiar figure of General Lannes sitting in a chair beside his bed, holding a bunch of flowers.

'The first thing I want to tell you is that I know things didn't go exactly as planned, but the result was splendid,' Lannes said. 'We have the whole bunch in custody and the Kremlin has no grounds for complaint. Their agents shot an unarmed traffic cop, failed to obey traffic regulations while carrying illegal arms and they were in possession of false papers – we've been able to tell the Russian Embassy that the civil authorities have made the arrests and brought the charges and there is nothing we can do. The Brits have also filed extradition proceedings against one of the drivers for conspiracy in the murder of that Englishwoman who died of the Novichok poisoning in Salisbury.'

'What about the soldiers?' Bruno asked. 'Any casualties?'

'Two wounded, one seriously, but he'll recover,' Lannes replied. 'Captain Duvalier is getting a medal and you're in for the Légion d'Honneur. Kerquelin returned with Sonny, and the technology deal has been signed. The doc says you'll be fine. You have a smashed shoulder and a nasty flesh wound but they've used a titanium section to rebuild your collarbone and you'll be playing tennis again next year.'

'What about Dular? How's he?'

'He's in the military hospital at Piqué with a leg broken in three places and a hairline fracture in his skull. His cover is perfect and his so-called cousin in Canada is still waiting for a compassionate visa to come and take him home, but the doctors say he's unfit to travel for some weeks yet. Altogether, and with great thanks to you, it was a perfect operation.'

Bruno tried to acknowledge Lannes's words but he felt terribly tired.

'I have to go,' Lannes said, stuffing the flowers into a water jug on the table by Bruno's bed. 'There's a waiting list of people to see you, most of them very attractive women, and I'm sure you'd much rather see them than me. And by special dispensation, I was allowed to bring in this fellow, but he's not allowed on the bed.'

Lannes bent down, grunted with the weight, and brought Balzac into Bruno's line of sight and grunted again with the effort of holding back nearly forty kilos of very affectionate basset hound. Bruno was able to extend his good arm and feel the familiar lathering of Balzac's loving tongue.

'Your friend the Baron is taking care of him,' Lannes said, rising with Balzac in his arms. 'And now I should make way for your next visitors. Well done, and thank you. And here's a note from an admirer.'

Bruno dozed again and when he came to he realized that there was a hand on his cheek and a fragrant kiss on his brow and two little faces peeking over the edge of the bed at him, their eyes enormous with surprise. Daniel and Dora, he thought.

'Daniel and Dora, how good to see you,' he said. He moved his head and saw Florence standing at the other side of his bed, her hand still on his cheek, her eyes full of concern.

'We're so glad to see you and hear that you're recovering very well. I have to confess that we've moved into your house. My parents arrived and they have one spare room, the children have the other and I'm sleeping in your bed. I hope that's all right. We'll all be out when my parents go home but it's been a very good visit and I can't say how grateful I am that we are all back on good terms again.'

Florence bent to kiss him again, this time a dry kiss on the lips, and then rose and said, 'We can't wait to see you back again.'

She walked around the bed to the side where her children were still staring, picked up Dora and held her so she could give Bruno a loud and smacking kiss on his cheek. Then she lifted Daniel who did the same, and said, 'The Baron comes around every day with Balzac so we can take him for a walk with Granny and Grandpa.'

They left and Bruno dozed again, waking when a nurse brought a tray of food, extended the legs and put it over his lap.

'This fell on the floor,' she said, handing him a letter in an envelope. 'There are more on your bedside table and lots of get-well cards. But first you have to eat. Food before letters, that's the rule here. You need sustenance. Shall I help feed you?'

'Yes, please,' he managed to say.

She spooned into his mouth some tomato soup, followed by potato and what tasted like chicken, and finally some slices of apple, all washed down by a glass of mineral water. Then she left, putting the other letters on the side of his tray. Bruno picked up the first one with his good hand and read the type-script: 'Thank you again for that splendid spaghetti à la Bruno. Next time I cook for you. Dular.'

The second one was from Guyon, wishing him well, and describing his happy surprise when the retracting knife that had disappeared from his locker had been anonymously returned to him at the Castelnaud address. If it was not the same one, Guyon added, it was the same make, with the velcro adhesive tape on the handle to ensure that it stuck to clothing. Had it been Kerquelin, the General or the mysterious Dr Barrat from Domme who had made that thoughtful gesture, Bruno wondered. Or perhaps Nadia, who knew Guyon well from the rehearsals of the re-enactment.

The third one was handwritten, and said:

Thank you so much for all you did for us and for Papa. I know he wants to come to visit you and thank you in person, but I'm flying back today after a very successful visit, thanks to you. This is to tell you that you have an open first class ticket to California and for your convalescence at a luxury spa that specializes in helping patients to a full recovery. And you can be sure of a very warm welcome from me, Claire.

There were cards, from Alain and Rosalie, from the Baron and the Mayor, from Jack and Pamela, Yveline and the St Denis gendarmes, from J-J and Patsy, and a big vase of flowers from Kerquelin and Nadia.

The nurse came back, holding another envelope. 'The man who was here before with the dog, the general, he forgot to give you this. I'll open it for you.'

She did so and took out a postcard with the photo of a sixteenth-century painting that Bruno and Isabelle had seen and enjoyed together in the Louvre. The painter was unknown but had depicted two handsome nude women in their bath, sitting up to face the artist, one of them, Julienne, Duchess of Villars, playfully tweaking the nipple of her sister to salute the new pregnancy of Gabrielle d'Estrées who was delighted to be bearing the child of King Henri IV who had pledged to marry her. Sadly, she died in childbirth.

Still living dangerously, dearest Bruno. You are now one wound ahead of me in the service of our dear France. I will come down to see you as soon as I can. You should know that while Balzac remains my favourite creature on the planet, you are always my favourite man. Isabelle.

How does she do it? Bruno asked himself. The perfect timing, the reference to the dog they shared, a painting they had admired together, the tantalizing sentiment that was always seductive but never quite commitment?

Leaving the food, he put to his mouth the hand that still had the scent of Balzac, and slept.

Acknowledgements

This novel was being written when Russia's President Putin launched his 'special military operation' against Ukraine at 5.30 a.m. Moscow time on February 24, 2022. To anyone who had followed Putin's career, listened to his speeches attacking NATO expansion and read his 2021 essay 'On the Historical Unity of Russians and Ukrainians,' it came as a terrible and tragic act, but not as any great surprise. So all the references in this novel to various operations in the West by Russian intelligence units, from cyber-attacks, assassinations, the establishment of an informal base in southern France, are all based on documented facts. Overall, however, this novel remains a work of speculative fiction, set in the delightful peace of the French countryside.

There is nothing, however, that has been invented in the splendid work of restoration that has brought the Château de Rouffillac back to elegant life. The owners, Kirk and Cassandra Owens, along with an extraordinary team of French artisans, have revived a jewel of the Périgord. The moment I saw what they had achieved, at the party they threw to thank their artisans, I knew the place was a perfect setting for a novel. They have become friends and are among the most generous hosts

I know, in a part of France that is renowned for its hospitality.

All the other characters are figments of my imagination, except for Harrison and Lori Coerver, friends from Florida, who donated a handsome sum to a local charity for the right to have their names in a Bruno novel. And we spent a splendid day together, wine-tasting among my favourite Bergerac vineyards. There is one other exception. The deputy mayor of Sarlat has the name of the gifted historian, teacher and local publisher who held that post. Romain Bondonneau is a good friend who kindly lent me his treasured copy of *Les Chroniques de Jean Tarde*, an ecclesiastical and political history of Sarlat and its diocese from its origins to the seventeenth century. A churchman, scientist and astronomer, Tarde died in 1637, after doing pioneering research into sunspots.

The global reach of the French electronic intelligence is much as described in the book. The Dassault Falcon 10X is so far only a prototype rather than production model, but with its extraordinary range a commercial version seems inevitable. Krish's lecture on Chinese demographics and Asia's water shortages are drawn from my own researches.

This book is dedicated to a remarkable young woman and colleague, Natalia Antelava, whom I first knew when she was a child and her father was a leading journalist in Tblisi, when Georgia was still part of the Soviet Union. At the time, I was the Moscow correspondent for Britain's *Guardian*.

We met again much later when she was studying journalism and Natalia quickly became a close friend of our family, almost an adopted daughter. She enjoyed a striking career covering Central Asia for the BBC, and has now founded Codastory.com, a remarkable and prize-winning venture to continue exploring stories once the headline journalists have moved on. Based in New York and Tblisi, it has become a remarkable success, and I'm proud to be associated with the group, and delighted that her husband and children have also become good friends who regularly come to stay at our Périgord home.

As always, for this sixteenth novel in the Bruno series, I am indebted to my literary agent, Caroline Wood, and to my editors in London, New York and Zurich: Jane Wood, Jonathan Segal and Anna von Planta. The food and recipes in this novel come from my magnificent wife, the veteran food writer Julia Watson, who did most of the work on the prize-winning Bruno cookbooks, which are to be published this year in English. Her new weekly food column on Substack.com has also become a striking and well-deserved success. Our elder daughter Kate was a great help with the editing. Finally, my fervent thanks are due to my friends and neighbours in the enchanting region of the Périgord, who have taught me so much and enriched our family's lives in so many ways.

Martin Walker, the Périgord, 2023

About the Author

Martin Walker is a prize-winning journalist and historian who has worked for the *Guardian*, the *New York Times*, the *Washington Post* and the *New Yorker*. He is the author of several acclaimed works of non-fiction, including *The Cold War: A History*, and *The President They Deserve: The Rise, Falls and Comebacks of Bill Clinton*. He is best known, though, for his internationally bestselling Dordogne Mysteries. Martin and his wife, Julia Watson, have two grown daughters. They spend their time between the Dordogne, London and Washington, DC.